Again
and
Again
Back
To
You

A Novel

Andrea Ezerins

SHE WRITES PRESS

Published 2024
Printed in the United States of America
Print ISBN: 978-1-64742-748-1
E-ISBN: 978-1-64742-749-8
Library of Congress Control Number: 2024906800

For information, address:
She Writes Press
1569 Solano Ave #546
Berkeley, CA 94707

Interior Design by Tabitha Lahr

She Writes Press is a division of SparkPoint Studio, LLC.

Company and/or product names that are trade names, logos, trademarks, and/or registered trademarks of third parties are the property of their respective owners and are used in this book for purposes of identification and information only under the Fair Use Doctrine.

American Pie
Words and Music by Don McLean
Copyright © 1971, 1972 BENNY BIRD CO., INC.
Copyright Renewed
All Rights Controlled and Administered by SONGS OF UNIVERSAL, INC.
All Rights Reserved Used by Permission
Reprinted by Permission of Hal Leonard LLC

This is a work of fiction. Names, characters, places, and incidents either are the product of the author's imagination or are used fictitiously. Any resemblance to actual persons, living or dead, is entirely coincidental.

Again and Again
Back To You

For Edgar, Lydia, Emily, Alex and Eric

Prologue

1964—Sri Lanka, formerly Ceylon

Cholan approaches his small wood hut, and he can clearly see that his mother is vexed. When she sees his empty bucket, she shakes her head in exasperation.

"What! Where is my water? You've been daydreaming again, haven't you? Now the making of roti will be delayed and so will dinner."

Cholan is known as the *mekankalitl talaiyutan ciruvan*, the boy with his head in the clouds, though now his head droops and his eyes scrape the brown earth. He kicks his sandaled toe against the dirt floor. His mother, usually forgiving, is not so this day, and he wonders why. A slight shiver runs up his back; he senses the gods and mortals are out of sync. *That is never good*, he thinks.

"Sonam," his mother calls. "Go fetch me a bucket of water, quick!"

Cholan's older brother yanks the bucket from his hand, snapping the bucket handle in Cholan's direction before storming off.

Still visibly annoyed, his mother says, "Cholan, you can start the fire for baking the roti."

Cholan bites his lip as it begins to quiver. This is a real punishment; he has an unreasonable dread of fire and smoke, and his mother knows it. She normally keeps him from any tasks that involve one or the other. But not today.

Head down, Cholan pulls some of the logs from the woodpile outside their hut and slowly approaches the large, open stone hearth in the kitchen. He scrapes at the ash and uncovers a few glowing embers, then fashions a teepee with the smaller pieces of kindling and starts blowing softly on the pile. His unease increases as he smells the bitter smoke working its way up the rough chimney. Some whorls make their way into the room and circle his head tauntingly. He glances at his mother, who is impatiently mixing the rice flour in her wooden bowl, and she quickly averts her eyes.

"Don't make cow eyes at me," she snaps, continuing to stir with much more vigor than necessary to mix the bread.

Head bent, Cholan coughs sadly and continues his task.

As the fire begins to blaze, Sonam returns, noisily banging the bucket and sloshing water onto the dirt floor. He walks by, cuffing Cholan, who looks up in surprise. *The gods are getting angrier, not calmer,* he thinks. Then he notices the swollen lip marring Sonam's normal good looks and easy smile.

Cholan asks quietly, "What happened?"

His mother pops up, takes a rag from the basket, and tries to dab Sonam's lip.

He ducks his head and mutters, "It's fine. I just slipped on a rock getting the water Cholan was supposed to get."

Guilt washes over Cholan, and with slumped shoulders he wanders outside. Sitting on the flat stones beside the hut, he surveys the village. Everything looks right, and the tension between his shoulder blades eases slightly. He hums to himself, willing the world back into proper alignment. After a minute or two of humming, the world feels a little righter, but still not completely right.

Sonam emerges from the hut and gives him a crooked smile. "Want to head into the forest and pick some mushrooms? Maybe it will make Ma happy."

Cholan's worry flares back up. If his brother can feel something is wrong, then things truly are bad. Sonam typically is oblivious to the spirits that Cholan feels all around.

He trots over to his big brother and puts his hand out, offering to carry the old wooden gathering bucket. They head up the trail toward the mountain.

After an hour of picking and wandering, Sonam turns and sniffs the air. "I think the roti is ready. I'm heading back. Are you coming?"

Cholan shakes his head. "No, I'm not hungry."

Thirteen-year-old Sonam is always hungry, while ten-year-old Cholan often forgets to come in for meals. Sonam picks up the bucket, waves, and heads down the trail.

Cholan is not sure how much time has passed since Sonam left him to his own devices, but he suddenly thinks, *Oh dear, Ma burned the roti*—and the sharp acrid smell causes every hair on his body to stand on end. As he stares at his forearm in fascination, a roar erupts to the left of him.

Spinning, he sees a wall of flames pulling everything into its vortex. His head becomes dizzy with fear. *Agni! Could the fire god be this angry because I forgot the water?*

He takes off in a sprint to get away from the angry fire god. He runs and runs, his lungs sucking in smoke and the heat becoming unbearable. A sharp pain knifes into his back—the exact spot where he felt the tension sitting in the village. That tension clearly prophesied this horrific event. The burning branch bounces off his back and lands to the side. He stares at his hands and arms and the skin is angry with red welts and blisters. The pain is now all over him.

And then, suddenly: Vishnu takes over!

With a swipe of his hand, Vishnu hurtles Cholan through time and space to a different afternoon. The air is no longer filled with smoke and ash; instead, the day is cool and crisp, void of any sign of Agni. Cholan sees his brother running up ahead and knows they are in one of their many races down the trail to the village. The trees on either side of him are a sweet, mottled green and so alive. There is no pain or misalignment of the god world with their world. Cholan sees his brother stumble and then slow. A surge of pure adrenaline shoots through him. *I'm going to beat him. Finally!*

With the many hands of Vishnu pushing him, Cholan's legs pump like pistons against the strong earth. Feeling pure and strong, hope surges through his body.

His eyes and his mind are back in this other time. A time without fire, without pain. He doesn't see the hopelessness of his current situation, the scorching of his skin, or how his smoke-filled lungs struggle to take in enough oxygen to his body. His mind is singularly focused on bright skies and Sonam.

Cholan bursts through the wall of flames just as he is overtaking his brother in their race of another day. His mind snaps back to the present when he hears his sister Sateen scream, "Cholan!"

The villagers are huddled at the riverbank and his father starts moving toward him—first slowly and then, as recognition dawns on his face, faster.

Cholan folds into a heap on the unscorched grass. One's mind can only do so much when the body is failing. Still, Cholan is able to smile as his father kneels beside him. He revels in the thought that he has just beaten Sonam, blissfully unaware that he will never run again.

Phurbu, the village Ayurvedic doctor, gently pushes Cholan's father aside as he is struggling to figure out where to touch Cholan with his red and blistered skin. Phurbu slides his hands under the small boy and carries his damaged body back to his hut, where he carefully cuts Cholan's remaining clothes off his body.

Phurbu nods. "Only your extremities. That is good."

Cholan tries to speak, but nothing comes out of his singed throat. He lies back exhausted; the pain is squeezing all thought from his head and he moans in agony, not sure he can bear a moment more.

✧ ✧ ✧

Cholan lies in the hut, counting the sapling trees that make up the outer walls of the hut, trying anything to take his mind off his suffering. He prays for Vishnu to come and snap his mind somewhere else again as he did yesterday to save him. He thinks his prayers have been answered when he begins to experience strange jumps through a sort of dream state. It isn't quite like yesterday, but he is happy for any respite from the dull, aching, never-ending pain.

On the days Vishnu does not come, all Cholan has are the 148 saplings that make up the walls of his family's hut and the memory of making the tightly woven fibers that tie the saplings together. He made them with the other village children by picking the thrushes that grow near the stream. They stripped the thrush down to thin threads and then braided them together to make strong binds that hold together their huts, even during the fiercest of monsoons—the ones that come twice a year. Cholan fondly remembers making the binds, although at the time he hated every minute of it. Looking down at his hands, which look like shredded goat meat, he wonders if he will ever be able to plait thrushes again.

Lying on the rough fabric of his mattress, Cholan's eyes slide from the saplings to his brother and sister's mattresses, hung on the large hooks they use to keep them off the ground during the day. *My mattress will never be hung up again.* His eyes, hair, and skin have become the same color as the mattress, a burnt-bread color. As the days continue, he imagines he is melting into it and thinks that one morning there will be nothing left of him except his two brown eyes as he disappears into the mattress altogether—gone forever.

CHAPTER 1: Magic

1976—Brunswick, New Jersey

K evin, after all the prior years of indifference toward Marta's very existence, notices her—really notices her.

Maybe she changed during the three months off over the summer between seventh and eighth grade. Maybe the world tilted just so and there was a sudden alignment of the cosmos. Or maybe the matching casts encircling their arms were mixed with magic and pulled Kevin finally into Marta's orbit. Who knows? Whatever the reason, a shiver runs down Marta's spine when she sees Kevin enter the nurse's office and their eyes meet. Time stops for one beat, and her heart tumbles in her chest. She knows her world will never be the same, as he really sees her.

She gives Kevin a quick smile, her hazel eyes framed by bangs, chestnut hair swaying about her shoulders ready to mask her face like a velvet curtain if needed. Kevin parts his lips to speak, but Marta quickly turns back to face Mrs. Watson, a soft smile on her face. He looks the same as he did last year; his hair is like golden straw. Her quick glance confirmed he still has his cowlick in the back. His longer hair hides it well, but she can see where the wing of his blond hair wants to take off and fly.

2 ∗ Again and Again Back To You

The nurse's office smells of disinfectant and something Marta imagines is what anesthesia smells like, though she knows the nurse doesn't perform anything more complex than putting Band-Aids on cuts. After a bit of silent standing and waiting, Kevin says, "Looks like no gym for us for a while. Does yours still hurt?"

Hugging her arms awkwardly around her body, feeling the cast press uncomfortably against her ribs, Marta glances back at Kevin.

She says, "Not so much any more. But I have Tylenol just in case."

"Me, too. Here is my plan. If I'm in some dumb boring class, I'm going to say I need some Tylenol and I'll pop back here for a visit with dear old Mrs. Watson," he says conspiratorially, nodding toward the nurse.

Mrs. Watson peers with raised eyebrows, and Marta shrinks into herself, biting her lip, worried she will get in trouble due to Kevin's audacity. Kevin gives the nurse a quirk of an eyebrow coupled with a beaming smile, and she smiles warmly back at him, shaking her head.

Having cajoled Mrs. Watson into forgiveness, Kevin turns back to Marta and asks, "What happened to you?"

"I fell off a pickup truck in my yard and broke my wrist. Chipped my tooth, too." She smiles at Kevin again and taps her front tooth. "See? Good as new. My tooth is what my parents freaked out about. They didn't pay any attention to my arm until it stayed swollen and started turning a deep purple two days later. Finally, they listened to me and took me for x-rays." She finishes her story in a rush.

Kevin gazes into her face and holds up his cast as he replies, "I slipped on my dock, diving into Brunswick Lake. God, it hurt when I hit the wood instead of the water."

Marta notes Kevin's cast is much more disheveled than hers, as if he has taken a file to both the arm hole and the thumb hole to make some self-prescribed adjustments to the fit. Kevin asks her about her schedule, and as luck would have it, they have several classes together. Of course, this isn't some unbelievable stroke of luck, as Brunswick is a small school, but Marta has a fleeting thought that this is all part of the plan the gods came up with to bring them together.

They discover they share homeroom and they walk side by side to room 232, chatting like old friends. Marta can't believe how comfortable she is talking to Kevin. It is as if they have been doing this forever.

That night, flipping open her diary, Marta stares off in space before writing:

> *It happened. I really talked to him, and it was so easy. I knew he was nice, but he seems so sweet too. I think he may like me—not like I like him but still I think he does. I am so happy I broke my wrist, we are both stuck in our casts for another couple of weeks. Who knows what will happen after that? Judy Blume is right. Good things can and do happen!*

By the third day of school, they have fallen into a routine. They meet at Marta's locker and head to homeroom together, then when lunch finally rolls around, they go through the line and then sit together. Patrick and Nancy, their designated "tray carriers," sit with them, as do a couple of other friends. This will become their table for the year, equipped with a seemingly magic aura, and they bond into a tight-knit group. After years of teetering on the periphery, Marta is securely in the core of this circle.

Gym class used to be a nightmare for Marta, but it has become a magical fifty-two-minute slice of heaven. Mr. Morgan doesn't even try to find something for Kevin and Marta to do to fill the time. He has limited use for kids who can't run and jump like Superman, and injured kids fall well below that, so they get to sit on the stack of red mats on the stage and watch the uncoordinated kids struggle through the class, sweating and fearful as they try to throw, catch, or hit various balls.

During these gym sessions, Marta and Kevin can talk freely.

One day, Kevin admits to Marta, "I can't believe I didn't pay attention to you sooner. I must be some kind of idiot!"

"It's because I'm like a little mouse," Marta says with a giggle. "Not many people notice me, usually. But I always saw you." She ducks her head as she makes this confession. "I've always felt you were special, even though you never said more than a handful of words to me in all these years. I remember the first time I met you, the first day of first grade . . ."

1969—Brunswick, New Jersey

Marta is excited and, as usual, very worried. Kindergarten was wonderful, but she isn't sure that means first grade will be. She chews her lip; maybe kindergarten wasn't real school and only now it really begins. There have already been some worrisome signs in these first few minutes in class—namely, none of the other kids seem to notice her, and she isn't sure why.

Sliding carefully into her chair with the attached desk, Marta adjusts her new blouse and pants she got for back to school. They are both a little big, as her mother wants them to last the whole year, if not longer. Marta worries the clothes are swallowing her up. *Marta* is printed in clear block letters on a crisp piece of folded cardboard on the front of her little desk, and she furtively scrutinizes the other girls' names and wishes she was a *Michelle* or *Ann* or even *Pam*, anything but *Marta*. *Marta* is so foreign sounding. The room is bright and colorful, and there are more books than she has ever seen. A petite red-haired teacher stands up from her desk and beams at each of them. Marta smiles back tentatively.

"Hello, children. I am Miss Talikin. This is the year we will embark on a wonderful journey together: we are going to learn to read. Some of you may already know some words or even may be reading; others may not. That is okay; we have a whole year together to learn the magic of letters being combined to form words and those words to form sentences and those sentences to create stories for us to explore and enjoy. How does that sound?" She ends in a rush, as if she wants to jump right into the magic.

Marta sits up straighter, her too-big blouse forgotten. The boy in front of her says, "Cool," and Marta thinks, *Exactly*.

Miss Talikin continues to explain and describe all they will do this year. Marta is spellbound.

When Miss Talikin pauses for a moment, the boy in front of Marta turns around in his chair and says, "Hi."

Gazing into inquisitive, bright blue eyes, Marta replies, "Hi." His eyes are so shining and clear, she can't look away; she doesn't drop her eyes as she normally does. She notes he has a gap between his front teeth, and she peeks at his name card on his desk. It says *Kevin*. Once he turns back to face forward, she stares at the back of his head and his blond, wavy hair until, blushing furiously, she forces herself to bring her eyes down to her desk.

Miss Talikin distracts her from her embarrassment when she holds up several books. "These will open new worlds to each of you. Worlds you control by what you choose to read. You can travel to the moon or stay closer to home; you can travel to Whoville or the planet Uriel from *A Wrinkle in Time* and anywhere in between. This is the year your world expands."

Marta wonders, *How can reading do all that?*

The next day, Kevin slides into his chair and says cheerfully, "Hi," in her general direction.

"Hi," Marta squeaks out.

This morning his blond hair is sticking out in the back with a cowlick that is damp, as if he has tried to tame it with some water. She is comforted by those hairs, which—since he keeps smoothing them down throughout the day, knowing they are misbehaving—she can only assume he is embarrassed by.

Miss Talikin does just what she said she would do yesterday: she opens new worlds to Marta and the other students. Some don't seem as impressed by the feat or in need of magic as Marta is, but they all learn to read.

Each day she goes home on the bus with a new book in her book bag, and once she is done with her chores and dinner, she sits and reads. Slowly working her way through *Hop on Pop*; *One Fish, Two Fish*; and all the other Dr. Seuss Learn to Read books. She watches Kevin work his way through them as well. She waits each morning for his morning *hi*, sure that it is aimed directly at her for a reason.

As the months go on, however, Marta faces the fact that Kevin talks and is friendly to every kid in class—he does not treat her any differently from their other classmates. He has an easiness about him, and Marta marvels at how comfortable he seems to be. Not a care in the world. Just the opposite of her.

Marta moves onto *Frog and Toad Are Friends* halfway through the year and can't help but reread the story of Toad and his funny-looking bathing suit. She connects to his worries about his clothes, as she, too, is concerned that her clothes, while not quite as bad as Toad's bathing suit, could result in a similar embarrassment.

1976—Brunswick, New Jersey

As these memories of first grade flash through her mind, Marta muses out loud to Kevin, "You were like a beautiful cloud—something I could watch and enjoy but I knew I could never actually touch or hold on to. I realized that even back in first grade."

"Until this year," he replies. "Until that first day in the nurse's office, when our broken arms magically brought us together."

"Oh my gosh, I had that exact thought on the first day at the nurse's office. Oops, I can't believe I just told you that. Honestly, I didn't mean to." Marta turns beet red.

"Hey, it's totally cool. Magic is real. You need to believe that, or what is the point?" Kevin chuckles and continues, "Just hope it is not in the plaster, 'cause I get mine off in a few weeks and I don't want to forget about you."

Marta glances up, stricken.

"Whoa, totally jokin'," he says quickly. "I will never forget you ever. Not if I am a million miles away on some far-off planet. Okay?"

Collecting herself, Marta lets out a deep exhale. "Yeah. Of course, I know you were joking." She shrugs nonchalantly, smiling bravely. "Even Mars?"

Kevin hits her shoulder with his good hand and states vehemently, "Even Mars."

He then turns serious and reaches for her hand. Marta stiffens and clenches her fingers into a fist to keep the calluses on her hands hidden from this boy. She shrinks into herself, no longer smiling. A flash of worry passes over Kevin's face when his hand contacts her tight fist. Marta sees it and her heart lurches. She didn't mean to make him feel bad. She forces herself to not pull away further and instead tentatively brushes his hand lightly with her fingers. Relief washes over Kevin's face and Marta feels a surge of happiness fill her. Looking down at their entwined hands, she feels the slightest rub of her rough inner palm against his own palm and she tries to ignore it. She is happy she saved him from any embarrassment of his own.

A warmth spreads through her chest, not an uncomfortable heat from a blush but more like the warmth of a blanket enveloping her. She has never been good with banter, but suddenly it is just rolling off her tongue. Their hands rest loosely between them and she feels a secret undercurrent to their conversations; it's clear to her that under the surface, rippling through some magic space, they are communicating something much more profound than the actual words they're speaking. She knows she will always be connected to this boy sitting next to her, no matter what.

CHAPTER 2: American Pie

1976—Brunswick, New Jersey

Kevin is thrilled with his new relationship with Marta. She is witty, shy, smart, and as pretty as Marcia Brady—so many great qualities, all rolled into one.

"What's your family like?" he asks her one day.

The two spend time together every day now, in school and outside of it, and they talk about everything. Kevin has already learned that Marta lives on a small farm and has a pet cow and a pig. He is pretty sure her father doesn't fully consider her cow and pig to be official pets, but Marta glosses over such things and seems to be a believer in *if you don't say it, it won't be real.*

At his question about her family, she shrugs. "I have a younger sister who is two years younger than me."

"My brother's also two years younger," he says. "And then there's Debbie, five years younger. We get along most of the time, though my mom and dad are a bit nuts. They're old-school hippie sorts. I'm always afraid they're going to pack us up and move us to a commune in the woods. They don't like the government and talk about home-schooling us way too much for my liking. They think school doesn't let us grow enough creatively, and other stuff like that. They're big readers of Jack Kerouac and any other antiestablishment rubbish."

Marta laughs softly. "My parents are the exact opposite of yours," she says, but doesn't share much more.

Kevin finds Marta a little mysterious, and that is a first: most of the girls he knows are pretty straightforward. Weird, certainly, but not mysterious. But he finds everything about Marta interesting, right down to her habit of holding her breath when she is worried or embarrassed or experiencing any number of the other emotions Kevin sees play across her face during their conversations.

Determined to know more, he peppers her with questions and gathers little kernels of information like a detective gathering clues.

"So, what's your favorite TV show?"

"Well, we only get to watch educational stuff," she says. "My dad only agreed to buy a TV after we rented one to watch the moon landing. Oh and of course we watch *Kung Fu.*"

He shakes his head. "*Kung Fu*? Really, that's educational?"

"I don't think so, but my dad likes it, so we don't question the educational benefits," she says. "I'm just glad to be watching anything. So that may be my favorite. Everything else is either the nightly news or PBS stuff."

Kevin squirrels away this information with all the other tidbits he has gathered, such as her parents are strict and keep her and her sister working on the farm most of the time.

"So, what is your favorite thing about living on a farm?"

She brightens. "Oh, definitely the animals. I love our cows. Staring into their eyes, they always seem so sad. Like they know something, and it is not good. I sometimes stare into their eyes, trying to figure out what they know, but then I get worried about what it might be and have to stop."

Kevin grins. Then he gets serious and asks, "Okay, least favorite thing?"

"Oh, that's easy. The chores. Specifically, feeding the chickens. The dust, the smell, the chickens . . . it takes me even longer with my cast. Hate that for sure."

"What? You don't get out of doing chores with a broken arm? Boy, your dad is a hard-ass. Even Mr. Morgan let us out of gym class.

Maybe see if the doctor will give you a note to get out of chores."

Marta grimaces, then puffs out her chest, puckers her eyebrows, and, with a stern look on her face, states in a deep voice, "Marta, what does this doctor know about a farm? Are those chickens going to feed themselves? Now get out there and do your chores."

Kevin barks out a laugh, sure her impression of her father is spot-on.

She tells some funny stories about the things she and her sister do to entertain themselves when left to their own devices and not under the watchful eye of their father. Marta is leaning back against the gym wall with her feet tucked under her and Kevin is holding her hand, tracing her fingers with his own.

He holds up her right hand and says, "Look, your finger is kinda crooked."

She giggles. "Oh, yes, that was sweet."

He continues holding her hand up to the light as though he can see right through to the bone and see the story that explains the bent finger.

"Me and Ada were picking rocks in a field in the back of our property. We have acres and acres of land, and all of it is rocky. I was swinging my arm back to get enough speed to hurl the rock into the dump truck, and Ada was right behind me, throwing hers forward. The two rocks smashed into each other."

"Ouch!" he says sympathetically.

"I screamed and blood was all over the place and my middle finger immediately swelled." She looks triumphant.

"And that's good?" He can't believe she thinks the pain of smashing her finger with a rock is a good thing. Then it dawns on him this means the work is really tough. He considers the slight girl, her back against the gym wall before him, and figures she is some kind of strong. And she doesn't even know it.

"Yep. The only way to get out of a day of picking rocks is an injury with blood and guts. Ada was so pissed. Her fingers weren't even scratched. She cursed and I cheered. It was definitely my lucky day."

She continues with a big smile on her face, "My hand was throbbing. I jogged to the house—slowly, cradling it, as it really was beginning to hurt bad. Turns out it *was* bad . . . I had to go to the emergency room to get a hole burned through my fingernail to relieve the swelling. Got out of chores for a whole week, though—well worth a little pain. I think I got to read two Black Stallion books during my week off, so a fond childhood memory for sure."

Kevin hoots in laughter and immediately stifles himself when Mr. Morgan turns an icy glare in their direction.

"I hate stone walls," Marta confides. "People love them and think they are so quaint, but I know someone dug, hefted, and then deposited all those rocks a hundred years ago, and I feel their pain." After saying this, she hesitates and blushes.

Kevin chuckles and takes her finger to try to straighten it. As he does, he thinks, *I would like to fix anything and everything that has ever hurt this girl.*

She continues idly, "My dad buries most of the stones in a pit in our back field. I guess he doesn't like stone walls, either. He is more of a barbwire-fence guy. Honestly, I think I have picked the same stones over and over—it's like they somehow work their way back to the surface after being dumped into the pit. I've always wanted to share that idea with my dad—the rocks being regurgitated back up by the earth—but I know he wouldn't get it. You get it, right?"

He nods his head vehemently. "Absolutely—the rock monster lies just below the surface and thinks it's a game you are playing! You pluck the stones and toss them in the pit, and he is tossing them back. It's all in good fun, you know, a big misunderstanding." He grins at her. "We should discuss this with my dad. He loves discussions and arguing different points of views, particularly if one's point of view is based on something fantastical or whimsical. He once took the troll's point of view and argued how the Billy Goats Gruff were in the wrong. Told you my parents are nuts."

Marta giggles. He can tell she is more relaxed around him now. He used to feel a distance between them even when they were sitting shoulder to shoulder, but he doesn't feel that so much any-more. Maybe he has uncovered all her secrets. He knows her life on the farm is tough, her parents aren't your normal loving parents, she gets lost in books, and she feels a little out of step with the world. He hopes he is helping her find herself and that she's starting to see herself as he sees her: a magical flower that with a little sunshine and magic will become the most wonderful thing the world will ever know. Kevin stares down at Marta and his cheeks are stained a bright pink when she catches his eye. He blinks his eyes to clear the words of poetry that are echoing in his head. Marta's hazel eyes dance up at him and he wonders if she can see the bright sturdy sunflower he had in his mind's eye a minute ago.

As the year continues, Kevin uncovers more and more layers of this special girl. Marta is soft-spoken but funny. She blushes frequently and gets flustered easily, but Kevin also sees a confidence deep inside her, an intriguing contradiction. She is smarter than him and very well-read. She sometimes uses words that he has to ask his mom the meaning of when he gets home. She is studious, and he learns that by showing up happy and focused, grades miraculously improve. He is doing better in school than he has in any year prior.

Marta rubs off on Kevin in other areas as well. Teachers seem to like him better, and kids do, too. He even grows four inches that year, and while he is pretty sure Marta didn't cause that, he can't rule it out.

Eventually their casts come off, and Marta resumes playing some sports. Kevin goes to Rec Park any time Marta is there to play softball or soccer. While he isn't into team sports, he is strong, with a sinewy strength that comes from swimming all summer, hiking in the fall, and doing all the activities his parents think is good for the mind and the body. Rec Park is two miles from his house, and Kevin skateboards or bikes there all the time. Kevin and Marta have figured out a way to steal more time to themselves now that they are back to the gym grind. Marta tells her parents a later pickup time or tells her coach she is being picked up early and jogs away from the practice field into the parking lot, where Kevin will be waiting, and they either walk in the woods or go to his house, where he introduces her to music and bands she has never heard of. Their special song is "American Pie" by Don McLean. They sing the lyrics at the top of their lungs. Kevin loves to watch Marta sing. She loses herself in the music, which is the only time Kevin thinks he sees into her soul.

> *So, bye, bye, Miss American Pie*
> *Drove my Chevy to the levee, but the levee was dry*
> *And them good old boys were drinkin' whiskey and rye*
> *Singin', "This'll be the day that I die,*
> *This'll be the day that I die"*

On one of those visits to his house in October, Kevin's parents are discussing some spiritual reckoning, and his dad turns to Marta and asks, "What do you think about the importance of being stewards of the earth?"

Marta blushes. "I don't really know," she says slowly. "Is that something from church or the Bible?"

Kevin's mother grins and shakes her head. "Church? What does church teach you about being good stewards? It just teaches you to blindly believe in your god over anyone else's god. Formal religion has been the cause of all wars since the dawn of time."

Kevin tries desperately to catch his mother's eye, as he can tell she is getting on one of her rolls, and he wants to stop the tirade. Marta is clearly confused and uncomfortable.

"I go to the Brunswick Congregational Church," she says. "Where do you guys go?"

Kevin's mom smiles conspiratorially at Marta and wraps her arm around her tightly. "Why don't you come to our church this Sunday and you can find out?"

Kevin groans loudly.

Marta glances back and forth between the two, looking even more confused. Kevin's mother is now smiling like an angel. He knows that is never good. She loves riling up things and people, and she clearly has Marta in her sights. But he knows he can do only so much when his mom latches on to something. His parents' progressive thinking sometimes is too much for him to deal with, and he has been hearing it his whole life.

"I think my parents would let me do that," Marta says. "I got to go to Nancy's Catholic church last year to see what it was like, so I think they would let me."

She doesn't seem to notice that his mom dodged the question of what church they go to. Kevin sighs. He loves his parents, and maybe it will be okay for Marta to hear some of their free thinking. Hopefully she won't think his family is too kooky and run back to her un-crazy family.

CHAPTER 3: Pickle Jars

1976—Brunswick, New Jersey

The following Sunday, the Dixons drive over to Marta's house and pick her up at ten thirty. Marta squeezes in the back seat between Kevin and his brother Mark. His little sister, Debbie, is in the way back of the station wagon.

Mark peers over at Marta and elbows Kevin. "That your girl-friend, Kev?" he asks with a smirk.

"Shut up, Mark."

Marta glances up toward the front seat, worried. When nothing happens, she looks over at Kevin and whispers, "I would have gotten in big trouble for saying that."

"Saying what?"

Marta whispers even lower, "Shut up."

"Oh lord, if I got in trouble every time I told this knucklehead to shut up, I'd always be in the doghouse," he tells her, laughing.

Marta giggles and relaxes back into her seat. Raising her voice back to a normal volume, she says, "Oh, I almost forgot—what church are we going to? I told my dad it was the Baptist church because I had to tell him something. I couldn't remember what your mom said."

"Oh, she didn't say," Kevin says with a wink. "But you'll find out soon enough."

✧ ✧ ✧

They drive to the entrance of Newcastle Falls Park and, to Marta's surprise, park and everyone tumbles out of the car. Marta stares at Kevin's family, who are in cut-off shorts, sundresses, and dirty sneakers. She stares down at her yellow pedal-pushers and collared blouse, dismayed at her choices.

"Is this your church?" she asks. "A park?"

"Yeah, sorry 'bout this," Kevin says, a contrite look on his face. "I told you my parents are old hippies. They don't believe in any formal religion unless you count Wiccan. I think they could get behind that. But here we just go to the falls and connect with nature. Nothing to worry about. It's kinda fun."

Marta bites her lip and begins to worry in earnest about what she will tell her parents. "Wiccan" is definitely out.

They hike for a few miles, with Kevin's parents espousing the beauty of nature and stopping periodically to smell flowers or turn over a log, marveling at the perseverance of life when they find mushrooms or salamanders underneath. They pick mushrooms as they travel up the hilly path. When they get to the falls, they spread out and sit down on natural stone benches, watching the waterfall as it cascades into the pool of clear, crisp water below.

Marta feels something calm inside her. She breathes more freely. *I really like this church*, she thinks. It is certainly better than her church, which entails a lot of sitting, standing, and opening of different hymnals, where singing loudly is a requirement. She is much happier sitting on the rough stone, watching the water splash below.

Debbie wanders off and starts doing cartwheels in an open area near the falls. Marta is itching to join her, as she looks so free and wonderful.

Kevin, as if reading her mind, says, "I bet you can do a mean cartwheel. I watched that girl in the Olympics score a perfect ten. She reminded me of you."

She looks up at him in surprise, as the Olympics were in August, before they "met." She says quietly, "That's funny. I watched Nadia Comaneci too. We're Romanian, so my father was really into it. You'd think she was his daughter, he was so proud and excited. I watched her and thought I looked like her too—I mean, I can't do anything like she can do." Her cheeks turn pink. "Did you hear what she said when people asked her why she never smiles?"

He shakes his head.

"She said it's because she is always running routines in her head, getting ready for the next competition. She couldn't even enjoy winning the gold medal because she was starting to worry about the next one." She peeks at Kevin, biting her lip, as she always does when her chest tightens with anxiety that springs up from nowhere and everything.

He takes her hand and leans his head into hers. "My dad has a quote he always says: 'All the things that truly matter—beauty, love, creativity, joy, and inner peace—rise from beyond the mind.'" He taps Marta's forehead and smiles. "It is some Zen philosophy he loves to spout. Some of his stuff is crazy shit, but some of it makes sense, and this saying makes sense to me. I think he is trying to tell me not to worry about stuff I can't control, and that sometimes the stuff in your head isn't really what matters. That is your sermon for the day." He flashes a mischievous grin, then turns to watch his sister.

Marta mulls the words over in her head. They make sense to her, too. After a few minutes of internal debate, her chest loosens, and she gets up and joins Debbie in doing cartwheels until she is dizzy with laughter.

Walking back toward the stone benches after she's finished cartwheeling, Marta glances around, and a tinge of anxiety winds its way up her spine, but no one is paying her any attention. Kevin's father is reading a small book of Buddhist teachings. Kevin's mother has her eyes closed and is wearing a faint smile on her face. Mark disappeared down toward the falls. Marta pushes the worry away and slides back onto the bench next to Kevin, taking a deep breath. At this moment, sitting in these woods, next to this boy, she feels happy.

The next moment, anxiety unfurls inside her gut as if angry that she even attempted to tamp it down.

She blurts out, "What will I tell my dad I did for church? He won't get any of this." She spreads her hands at the lush, green trees and the water surging by.

"Maybe tell your dad it was a naturalist church called Newcastle Church, in the middle of the park," Kevin suddenly says. "You can make it sound legit. Tell him we all picked up trash around the park. We sometimes do that, too. I think there should be a church like that, so make one up. You're good with stories."

Marta looks up, feeling relief and surprise. Again, Kevin has displayed this uncanny ability to read her thoughts. She especially likes the fact that he thinks she is a good storyteller. That almost makes the idea of telling a lie to her parents something good. *Just tell a story*, she thinks. *I can do that.*

Back at their house, Kevin's mom puts on Bob Dylan's *Hard Rain* album, and they all gather in the living room to listen to "Shelter from the Storm." Sitting with his family, listening to Bob Dylan wheezing out his pain, Marta again feels as she did in the park, as though there is a higher god who occasionally lets you know what perfection feels like. She stares at Kevin's parents. They look ordinary, but they are truly extraordinary in how they spend so much time opening their kids' eyes to the beauty in the world around them. Marta thinks of her parents and how they never look up but always down. They miss so much stooped with the weight of the world keeping them from seeing or hearing the beauty all around them.

Turning, she glances at Kevin. He is staring at her intently and he whispers, "I can see the music moving through you."

Marta scrunches her forehead. His warm shoulder is pressed against hers, and Marta feels a direct connection to this boy, the earth, and the song. They will be each other's shelter from the storm.

Later, they make lunch together in the Dixons' large and chaotic kitchen. Marta is in charge of putting pickles on all the plates. When she uses the last of the pickles, she rinses the cap and jar and asks, "Where do you keep your pickle jars?"

Kevin's mom asks, "Keep our what?"

"Your pickle jars. This one is empty."

Kevin's mother looks at Marta quizzically, reaches for the jar and its cover, and drops them both into the trash bin. Marta stares at the trash until Kevin nudges her in the ribs.

They eat their sandwiches and pickles; everyone is talking at once and laughing. Mark even punches Kevin in his ribs. A box of Oreos is passed around afterward. Marta marvels at the difference between this meal and the Sunday dinners at her dull, quiet house. She can't imagine chattering on like Debbie is doing over the plaintive cry of Bob Dylan. Sunday dinner is normally a pot roast that her mother bakes in the oven for hours with potato and cabbage. Marta doesn't mind the food her mother cooks up. It tastes good with her mother's spices and the ground mustard her father makes, but the sandwiches they made and ate were so . . . American.

Back at her quiet, dark house that night, Marta thinks about the pickle jar lying in the trash at Kevin's. Her family saves every item and reuses it forever; pickle jars are the perfect containers for the pickling or canning of peaches or applesauce in the fall. Their pantry and the cellar storage are filled with pickle jars of every size and shape. Years and years of scrimping and saving every penny, but they never get ahead.

Lying on her twin bed with the vinyl mattress under the faded sheet, she decides she doesn't want to work so hard for so little. Other kids' families, including Kevin's, throw out plastic bags and pickle jars. She has a wild urge to go down to the cellar, grab a few random jars, and hurl them against the wall, smashing them into smithereens. Her lip quirks up in a smile. She knows she would never, as her parents would think she had completely lost her mind. But one day, she promises herself, when she is a braver Marta, she will break a few pickle jars. She pauses as a memory flashes through her head. She realizes she met that braver Marta once already. It was all the way back in sixth grade. She didn't break a pickle jar, she did something even more fearless.

CHAPTER 4: The Thief

1973—Brunswick, New Jersey

In September, eleven-year-old Marta gets off the bus with Ada and they both smile at their father, who is in the yard working on a piece of equipment. He looks up and inclines his head at the two girls but doesn't return a smile.

Looking away, Marta watches a bird soar up in the blue sky. *To be able to take wing and fly, what freedom.*

"Marta, stop dreaming and go get changed. There're chores to be done, and nothing gets done just by wishing it," her father says gruffly.

Turning red, Marta stares down at the ground. She hates being reprimanded, especially over something as silly as wanting to be a bird. If her father ever knew, he would think she was a nitwit. Work and hard work is all he dreams about.

Heading inside, Ada and Marta grab a handful of grapes from the bucket next to the sideboard and change into their farm clothes. Marta looks longingly at her backpack as she steps out of her room; all she wants to do is to snuggle up with *The Black Stallion*, which she just checked out of the school library today.

Outside again, they stand quietly, watching their father putting grease into the chassis of the mower. Marta notes how much older he seems than the parents she sees at the various sport or school activities. He is stooped, with the weight of the world resting on his broad shoulders.

Marta and Ada are his only help on the farm, as their mother is always busy inside doing the canning and cooking when she's not at the nursing home down the street where she works three days a week. Chores are their only connection with their father; he doesn't know what else to do with two young girls. They chop wood, pick rocks, and tend the chickens and cows. They have a football field–sized garden and a roadside vegetable stand from which they sell the overflow produce.

Marta glances at the farm stand, which is directly in front of their house. She hopes she gets to tend it today, as she always smuggles a book out to the stand even under her father's watchful eye. She feels a tug at her heart remembering picking up her new book from the library shelf today and staring into the horse's liquid eyes, eyes that pierced through all her defenses and hit her right in her heart.

Someone must always tend the stand, because their father doesn't use an honor bucket to collect the money from the neighbors and strangers that stop by—he doesn't trust people, and Marta gets it, as their subsistence at least partially depends on how many quarters they collect from the stand over the summer and fall.

Glancing at her sister, Marta frowns at her eager face. Ada also loves minding the farm stand but for a totally different reason than Marta. Ada craves talking to anyone who happens by. Ada will yell, "Get your peaches, corn, and tomatoes," throughout her shift, waving down cars loudly and energetically. Last week she was so far out in the street that their mother had to rush out and pull her back to the yard. She was made to sit in a chair for the rest of the afternoon. Marta, on the other hand, considers customers nothing but a nuisance—an interruption that takes her away from her reading. Today, she is itching to be transported away to another time and place.

Setting the grease gun down, their father nods to Marta and Ada. He states without any fanfare, "Ada, the farm stand. Marta, you and I will feed the chickens."

Marta groans in disappointment. Marta wanted to find out why she sees pain and compassion in those liquid eyes.

Her father stops and frowns, giving her a stare.

Dropping her head, she mutters softly, "Sorry, Papa."

Together they trudge to the chicken coop. As Marta lifts the hods and pours the grain into the feeders, she tries to avoid the cloud of dust that rises from the dry grain. She worries tomorrow in school the kids will smell it or, even worse, spot a shell of grain stuck in her hair. After each delivery, she shakes her head vigorously to dislodge the dust and flecks of cornmeal. Her haircut, a straightforward bowl cut her mother trims each month, is already reason enough for the other kids to tease her; a piece of cornmeal in the unflattering cut would pretty much seal her fate of becoming a target of ridicule. She shivers at the thought of being the center of attention for the wrong reasons.

Pouring the grain from the next hod, the dusty coop fades away. She is now up on the back of her beautiful black stallion. She rides him out in their fields. She sees some of the kids from school hanging on the fence watching her. Their jealousy is palpable. She is surprised when she slides back to the coop. Her father is taking the hod out of her hands. Blinking, she peers around. The chickens are fed but she was out in the meadow on the broad back of the horse the whole time. She feels strange at losing time, but the bubble of joy from her marvelous horse ride stays with her right up to when she snuggles up in her bed reading the book and becomes lost again in the world of Alec and the Black.

This time she is pulled out of it when Ada jabs her shoulder. Again, Marta slowly blinks her eyes, and the desert island melts away and the small, austere bedroom takes its place. Jumping up and down in front of her, Ada yells, "Momma, Marta isn't listening again. She is reading and won't come down for dinner."

"Oh, for heaven's sake, Ada, keep quiet. I am coming." Marta pauses. Worried now, she asks, "How many times did Momma call me?"

"Only three times this time. You're lucky I'm here to wake you up from wherever you were this time."

Marta breathes, "On the Black."

It is near the end of the school year when Marta learns that love can make you do crazy, unexpected things—otherwise unthinkable things like break a pickle jar.

She's moving to middle school next and is sad to think she won't be able to visit her favorite place in the world any longer, the place that has shown her the world: the school library. Mrs. Goodwin promises that the middle school library is even better, but Marta can't believe that. One week before the end of school, it is the last day to check out books, and she picks up *The Black Stallion*. This book has been solely responsible for making this uneventful year fill with wonder. She barely felt the pangs of loneliness or boredom that are her life because she spent so much time feeding seaweed to this horse and clutching wildly on the reins as it thundered down the racetracks. She wants to check it out one last time. But as she approaches the check-out desk, she does the unthinkable. Her hand clenches the book, and in an act of love and desperation and sheer audacity, she slips the paperback into her book bag.

Marta has never stolen anything in her life. Shocked, she stares at her empty hand and thinks, *Who put the book in my bag?*

She glances around. As usual, the other students aren't paying her any attention. For once, Marta is glad to be invisible. Stepping out of the line, she looks around furtively. With shaking hands and a chest so tight she is sure she has completely stopped breathing, she marches through the library doors and out into the hallway. She has no idea where she ever got the nerve.

As soon as the door closes behind her, she sucks in a deep breath, staring down the hall, expecting to see Principal Bauman marching down the hallway to drag her to the office—but no one is around. She exhales and feels a lightness in her being that lets her know everything is going to be okay. She needs that book like she needs oxygen, and the world is okay with what she's done. Or, rather, what the other, daring Marta has done, as she still can't quite believe she is the one who stole the book.

Rushing home a bundle of nerves, she sets about making a treasure box out of an old shoebox and lays *The Black Stallion* into it. She finally has a treasure that is all her own. She keeps the box and book hidden from her mother and others, as the library envelope on the inner page declares her crime too clearly to leave it lying around the bedroom she shares with Ada. A pickle jar in the form of a book.

1977—Brunswick, New Jersey

Marta decides to share her story of her thievery with Kevin, marvels when he doesn't miss a beat, is completely amazed when he jumps up and yells to his mother, "Ma, can we plan to go horseback riding this weekend? Marta has never been before."

"Sure. I don't think we have any plans. Great idea."

Saturday dawns sunny and clear and Marta is on pins and needles. On the drive to the stable, Kevin nudges her out of her trance.

"Remember, you won't be hanging on to the reins for dear life with the old horses we get to rent," he says. "But you never know—maybe you will get the Black to ride." He laughs easily.

Marta's feels a further easing in her chest. Her deep, dark secret has finally been brought out of the darkness and without any repercussions. Life continues to surprise her.

CHAPTER 5: First Kiss

1977—Brunswick, New Jersey

The leaves on the trees are just starting to unfurl in the warmth of early spring and Marta and Kevin are at Rec Park, walking on the trail that loops around the baseball and softball fields. They come to an open area where the sun breaks through the tree cover—a secret meadow where the sun is shining just for them. Kevin is sure they have been here before, but for some reason, it looks different this time. He glances up at the sky and figures the angle of the sun must be what's making it appear so magical. He gazes down at Marta and then stares at their intertwined hands. Perhaps it is love that is making everything shiny and new. He thinks, *When did I become such a sap?*

Suddenly, Marta releases his hand and runs right into the center of the secret meadow. She spins around with her arms flung wide, the sun bouncing off her hair and face.

Standing motionless in the shade, Kevin feels a direct connection to the carefree and happy girl twirling in a shining flash of light. She is expressing his exact emotions; it's as if she glimpsed into his heart, and because words can't capture it properly, she had to express his feelings through motion. He feels a surge of pure joy from her.

Kevin takes off running—not thinking, just doing, entirely connected to her actions. He slows slightly as he nears her, and she flops down on the ground, a slight smile on her lips, her eyes closed. As he stands peering down at her, he realizes she is in her own special world and isn't even aware of him. His connection to her is flowing right through her and on into the sunlight above. He stands for some time, simply gazing at her: light brown hair fanned out around her head; lips curled into a smile, as if she is laughing quietly to herself; cheeks flushed. And suddenly he knows he is going to kiss her.

As *kiss* floats up into his consciousness, Marta's eyes flutter open.

She puts her arm to her forehead to block the sun. Her hazel eyes appear blue now as they reflect the sky above. She squints, crinkling them. Their eyes lock. He drops to his knees. He feels lighter than air; all worries float away. A wild lion suddenly appearing couldn't deter him now.

Placing his hands on either side of her head, he leans into her without touching her. She smells like grass and vanilla. He leans in farther and brushes her lips with his. That seems too soft, so he presses his lips a little harder, and they both shift their heads to complementary angles.

He isn't sure how long they've been kissing, but they are both barely moving or breathing. He pulls back slightly, and Marta whispers, "Cool."

He doesn't need any more encouragement. He lies down beside her and pulls her close to his body. She immediately wraps her arm around his neck and pulls his mouth back to hers.

This kiss is an exploration, a kind of dance—sometimes moving forward, sometimes moving back, searching, reaching, and pulling. His hands become entwined in her hair. He shifts and she fits herself to him. He rolls on top of her, and in the next moment she is on top of him. Time has rolled to a stop; it is bliss.

They both pause and smile shyly at each other. It is one thing to have your eyes closed and let your tongue and lips take over. It is another thing to look at the person you just ran your tongue over and try to talk coherently about the experience. But they don't need words, as they are in complete harmony.

"You're still breathing." Kevin whispers.

"I can't believe it myself. It just happened and now I don't want it to stop," Marta responds, and she quickly covers her mouth with her hand and a crimson blush stains her cheeks. Kevin takes her hand away and leans in, kissing her red cheeks and the corner of her mouth.

After that first kiss, all Kevin has to do is reach out to her and she falls willingly into his arms, melting against him. The sweetness and the yearning she feels each time is like a flame that ignites within her. Life is no longer something she reads about between the pages of her books—it's real. She flips through her journal, reading all the goals she has jotted down over the years. Once written as desperate wishes, now they all feel possible. More than possible, *probable*. Worrying about things doesn't make them happen or not happen. Doing and living is what seems to be the secret. That and a boy who hears you and listens to you and believes in you. A boy that is mystical and sent to Earth to save you.

She can't imagine this magic ever ending, and she knows Kevin can't, either. They discuss their future together, and boy, is it sweet. They continue to walk the paths of Rec Park, talking and dreaming about all the possibilities in front of them.

One day Marta shyly states, "I really want to be a teacher, but not the ordinary kind of teacher. I want to be a Peace Corps teacher and then maybe a writer . . ." Feeling nervous, she takes a well-worn brochure out of her backpack and hands it to him to read.

She picked up this brochure from the school library last year, and the pictures of children sitting in a rustic classroom somewhere in Africa spoke to her. When Mrs. Talikin taught her to read in first grade and in doing so opened a magic window to the world, Marta decided she wanted to be a teacher. Then in third grade she discovered *Harriet the Spy*, she added to her dream of becoming a teacher and decided to be a teacher *and* a writer. She smiles remembering her Harriet rebellion back then.

1971–1972—Brunswick, New Jersey

Kevin is in her third-grade class that year, but she doesn't have the perfect view of his cowlick like she did in first grade. Mrs. Jones has them sitting alphabetically, so Kevin Dixon is in the row behind Marta Carini and off to the left. Still, she watches him out of the corner of her eye. She is too far away to be a direct recipient of his cheerful morning *hi's*, but close enough to feel connected.

As the end of that year draws to a close, Marta finds the paperback with the cover image of a slouchy girl walking down a dangerous-looking sidewalk with her trusty notebook in hand. Marta discovers *Harriet the Spy* nestled in the elementary school library shelf and she starts copying Harriet. She decides she will only eat white bread and tomato sandwiches with mayonnaise, like Harriet.

"It must be white bread that is as soft as cotton and smooshes together when eaten," she pleads with her parents. She refrains from adding that her mother's homemade bread could easily be mistaken for cardboard.

"My sourdough bread is just fine," her mother insists. "If you squint at it, it almost looks white."

"It *must* be Wonder Bread," Marta whines. "That's what Harriet eats."

"Enough, Marta!" her father finally snaps. "If you want the same bread your friend eats, you can buy it yourself and throw away your own money, not mine."

He doesn't expect that Marta's conviction will extend to using her hard-earned pin money, religiously saved from the tips customers give her when she helps her father deliver newspapers every Saturday and Sunday morning, to buy the bread. But then, he also doesn't realize how important Harriet is to his daughter.

Marta marches to the local grocery store and with her own money buys the blue-and-red-dotted bag of Wonder Bread. She eats Harriet sandwiches for the summer between third and fourth grade, but when the garden stops producing plump, juicy tomatoes, Marta stops her *rebellion* (as her parents call it)—she can't afford store-bought tomatoes *and* Wonder Bread—and begrudgingly goes back to eating peanut butter on sourdough bread.

While the food regimen falls by the wayside, Marta continues following in Harriet's footsteps with her spy activities. She buys a notebook with pink paper, and she writes down everything she sees. She fancies herself a great observer of people. She sees the friendships and the bullying and writes it down and dissects it, which helps get her thoughts and feelings out and shared, even if only on the page.

Marta emulates Harriet's observational skills, and fortunately her writings don't get her in trouble like Harriet's do. They are an essential part of her growing up. Her entries often conclude with her noting the many differences between herself and other kids; journaling helps ground her and clear the negative voices from of her head, at least for a bit. Marta is different from the other kids in school, but laying out that fact on her pretty pink paper makes it less worrisome.

1977—Brunswick, New Jersey

Holding her breath, she watches Kevin. She could picture herself there in that place shown on the brochure, pumping water from the well and helping the children learn their letters until the world of reading opened for them as it had for her in first grade. All this would give her fodder for her stories she would write one day. She knew she had found a path that would take her away from the farm and out into the world. Last year, she wasn't sure she would ever be brave enough to pursue any of this, but now, with Kevin, it seems possible, and she wants to conquer the world.

After scanning the brochure, Kevin pauses just a beat and then bursts out, "Cool! Hell yeah. That is too perfect. We get to see the world and save the world all at the same time."

Marta releases her breath and laughs at his exuberance. She was hesitant to share this dream with Kevin, worried he would not want to do it with her. She should have known he would. He is the brave, adventurous one. She feels a surge of pride that it's she who thought of something so crazy in the first place.

Then Kevin stops dead in his tracks. "What a minute. My parents did this, too. Oh man! They will love this. Wait until you hear their stories about digging wells in Kenya and setting up schools. I've heard them all before, but now I may really listen instead of tuning them out. It does sound pretty cool." He reaches for Marta's hand and flings it high in the air, and they run over to their favorite rock to sit and plan.

"Okay," Marta says thoughtfully, "so it will only be my parents who will be against this. That could be manageable. We will go to college first, right? Remember what Mr. Wallace told us in sixth grade?" She feels exposed all of sudden and ducks her head down, unable to meet Kevin's eyes. What if he doesn't think she's good enough for college?

Kevin reaches over, takes her chin, and raises her face. She is forced to meet his twinkling eyes.

"I don't remember anything he said about such stuff. Remember, I wasn't the teacher's pet like someone I know." He gives her a teasing wink.

She bats his hand away from her face. "I was not." She fake-scowls at him.

"Oh, you definitely were, big time. But forget about that—what did he say about college?"

Marta can't believe Kevin could forget this moment, as it is seared into her own memory. "But you *must* remember what he said—don't you? He told us if we do well in school, we can get a scholarship or something to pay for college. That changed everything for me; that's when I got serious about school."

Kevin playfully punches her arm. "Really? You seemed pretty serious before that."

"I can picture Mr. Wallace exactly, sitting on his desk with his feet propped up on his chair," she says, undeterred. "He said, 'Education helps you make sense of the world and where you belong in it.

It is the great equalizer and makes anything possible. It can lift you up and out of poverty and show you new horizons.' I was so embarrassed because he was looking right at me. I didn't know until that moment that he knew I was poor and stuff," she finishes sheepishly.

Kevin drops his joking tone. "Hey, that is an awesome thing to tell kids. Honestly, I wish I was paying attention that day. He was a great teacher."

"So, I'm hoping I can get that free ride Mr. Wallace talked about back in sixth grade," Marta confides softly. "That's the goal. You can do that, too, right?"

Looking momentarily worried, Kevin then proclaims confidently, "Damn straight. I will buckle down. Grades don't start counting until high school anyway, right? No problem." He leans over and kisses Marta. "Besides, with you by my side, I can do anything."

Marta's imagination races on. "We should adopt some kids after a couple of years but also have some of our own."

Kevin nods in agreement. "We can stay in Africa or wherever until our oldest turns five or six, then return to the States and settle down. You know, buy a house and all that stuff. Wow, that sounds so cool."

For the first time in her life, Marta feels strong and confident. With Kevin cheering her on, she is the braver, more adventurous version of herself. She can see herself laughing and enjoying herself as she makes her way through life. What a wonder to not feel small and timid but instead tall and brave. Life is good, and she can breathe.

They see their whole life in front of them: traveling the world, fighting for justice, and creating world peace. They talk and dream and plan—right up to the day Kevin and his family move to Vermont, shattering both their dreams and their hearts.

CHAPTER 6: High School

1977–1981—Brunswick, New Jersey

The day before Kevin leaves, they are sitting on their favorite rock in their secret meadow. Both are somber and shell-shocked.

He reaches into his pocket, takes her hand, and turns her palm upward. He places in it a beautifully smooth, oval-shaped, gray granite rock.

"This is a worry stone," he says. "I'm scared you may forget to breathe one day and drop dead. So, this is to help you remember to breathe and to never stop listening and dancing to music."

She turns the stone over and sees that the word *Breathe* is etched into the river stone with shaky lines. Gazing up at him, her heart is in her eyes.

She quietly says, "Thank you."

"I used my dad's tools," he says self-consciously. "I know it doesn't look so good, but the rock was really hard."

She frowns—at his self-doubt, and at their impending separation. "I love it. I love you. You leaving is just . . . unimaginable. I don't really have words for it. All I know is I'm not sure I want to continue breathing. I can't believe it's over." She trips and stumbles over the words.

"This is not the end," he says quickly. "Don't worry about that. We'll write; we can talk on the phone. I know your dad is strict about the phone, but I will see if I can call you, maybe like once a month."

Gazing into Kevin's earnest eyes, Marta almost believes him.

The next day, Marta sits at her desk with a blank piece of paper set in front of her. She chews her lip, struggling to find words to capture what she is feeling. A single tear drops onto the page. There are no words for the blackness that has enveloped her. She can smell it, and it smells rotten, like when one of their potato bins has rotted during the winter. She folds her arms over the top of her desk and drops her head in their cradle. The hollowness is a physical pain, and it feels as if her insides are being scraped out by a metal spoon. She feels her body start to dry and wither as she curls inward, no longer connected to her physical self. She is a leaf in autumn that has dried little by little as the days shorten and now is tumbling down from its perch high in the oak tree. She is falling through time and space. She thinks she is awake but can't open her eyes or move.

She stops fighting and gives in to the floating sensation.

Now it is almost peaceful being hollow and dry. As her shell of a body floats through the cool air, she peers down to Earth. She sees a vista filled with skyscrapers and spots the Statue of Liberty out on a golden harbor. No emotion breaks through her shell—no patriotic swelling of pride, no love of country. She is just glad the pain is gone.

She continues, traveling over highways with cars that look like ants crawling along them, then to forests and over towns with their white steeples jutting up into the halcyon sky. There is a quickening as she approaches the vast Atlantic Ocean. She smells the bracing salt air and hears waves crashing.

Turning westward, she lowers toward the earth. She tries to guess where she is, as her trip could have taken minutes or days;

she is no longer in a realm where time is linear. Then she spots Kevin's family car in the driveway of a gray and white ranch house. Of course, this is where her leaf would take her: to Vermont.

She crackles in her dry shell, trying to emerge, but is unable to break from the confines of the dead leaf. No movement from within is possible. All movement comes from the outside, from the wind. She drifts on the air currents, bobbing up and down, staring at what must be Kevin's new house. She sees a blond girl come out of the house next to Kevin's ranch. The girl walks idly down her driveway toward her mailbox. She glances at Kevin's house several times during the short walk, and Marta feels a kick to her gut—no longer devoid of all emotion, it seems.

From far off she hears, "Marta, dinner!"

Marta's leaf pulls back and reconnects, shifting into flesh and blood, and her errant body settles back into her chair at her desk. Her heart starts to beat loudly, and now that she is back in her own body, she feels as if her heart is taking up a little more space in her hollowness than it did before her journey.

Lifting her head slowly, she is confused by the sensations she's experiencing now that she's returned to her body. She blinks. Her eyes drop to the blank piece of paper; her teardrop has dried but she can still see the slight mar on the white paper where it fell. She shakes her head and wearily stands. She stretches her body, as it is stiff from being locked into an unforgiving shell. She wonders how long she has been gone. Walking quietly out of her bedroom, she heads to the dinner table, not sure she will be able to eat a thing.

After a good night's sleep, Marta sits before the blank paper and tries again, hoping for no repeat trip to Vermont. Today, the words tumble out of her. She decides her strange leaf dream of the blond girl next door was just her imagination conjuring up her worst fears, so isn't going to ever tell Kevin about it. She doesn't want Kevin to think she has gone completely crazy after only one day without him.

Ada watches intently from her bed as Marta composes a letter:

Kevin,

I know you may not even be to Vermont yet, but I had to write. God, I miss you so much. It's as if a part of me has died. I am going through life but I'm not really there. The good news is I really am not so worried or scared about going to high school. You know me, normally I would be crazy with worry. But when the worst thing has already happened, you don't worry about the other stuff.

I can hear your voice in my head, telling me to breathe, and I carry my Breathe stone in my pocket wherever I go. It helps. I feel close to you when I hold it.

I just needed to write, as it makes this whole thing real. I picture my letter floating up to Vermont, finding you, and you reading my words, and for that moment, we are connected.

Love you, miss you,

Marta

Four days later, Ada comes running into their room and delivers a slightly wrinkled letter to Marta as she sits reading a book. Marta tears it open and reads it hungrily.

September 3, 1977

Hi there,

I was so happy when I got your letter. I knew you were going to write, as you are so good with words, but you must have mailed it before we even started the drive. I had to unpack a bunch of boxes to even find pens and paper, never mind envelopes and stamps. It is a disaster up here.

When you said something died inside, you know what I picture? You and me going through life with an arm cut off and no one can else can see that we are missing a limb, so no one else knows the pain we are in.

Oh, here is the other thing I picture or hope for. One day when you are rubbing the stone, it makes me magically appear and we can be together even if it is only in a dream. I think my mom read me a story about a genie when I was little, so I think it can really happen.

So keep rubbing, but don't rub the word off the stone. I am not sure how deep I made the cut.

High school starts next week and I'm kinda nervous. But you are right, the worst thing already happened, and the world can't pile more shit on us by making high school miserable, can it? Hope not. My mom is trying to cheer me up, too. She is letting me mope about and is making my favorite meals. So, I may get to eat hamburgers with bacon and pickles for the rest of my days. I'd trade all the baconburgers in the world if I could be with you.

Miss you lots,

Kevin

Tucking the letter back into the envelope, she puts it in her desk drawer, pointedly looking at Ada to ensure she knows it is off-limits. Ada rolls her eyes and looks away quickly.

Tomorrow is the first day of high school, and suddenly Marta doesn't feel as nervous and frightened as she did before getting Kevin's letter. Having him is like having a secret weapon protecting her from the scary things out in the world. She needs to just wait, and they will be together again one day.

At school on the first day, Marta sees Nancy and Pat holding hands in the hallway, and she feels a pang of jealousy. Although they make a cute couple, it seems so unfair that she can't do that with Kevin. Nancy and Pat started dating this past summer when Kevin and she were in their own little cocoon. High school would be wonderful if Kevin was with her.

Marta writes to Kevin and tells him about Pat and Nancy, and Kevin writes back that he is happy for them. But he doesn't have to see them snuggling and holding hands everywhere he turns.

The weekend after school starts, Marta and Ada are at Kmart with their mother buying the folders and notebooks she found out she needs. Marta wanders into the perfume aisle, even though she knows her mother will never buy her perfume. She sighs dejectedly. She is worried she may sometimes smell like the stinky chickens she has to feed morning and night. She is tired of trying to rid herself of that foulness before she heads to the bus.

Picking up the bottle of Jovan Musk, the bottle feels smooth and sleek in her hand. She casually scans the store and then, without a conscious thought, slips her hand into the pocket of her windbreaker, sliding the bottle deep inside the pocket.

She rushes away, a lump growing in her throat. She thinks it is *The Black Stallion* all over again. She wonders if she is becoming that brave version of herself, or if maybe she is just a klepto. Boy, she hopes she is turning into someone braver, but who knows. She writes to Kevin to see what he thinks.

As usual, his reply makes her laugh at all her worries.

Hi Marta,

I can't believe it. I'm going to be married to a hardened criminal! I'm totally joking. I can't imagine that the store would even miss something so small. Your secret is safe with me and I get it. I really do.

Hey, I kinda like cross-country. We get to do like two-mile runs through the woods and stuff. It's fun. Sometimes I run by myself and that is cool. I think of you. Other times I run with Frank and Pete and they seem pretty cool. I was thinking about that Buddhist saying I told you my father used to tell me. Remember when we went to the falls instead of church? Well, now I use it like a mantra in my head when I'm running. It makes the miles fly by. It was: All the things that truly matter—beauty, love, creativity, joy, and inner peace—arise from beyond the mind. Do you remember?

Love,

Kevin

Sitting at her desk, Marta is working her way through *Romeo and Juliet*, when she hears the phone ring.

"Marta, phone. And you won't believe who it is!" Ada calls gleefully from down the hallway.

Marta jumps up and runs out her door. When she gets to Ada, she snatches the phone from her hand and presses the receiver to her ear. "Hello?"

"Hi there," Kevin's voice says through the phone. "It's me."

"Oh my. What a great surprise." Her body hums with excitement. "How are you? It's so good to hear your voice. I mean—it's great to talk to you."

"Same here. What were you doing?"

"Just reading my English assignment. It's *Romeo and Juliet*. I couldn't believe it when Mrs. Shapiro assigned it. I was going to write to you about it. I think the universe is trying to kill me. Can you imagine having to discuss and write about doomed love . . . ahh, I mean a doomed couple? I may just lose it."

"The only thing that will kill you is you may be bored to death reading old stuffy Shakespeare from a million years ago. Yuck! I can't imagine." Kevin chuckles.

She laughs. "It isn't that bad. I kinda like it, except for the dying part that I know is coming." She relaxes into the phone. It is just like they never parted. She feels a comfort wash over her, as she always does when she's with him.

"You always were the smart one," he says. "So, how is field hockey going? I know you signed up for it just to get out of chores, but it sounds cool."

"Ugh! It's a lot harder than I thought. I may need to switch to cross-country next year like you're doing. That sounds much more my speed. I don't like checking girls, and for the life of me, I don't get offsides."

Kevin snorts. "It's only been a month, give it time. You'll get it, and I bet you'll be good at it. But seriously, cross-country is pretty cool. We get to run through the woods. Oh, I told you that in my letter. Did you remember that expression that my dad always quoted?"

"I was getting ready to write you back," she says. "Yes, I love your dad's expression. Sometimes when I'm nervous about something, I take a deep breath, rub the rock you gave me, and repeat those words. It really seems to help." She blushes, worrying that she is sharing too many of her worries, but then thinks, *Who else can I tell if not Kevin?*

"Oh, that's cool." And he sounds as if he really does think it's cool.

Marta lets out the breath she's holding. *Okay, he doesn't think I'm a total worrywart. How many more crutches do I need to get through life?*

Her father gets up from his chair in the TV room and walks over to the kitchen. He stands there, looking pointedly at Marta.

She gives him a frown and quick shake of her head, feeling emboldened with Kevin on the other line.

Her father clears his throat. "It's been long enough now."

Marta knows she isn't brave enough to argue any further.

"Hey, Kevin, my dad is making me hang up. I'm really sorry."

"No problem," he says quickly. "I know your dad doesn't let you talk on the phone long, even when it isn't him paying. I'll try to call you again around Christmas. I'll have my grades by then, so we can compare and make sure we're on track for our full ride, right?"

Glaring up at her dad, she says with a spark of defiance in her eyes, "That is the plan. Hey, I'm so happy you called. Bye."

"Bye, Marta."

With a pout, she starts to slam down the phone—but ends up placing it back in the receiver with the slightest of thumps. She feels a giddiness in her chest that even her father's stern demeanor can't dissipate. She gets up slowly and, in a trance, walks slowly back to her room with her arms wrapped around her body.

Ada is sitting on her bed, looking as though she may burst.

"What did he say? Does he miss you?" she blurts out.

"None of your business," Marta replies coolly.

Ada's face falls and Marta relents.

"He is great. It was super to hear his voice. I really was worried I might have forgotten what he sounded like. But he sounded just like Kevin. Phew!"

Over Christmas, Marta mails Kevin a package with a little R2-D2 figurine. Kevin wrote about *Star Wars* in one of his letters—how he and his brother saw the movie and he absolutely flipped over it. Kevin wrote that Marta had to see it, too, because he couldn't marry someone that didn't love *Star Wars*. So she took Ada to see it, to see what all the fuss was about. She thought it was kinda cool, but not quite as cool as Kevin did. Ada liked it more than Marta did.

She didn't share her opinion with Kevin and was just happy when he absolutely loved his Christmas gift. And he mailed her a present, too: a bottle of Jovan Musk perfume. He was so cute explaining in the card that this was to keep her from following the path of crime she was on.

God, he is so funny.

Snapping the book on her lap closed, Marta tries to keep the tears from falling, but she can't. Her eyes blur and the tears stream down her cheeks. She was so worried about reading *Romeo and Juliet* but got through that reading assignment with nary a tear. She had no such worries about *Great Expectations* when it was assigned after the New Year because she had no idea what it was about.

My God. The universe really is out to get me. This is a clear warning that I may be on my way to becoming poor Miss Havisham. I can see myself becoming a crazy spinster, sitting around in my wedding dress with all the clocks stopped. Did time stop for me the day Kevin left Brunswick? Maybe . . .

Brushing the tears from her cheeks, she struggles to rein in her wild emotions. She isn't going to become Miss Havisham. Kevin didn't jilt her; he is still her one and only. Shaking her head to dispel her crazy vision works to make some reason return. After a bit of time, she concludes that the lesson from *Great Expectations* is she needs to make sure she isn't sitting around pining for Kevin; instead she needs to continue living her life to avoid sharing Miss Havisham's fate. *But how do I do that?*

She wipes away the last of her tears and takes out her journal. Flipping it open, Marta is dismayed when it falls open to her entry about their first kiss. Marta rolls her eyes up to the ceiling but stifles a grin at the perversity of the gods. She takes a deep breath and scans the page and is pleasantly surprised when it doesn't make her cry. She touches her lips and can almost taste his lips on hers. *How sweet.*

Marta works hard to move forward and focus on her goals, no stopped clocks for her. She needs to be ready for when Kevin and she are together again in four short years. As the months go by, the tinge of worry in the back of her mind grows a little. *What if I or Kevin or both move forward and the other is left behind or takes a different path and we never reconnect.* She dashes off a quick note in her journal:

March 12, 1978—I love Kevin with all my heart.

Staring at those words on the paper, a vision of her older self, sitting in a small cottage on the coast of Maine, comes into view. She drifts to another place and time . . .

> . . . *I am in a small cottage on the coast. Every day I don my wetsuit and swim in the icy-cold September water. Unbeknownst to me, up the road, Kevin has a furniture workshop in a cottage overlooking the ocean that I swim past every day. One morning I misjudge the shore and swim into the barnacle-covered rocks that cover the Maine coast-line. Kevin sees a swimmer in distress from his window and runs out of his workshop, but to no avail. I slam headlong into the rocks, getting a nasty cut on my head and possibly a slight concussion. Kevin runs down the path to the water, pulling on his rubber fishing boots as he goes, and is able*

to pull me out. I have cut my hands and feet on the sharp rocks; I'm bleeding and dazed.

He carries me up to his old, rustic workshop, lays me down in front of a crackling fire, and starts to strip me out of my wetsuit, as I'm starting to tremble from the cold. I try to figure out what's happened but am very confused (concussion, remember?), so when he asks what my name is, I reply, "Tata," which is a family nickname. Kevin thinks I've said "Tara," and I'm too out of it to correct him. Kevin calls his neighbor Jennifer, who is a nurse, and she comes over and checks me out. She deems the cut on my forehead minor but says I need to be kept awake due to the chance of concussion. Jennifer refers to Kevin throughout her ministering as "Dix," because most of the folks around his town call him Captain Dixon. Captain of a boat—cool, right?

This mix-up is the perfect equation for identity confusion, which results in me and Kevin talking without realizing who the other is. We spend the afternoon at his workshop, sipping tea and eating sandwiches. We feel a strong tug of attraction and a connection. He passes me plates and cups at certain points, and whenever our hands touch, the shock and surprise of the connection shows on our faces.

We each realize who the other is when I take out the Breathe rock from my pocket and Kevin recognizes it immediately. We realize the undeniable attraction we have for each other and find it has only intensified over the years.

Marta slowly comes back to the present and her lips part in a wide grin. Her daydreams are back. They've been lost to her ever since Kevin left. She missed both Kevin and her daydreams over these past eight months. She breaks into a smile. At least one important part that had left her has returned.

✧ ✧ ✧

Rushing into the room, Marta quickly throws her field hockey uniform into her bag. She frantically looks around, yelling, "Ada, do you know where my rock is? I can't find it."

When Ada doesn't respond, Marta spins and glares at her. With her hands on her hips, she snaps, "Ada, come on—this is a big game, and you know it's my lucky charm."

"Your lucky charm for a stupid hockey game?" Ada fires back. "I remember when it was your connection to all things Kevin. What happened to that?"

Stopping short, Marta's eyes narrow.

Ada relents. "It's in your top desk drawer. I found it under your bed the other day and thought you might need it—you know, for your big game or something like that."

Yanking open the drawer, Marta takes out the rock. Looking wistful, she rubs it absentmindedly. She shoves the rock into her bag, and as she does, she spots an envelope on her desk. Turning, she glares over at Ada. Ada shrugs.

"I'm late already," Marta blurts out. "Nancy is going to pick me up any minute. I'll read it later."

Frowning, Ada raises her eyebrows at her.

"Okay, all right." Marta sits down, rips open the letter, and quickly scans it. Then she tosses it back down on her desk and, with a quick good-bye over her shoulder, rushes out with her bag.

Hearing the car door slam, Ada slowly gets up and takes the letter in her hand. She can't believe the callousness Marta has been showing lately toward Kevin's letters and the rock. Ada remembers how careful and secretive she used to be with both. Clutching the rock whenever she felt sad or scared, reading the letters over and over again. Ada had to be so careful when she snuck them from Marta's treasure box and read them for herself. Now Marta loses the rock regularly and leaves the letters out on her desk, clearly not caring that Ada will read them.

Shaking her head, Ada has become Marta's conscience, bugging her when it has been months since she's written Kevin, worrying on her behalf when Kevin's letters also have large gaps between them.

Sitting at her sister's desk, Ada carefully unfolds the letter. She presses it flat and reads:

October 16, 1981

Hi,

How are you? I'm sorry it has been a while. I've been really focused on cross-country this year. Senior year is great. I'm one of the most experienced out there and, like you said in your last letter, being captain has a ton of responsibilities. I can't believe you are co-captain of field hockey. That is so cool. I remember when you were thinking you were going to quit. Turns out doing all those sports over the years was good practice to get you ready for field hockey. Oh, Mark and I went to see Raiders of the Lost Ark. It was soooo good. You will love it. Take Ada and go see it. It is funny with lots of action and stuff. Almost as good as Star Wars, but you know that will always be my favorite, but Raiders is close.

Love,

Kevin

Setting the letter down, Ada feels slightly deflated. Their exchanges have not only been fewer and fewer recently, but now they no longer have the longing and the connection that their letters held those first years after Kevin moved. *Can someone fall out of love through letters?* Ada was sure Kevin and Marta had a magical love. She had watched it take hold of them both during that first enchanted year. They'd seemed cloaked in a glow that kept them in a special cocoon no one else could touch or disturb. After Kevin moved away, Ada watched as Marta disappeared into herself for a while, lifting herself from her despair only when she received a call or a letter from Kevin. *It was so romantic.*

Ada was glad when Marta slowly reemerged over the weeks, months, and tears. But instead of refocusing on Kevin, she turned her attention toward school and her goals. Performance and perfection became her primary desires, and while Kevin remained important to her, he wasn't everything to her anymore. Ada tried to hold them together by cajoling Marta and reminding her how important he once was to her, and that worked occasionally. Marta would finally force herself to sit down and pen a quick letter to Kevin, but sometimes she can't even be bothered to put it in an envelope and mail it—she'd leave that to Ada.

Ada's fingers itch to dash off a *real* love letter to Kevin. She knows just what she would say that would remind him, too, of their love. She thinks that maybe they need to see each other again and that will rekindle the love they had. She's determined not to let their love die.

April of senior year, Ada gets her wish. Kevin's father is taking the kids to Disney World for April vacation, and on their way, they plan to stop in for a visit.

The Dixons pull up in front of Marta's house in their old Subaru, and the family tumbles out. Standing off to the side of the driveway, Marta feels the sweat trickle down her armpits. It is unusually warm for mid-April. She smiles shyly at Kevin, who appears to be close to six feet tall and has longish wavy hair, still the color of sunshine. He is wearing cut-off jean shorts and a dark T-shirt. Marta has trouble connecting this tall, lanky almost-man to the picture she has of Kevin from Rec Park during their summer together. She frantically rubs her finger against the Breathe stone. She stopped carrying it with her every day a long time ago, but today she retrieved it from her treasure box. She hopes it helps her nerves. As Kevin approaches, she takes it out of her pocket and holds it out to him awkwardly. She is not sure what she means to do with it.

"It really helped me stay calm and breathe," she tells him.

"I'm glad," he says. "But I bet you don't need it anymore. Boy, you've changed."

"So have you. I'm not sure I would have recognized you. I didn't know you were so tall. When did that happen?" Marta says, fidgeting with the rock.

Both stand awkwardly, looking at each other and then glancing back at their families, who are standing in the driveway.

Finally, everyone else heads inside to use the bathroom and have iced tea, and Marta breathes a sigh of relief. The air seems a little less thick now that they don't have an audience. Glancing toward the house, she sees Ada's face in the window. Smiling, she turns toward Kevin—trying, for Ada, to connect with this boy who once meant the world to her. She isn't sure what's happened, as a part of her is still clinging to that love from so long ago, but another part of her is looking into the future, itching to start her life, and she can't see where this boy fits in anymore.

They gaze into each other's eyes and a flicker of their love rekindles—but they both quickly turn away. They are silent. They struggle to talk about the past, and they don't talk about their future.

A short time later, the Dixons pack up their old Subaru, and then Kevin is gone for a second time. After the Dixons' car pulls away, Marta's eyes cloud in pain, and she walks slowly around the back of her house. She doesn't want to go in, as she knows she will have to explain to Ada what just happened and isn't sure herself how to characterize it. *It is all so confusing.* She loves Kevin, but she isn't sure the boy who was just here was the Kevin she loves.

Wandering aimlessly, Marta glances up at the large maple tree in the center of the backyard. Its leaves have started to unfurl in the warmth of the spring, starting their process of rebirth. She remembers Rec Park this same time of year. She reaches up and plucks a new, green leaf from a low branch. It is soft and supple and seems to be bursting with potential as it starts its new life, taking sunshine from the sky and converting it into food for the mighty tree. She scrunches up her face, trying to remember Mrs. Jacob's science lesson on this topic. *Photosynthesis* pops into her head.

Twirling the leaf in her fingertips, she remembers her strange and magical journey as a leaf all those years ago when Kevin first moved away. She metamorphosed into a dried-up old leaf—no potential, no purpose. Staring at the fresh leaf in her hand, questions fly through her head. Has she transformed into something new and different over these four years? Did she *want* to grow and change, or did it simply happen? Did she have any more choice in starting anew than the leaf in her hand?

She recalls her fear of turning into Miss Havisham and thinks, *Maybe I did will this change.* She lets the leaf drop, wondering if this new leaf contains any part of the withered leaves that dropped from this very tree just last season. Has she traveled through the cold hard winter and through time and space to become something new?

Pressing a hand to her heart, she feels something click within her. *Maybe I can't go back in time, but maybe time is a circle like the seasons, and I will be able to come back to Kevin like the leaf comes back to the tree each spring. Someday, maybe.* Remembering her day-dream of the Maine cottage, she thinks, *It won't take that long, will it?*

CHAPTER 7: Goals

1982–1987—Brunswick, New Jersey

The rain is coming down sideways when Marta sloshes off the bus in May. Not wanting to get any wetter, she almost walks past her old silver mailbox but at the last second veers toward it and, with a catch in her breath, slowly opens it.

She immediately sees the large packet wedged inside. As she slowly pulls it out, she spots the Rutgers University emblem in the corner. She is glad Ada went over to a friend's house after school.

She knows by listening to all the other kids talk about their school letters that a big packet is good news, while just a regular-sized envelope is not. *Step one*, she thinks. She will have to open it to see if she's gotten the scholarship she needs.

Walking into her small house, she hurriedly takes off her wet jacket and shoes. She heads straight to her and Ada's room. Carefully, she tears open the envelope—then she waits. This envelope holds the answers to her long-held hopes and dreams, and she is too scared to look.

After a few more minutes of inaction, her fingers start itching and her nerves are stretched to the breaking point. She pulls out several pages. The first one says, *Congratulations, you've been selected for the class of 1986 at Rutgers.* She scans it and shuffles through to the letter with the Financial Scholarship header.

Quickly reading it, she hugs it to her chest. A tear slowly works its way down her cheek. She did it. Just as Mr. Wallace explained she could, all those years ago.

Letting her breath out in a long exhale, she relaxes. It feels like the first time she's been able to actually catch her breath and fill her lungs completely since starting the college application process a year ago.

A tinge of worry worms its way up her spine, and she straightens, as if a ramrod-straight posture will keep all little worries at bay. She pictures the Olympic gymnast, Nadia, and her worried frown, and just like her, Marta struggles to hold on to the joy and enjoy this victory. Despite her best efforts, she starts wondering and worrying, *What will college be like? Will I be able to do the work? What happens after college?*

And then, like it always does, up pops the thought of Kevin. She wonders if he is getting acceptance letters, too.

At dinner that evening, Marta announces, "I was accepted to Rutgers and got a full scholarship—that means college won't cost any money."

Marta's mother beams. "That is what you wanted, right? That's good. Isn't it, Ernest?"

Marta's father stares at her without a hint of a smile but he nods in agreement. "Yes, that's good. You're a smart girl. Work hard and do the right thing, and you will succeed."

Ada adds enthusiastically, "Marta's going to make the best teacher ever. You've read every book there is, so you will be great."

Marta's father interjects, "Teacher? No, Marta. Money runs the world, so go out and earn the money. Business. That's the answer."

Marta looks down at her plate, no longer hungry or excited. She glances sidelong at her dad as he continues eating. She gulps in a big inhale—and then, in a rush, says, "Dad, I really want to be a teacher."

She pictures the rustic classroom somewhere in Africa and, with a slight hitch in her voice, adds, "They make money, too."

"Marta, you have a good head on your shoulders," her dad says sternly. "You worked hard. Now you have to make the world take notice. Business is where you can make real serious money. It will change your life. Just like you want."

She's surprised her father understands that this is what she is striving for. She certainly has never shared that with anyone, except for Kevin. How does he know she wants a different life from her current one?

Maybe he's right. Maybe she *should* go after the money. That's the only way to guarantee she'll get a different life. But what about her dream?

Ada whispers, "You would make a great teacher."

That evening, when she and Ada are both lying in their beds, Marta shares, "I think I *am* going to do business. It will make me a lot more money than teaching. That way I can help you go to college, too."

"Don't you dare do it for me," Ada snaps. "I'm not going to college. I'm not like you, Marta. I may go become a medical assistant or something, like Patty is. Or Piggly Wiggly has a management course you can take on the weekends and then you can make a ton more money as an assistant manager or something. Mr. Barton says I just need to punch in for my shift on time and he'll put me in for it."

"Ada, that is just him trying to get you to come in on time at Piggly Wiggly," Marta scoffs.

Ada's bright smile dims.

"Sorry," Marta says hastily, "I didn't mean it. I'm sure you would make a great manager—it's just that you could be so much more, and I can help if I go into business and start making tons of money. Okay? So, no matter what, start focusing on school and getting your grades up."

Ada shakes her head slightly. "I'm not you, Marta," she mutters. "I don't have all these goals and dreams. I just want to be happy."

As Marta drifts off to sleep, she thinks, *I want to be happy, too.*

Walking into the first session of her last management organization class, Marta immediately notices Steve. He has short-cropped brown hair, a nice smile, and sad brown eyes. He is definitely not someone she has seen during her years in business school.

She sits down next to him with a friendly "Hi."

He responds in a rush, looking worried: "Hi, I'm Steve. I'm a sixth-year architecture student. I just need a business class to graduate, hoping this one isn't too tough. I got the professor to waive the prerequisites, but now I'm a little worried."

Marta smiles knowingly. "Don't worry. If you have half a brain, you should be fine. I heard Professor Galbraith isn't too hard. I can help fill in any gaps."

He returns her smile. His face has nice angles and a cute nose.

As they grin at each other, a vision of Kevin crosses Marta's mind. He is never far from her consciousness, no matter how carefully she has worked to construct her new and exciting life; he has come along for the journey. It is a comfort, like a warm blanket that is always there to slip into when she needs something familiar.

Over the past four years, she has built a life that is far from her parents' farm. She doesn't think of them much, although she does have pangs of guilt about Ada, who is still working at the Piggly Wiggly. Mr. Barton was true to his word: Ada got to go to their weekend management course, and now she is the evening manager. She married her high school sweetheart. They live in a small, cheap apartment near the farm, and while they seem happy, Marta wants so much more for her little sister.

On her second official date with Steve, Marta playfully grabs his hand, turns it over in hers with his palm facing up, and traces her finger over the surface. It is as smooth as can be. He has clearly never baled hay or chopped wood before.

Marta is relieved, as she wants someone whose back won't become stooped as they grow old together.

"Ever picked rocks before?" she asks jokingly.

"What?" He screws his face up. "No—are you mixing me up with a geologist?"

"Ever repair a fence?"

"Absolutely not. I'm not sure what end of a screwdriver to use most of the time." He chuckles. Then he turns serious. "If you're looking for Mr. Fix-it, that's not me. I know people think architects should be able to build stuff, but not me. I can create something and get it down on paper, but you wouldn't want me to build it."

Marta nods, satisfied; things are falling into place. Steve is serious and focused. He, too, is from a small town and hopes to land a good job that will give him long-term financial security. With him, she senses a compatibility that she's never had with any prior boyfriends. Steve is safe, not one to act impulsively; he will be steady, and that is what one needs to help keep the world a little at bay.

On a beautiful May day, Marta crosses that huge stage at the Prudential Center to receive her business degree. She remembers that rainy day four years ago when she got that envelope. It has all gone by so fast.

She has learned in these last four years to smile brightly even when she is worrying or has too many routines running through her head. Daydreams, which helped her pass the time doing chores when she was young, have continued to help her through college as she's worked to build a shield that keeps others from seeing her as she is. She's become adept at having others see the person she wants them to see. Someone a little braver and a little freer than she is inside.

She's not as happy as she would like to be, but she knows you can't have it all.

Walking across the stage, she sends out a special thanks to Mr. Wallace for showing her a way up and out. Mr. Wallace didn't just teach his students, he showed them how to use what they learned to become something they didn't know they could be.

With her hand clutching her diploma, she makes two silent promises to herself: *I will continue to work hard, so that one day I'll be able to throw away all the pickle jars I stumble upon in life,* she vows. *And for Kevin, I will try to hold on to some of the sparkle he inspired in me. Even if I never sparkle as brightly as I did in 1977, I'll keep trying.*

It doesn't dawn on her at this time that these could turn out to be competing promises.

Sitting on the periphery of the classroom in Sorella Corporation's training facility, Marta feels the sweat begin to gather against the new blouse she bought on clearance. It is the first day of training for the rotational program Marta was accepted into, and she nervously inspects all the bright, shiny new hires and wonders how she will fit in.

A girl rushes in late, grabbing the one open seat in the room—right next to Marta. Marta is relieved, as she was worrying she might end up the odd man out if they had to work in pairs or teams.

The girl flips her wild hair away from her face and gives Marta a bright smile. "Hi, I'm Tracy. Have we started?"

"No, not yet." Marta glances at her watch and immediately feels bad for being *judgy.*

Tracy lets out a loud, dramatic breath of air and stage whispers, "Phew! I could not figure out where I was going and wandered around the building for like ten minutes. This place is huge."

Marta nods and glances around, only to see multiple pairs of curious eyes pointed in her direction. She wishes someone a little quieter and more punctual had taken the open seat. She checked out the classroom yesterday to ensure she wouldn't be late like this Tracy girl.

When she and Tracy are paired up later in class, she lets out a quiet sigh.

But Tracy is friendly and outgoing, and for the first two weeks of class she works hard to break through Marta's reserve. Like Kevin did years ago, Tracy eventually succeeds in getting Marta to loosen up a bit, and Marta forces herself to connect with this bubbly, carefree girl.

The day they get their first paychecks, Tracy is all smiles. "I am psyched. You got yours, too, right?" she asks Marta.

"I sure did," Marta says, eyes wide. "I can't believe it. I've never gotten a paycheck that big."

"Want to go to Bergman's? I need a few things now that I am a career businesswoman." Tracy winks. "What do you say?"

"Sure, I'm in." Marta knows she needs a lot more items in her closet. She has been trying to cycle through her few new blouses and skirts in creative ways but always worries that someone will call her out on not having enough outfits in her rotation, just like in fourth grade all those years ago. Mean girls never really disappear, they just get older and cleverer.

When Marta and Tracy enter Bergman's, Marta goes straight to the clearance rack and grabs clothes until she has a huge pile.

Tracy quickly goes through her stash and rejects them as quickly as Marta can add to them.

Laughing, she says, "Slow down there. You want a few staples, and then you mix and match. Quality over quantity is what my mother always said."

Marta pauses and studies Tracy, noting again her flyaway hair and bold style of dress. She may not be the right person to take fashion advice from. Tracy insists that Marta select a few foundational pieces she can pair with different scarves and blouses for different looks.

Flipping over the price tag of the stylish black suit she has on, Marta exclaims, "There is no way I am paying three hundred dollars for a suit. I could get tons more clothes off clearance for that amount!"

Tracy laughs, regarding Marta as if she is the funniest thing—which, Marta soon discovers, means you have lost the battle.

Marta buys the suit—and though she initially bemoans the fact she's spent almost her whole first paycheck on it, she comes to realize Tracy is right. The confidence one gains from wearing a three-hundred-dollar suit is priceless.

And over the next few months of the program, despite being complete opposites, she and Tracy become inseparable—Tracy, with her wild, curly brown hair, which she is always in a battle to tame; Marta, with her pin-straight, light brown hair that must be cut in a blunt shoulder-length bob to give it even a smidgeon of body. Even a humid ninety-degree day doesn't give her hair one extra wave.

Tracy has an easy way about her and the ability to talk and draw out anyone. She is the perfect foil to Marta, who lives in her head way too much. Tracy shows Marta how to live on the wild side a bit, even when Marta thinks she can't. While she is sure Tracy is the one who has taken poor little Marta under her wing, Tracy insists that Marta, with her steadiness and clear intelligence, is the one who drew Tracy to her from the beginning.

Marta introduces Steve to Tracy one evening at happy hour. She wants the two to hit it off, as both are near and dear to her heart.

Tracy is on her second lemon drop martini when she asks, "So did Marta tell you how I almost got fired on our first official client meeting?" She winks at Marta.

Marta shifts uncomfortably in her chair. "Steve, do you need another beer?"

"No to both questions," Steve says. "I don't need a beer, and I don't think I heard anything about the meeting. Did you tell me the story, Marta?"

Tracy barks out a laugh. "Oh! You will love it. Won't he, Marta?"

Marta tilts her head to one side, not sure at all that Steve will enjoy this story. He doesn't like things that aren't thought-out and planned, so it's not likely that he'll appreciate this tale of a Freudian slip to the max. It is normally nice for her that he worries about things so much, as it means she doesn't have to, but sometimes it does mean missing out on the kinds of fun and funny things that happen with someone like Tracy, who's always shooting off her mouth.

"Well," Tracy begins, oblivious to Marta's discomfort, "Marta and I are at our first client meeting to get feedback on a new Sorella's evac system. We are meeting with six dentists and two hygienists from the Windham Dental Group. The restaurant is one of those stuffy old gentlemen's clubs with dark paneling and waiters in black-and-white suits who take pride in not needing a pad to write down anyone's order. Old Dr. Dean is lording over the table, and he asks, 'So what do you think of the new Wegman's? Kathy just loves it. Great selection and excellent service. Can't believe a grocery store can get people to flock to it just by offering some good, old-fashioned customer service. Can't ever forget the importance of customer service.' Blah, blah, blah. What an old windbag. Everyone seems to know what he's talking about, but I've never heard of Wegman's. Have you?"

Steve shakes his head.

"Well, I want to keep the customer talking. That's what they told us to do. Didn't they, Marta?"

"Yep, they sure did. I'm not sure they quite had *this* in mind, though." Marta smirks, now getting into the story.

"Very funny." Tracy tosses her hair, grinning. "Well, I ask, 'I've never been to Wegman's. Are they new?' Old man Dean nods his head, so I ask him, 'Which do you like better, Wegman's or BJ's?'"

More animated now, Marta pipes in, "There is dead silence around the table, and Tracy covers her mouth in horror and turns to me. I am frozen. I can't believe what just came out of her mouth. I can't think of anything to say to save her."

"Yeah, thanks a lot." Tracy rolls her eyes. "I thought for sure I was going to be fired over this. This was a serious bunch of dentists. But suddenly, I heard a snort from the end of the table. It was Kelly, one of the dental hygienists, cracking up—and thank God, 'cause then the rest of the table joined in. I was saved."

Steve frowns. "That does sound close. You really could have been fired, you know."

Tracy shrugs. "Yeah, but I wasn't. It wouldn't be a good story if I had been fired." She nudges Marta. "I owe Kelly big-time. Next time I go there, I got to make sure I bring her some Sorella's swag."

"That's a good idea," Marta says brightly. She notices just then that the head of their department is sitting at the table near the door. Desperate to change the subject, as Steve appears very uncomfortable, she blurts out, "Hey, look—that's Dr. Jenkins!"

Tracy bounces up. "Let's go introduce ourselves. I've never met him before. Have you?"

Marta sputters, "No, and I don't want to. Are you crazy? You don't just walk up to the department head and start a conversation like that." This is even worse than Steve's discomfort.

"I don't think that's a smart idea, either," Steve says. "He may not want to be bothered."

But Tracy is already out of her seat and tugging Marta with her as she marches off in his direction.

Not wanting to make a scene, Marta allows herself to be pulled along.

When they reach his table, Tracy confidently states, "Hello, Dr. Jenkins. Marta and I wanted to just say a quick hello. We are working in your division right now as part of the Sorella rotational program."

Smiling broadly, Dr. Jenkins stands and shakes their hands. "I appreciate you stopping over. Refreshing to see such gumption these days. Lots of people think folks at my level are unapproachable, but we really like talking and getting to know the next generation of Sorella's employees. How are things going so far?"

"We're both learning a lot and getting to take part in some key meetings," Tracy says. "We were just talking about our first client meeting."

Marta stifles a gasp.

"Wonderful experience!" Tracy continues smoothly. "As we said, learning a lot."

A man walks up to the table, and Dr. Jenkins introduces him as Sorella's head legal counsel. As they say their goodbyes, the department head says, "Tracy and Marta, set up some time on my calendar through Kathy Thompson, my admin. Let's continue our chat next month."

Marta can't believe it. She never would have been this brave without Tracy, and now she's learned that some top executives actually appreciate rubbing shoulders with the underlings—and something good may actually come from it. She's glad she didn't have time to listen to herself, or to Steve, before Tracy dragged her over here.

On the drive home, Steve says, frowning, "Tracy could get you in a lot of trouble. I think you should separate yourself from her."

Marta is silent. This thought has crossed her mind over the past months, but she doesn't want to give up her friendship with Tracy—plus, everything worked out fine, just as it normally does. Tracy helps her live a little more bravely, and Marta doesn't want to lose that.

From here on in, she decides, she will just carve out a middle ground for herself. Somewhere between Tracy's wild and sometime harebrained schemes and Steve's path of playing it safe and avoiding all possible risks. It will be Marta's road to happiness or something close to it.

After that night, Marta leaves Tracy out of her descriptions of her successes when sharing her work stories with Steve. Steve is very supportive of her dedication to her job and assumes she has cut her ties with Tracy, as he suggested. Meanwhile, he has landed at a small architectural firm and is getting to design some small buildings in the area. On weekends, they sometimes visit the buildings he's had a part in designing.

A year into her rotational program, Steve and Marta are standing in front of one of Steve's buildings when she hears him ask, "Will you marry me?"

He is down on one knee, looking up at her.

Steve is safe and secure, and in him she has found someone that represents the financial security she desires so deeply. They are both making good money. Marta is achieving her goals, and the future looks bright. She finds it easier to breathe now. She still has to work to not live in her head; every day, she tries valiantly to show the world the dancing, spinning, free-spirit side of herself—and she's getting quite good at it. Tracy is her role model.

Yes, the ghost of her first love has yet to stop haunting her, and it crowds her relationship with Steve a bit. But Steve is the one who's here, and he's what Marta needs.

She beams down at him. "Yes," she cries. "Of course, I'll marry you!"

Shortly after that, Marta is at her house for a visit with her mom and they are discussing plans for the small wedding she and Steve are planning in six months. Her father is reading the newspaper, ignoring them both.

"Let me show you the picture from our wedding. Have you ever seen it before?" Marta's mother asks.

"No, I've never seen any pictures. Did you have a big wedding?" Marta asks.

Marta's mom hurries out of the room.

The phone rings and her father glances over to her and with a sigh gets up.

"Hello? Ahh, yes, Kevin is it?" her father says loudly.

Staring at her father, Marta is glued to the recliner she is sitting in. She tries to process what he just said.

"Well, Marta doesn't live here anymore." There is a pause, "And she is getting married in a few months, so I don't think you need to talk to her now, do you?" And her father sets the receiver down in the cradle with a click.

Marta sits in stunned silence. *He called.* A flood of memories burst through some hidden barrier within her and with them comes a myriad of wonderful, expansive feelings—followed by the pain of all that was lost. She still can't move. Her legs are complete stone weights against the plastic vinyl of the green chair. Finally, when her mother rushes in, she breaks Marta out of her trance, but still not fully able to comprehend things, Marta drives back to her apartment. Her mind is a whirl. *Should I get closure with Kevin before I marry Steve? If so, how? I could drive north and find the address I wrote all those letters to years ago, but I can't imagine doing that.*

She knows that would require a lot more bravery and daring than she has inside her. She fears too many things. She is scared to lose what she has with Steve or even question it. But her biggest fear is finding out that the dream she held so close to her heart for so many years was never real. Discovering the love she had with Kevin was false or a trick of her imagination is something she could not bear; it's safer to sit and daydream.

So, she does nothing. She goes into her marriage holding firm to a memory that could be completely inaccurate and a dream that had so many iterations and embellishments that it would make any living person pale in comparison. She knows this and reminds herself of that sobering thought often.

Yet she can't help but cling to the other possibility: that the reality is exactly as she remembers it, and those feelings are as true today as they were back in 1977; that she and Kevin are soulmates, meant to be together.

CHAPTER 8: Flight of Fancy

2003—Newark, New Jersey

It is the bleakest of months, February, and Marta is finally leaving her customer meeting in Atlanta. It did not go as well as she would have liked. She just couldn't connect with the dentist group. Now, traffic is building as her taxi heads out of Atlanta toward the airport.

"Dammit," she mutters, "of course it has to be Hartsfield. I'll be lucky if I make it."

She glances down at her feet, and even in her annoyed state she can't help but smile a little. The brown boots she's wearing aren't just any brown boots, they are sheer perfection: soft brown leather with flat heels like horseback-riding boots. And the coup de grâce? They have a four-inch band of suede on the top that goes almost past her knees. They are just on the edge of being too funky for work.

These boots were love at first sight. She bought them on an impulse, ignoring all voices in her head about the expense or the practicality, and she doesn't regret the purchase for one minute. They are utter joy. And the sweater dress she's wearing with them gives her an extra boost of confidence as she smooths it across her lap.

Marta never wants anyone judging her because of the clothes she wears. She knows the importance of appearance. She has too many bad memories of not fitting in when she was growing up, not looking *quite right*. Now, she makes sure no one questions whether she belongs because of the way she dresses. She loves that this outfit fits the mold but still has an edge.

I may miss my flight, she thinks with a self-amused snort, *but I'll look good doing it.*

She makes it with a few minutes to spare and collapses into her seat, bone-tired. Traveling used to be a fun getaway for her. She could leave her stuff around the hotel room and come and go without anyone to check in with or worry about. Not that Steve does that too much, but he certainly doesn't like her to leave her things in an unorganized mess, which she likes to do when she is on her own. She's always felt she can breathe easier when she is away—but lately, even that has lost some of its appeal. Now she mostly just feels exhausted at the end of her trips. She worries she is sliding into middle age, where settling and being comfortable are the focus and any thought of really living takes a back seat.

She watches as folks board the plane. There is a lot of confusion over seat assignments, and the flight is pretty full. It seems as if things are more chaotic than just an overbooking situation.

Turning to the person sitting next to her, she asks, "What is going on? Is the flight delayed?"

Just then, the flight attendant announces some names over the intercom and asks those called to come up to the front with their belongings. Marta is in row 17 and can't see what is happening to the people who are getting up.

Her seatmate turns to her with a grimace. "I guess some major problem with the seating. I think the prior flight to Newark was canceled, so people got on this one, thinking it was their flight."

Just then a baby starts to wail somewhere behind them and the guy murmurs, "Poor kid."

"Poor mother," Marta says wryly.

"Or father," he retorts, grinning.

"Right," she says. "You must have kids."

He responds with a grin. "Yep, three great ones."

The smile doesn't quite reach his eyes—which, she realizes, are a beautiful blue. She feels a momentary wobble as the plane seems to shift slightly, even though they definitely haven't taken off yet. She is a sucker for blond hair and blue eyes—has been ever since eighth grade. She has never been sure which came first: her attraction to blond hair and blue eyes, or to Kevin. It's kind of a chicken-or-egg question.

This guy in the seat has blond hair that is just starting to recede a bit, and he looks a lot like Kevin does in the many daydreams she's manufactured over the years. Is her mind playing tricks on her, like some kind of *Shallow Hal* situation? Can she see Kevin in everyone now, as Hal could see everyone's true inner person? The guy is probably around her age, maybe a bit older. It is getting harder and harder to guess ages these days. She figures he must be tall, as his knees are almost hitting against the seat in front of him. Maybe six feet or so. He's wearing a nice pair of brown dress slacks with some darker stripes in them. She thinks they make a good combination in their matching color schemes. *A sign from above?* She dismisses the thought immediately, as she knows men's clothing offers guys few color choices. She can't be looking for signs when there is a high probability of finding one to begin with.

They sit on the tarmac for another thirty minutes as the commotion over the seats gets worked out. The baby's cries ebb and flow. Marta is getting annoyed—not at the baby but at the delay. Normally, she has the utmost patience in these types of "out of your control" situations, but this time she doesn't have her normal distraction, as she forgot her Kindle on this trip. Even the Delta in-flight magazine with its three Sudoku puzzles is useless, as she already skimmed the various articles and completed the puzzles on her flight down to Atlanta.

Marta doesn't generally chat it up with her fellow passengers, but she thinks maybe the universe is offering her a consolation prize of sorts. Since she is stuck here without any other good alternatives, it seems her only option is to chat with the nice-looking guy sitting next to her. Before she can figure out a good opening, however, the baby coos, prompting her to start to build a story around it and its mother, sight unseen.

The mother, who has hazel eyes and brown hair, stares down into the baby's blue eyes, which remind her of the baby's father. She is excited she is going to see him, finally, after all these months . . .

But she only gets this far in her narrative before dragging herself out of the daydream and back to reality. A feeling of melancholy sweeps over her. She opens herself up to it and shifts in her seat to keep from slumping. She must stop dwelling on babies. A deep pang shoots through her chest, and she works to tamp down the feeling of sadness that's making her eyes tear up.

Focusing on the spot in front of her, she tries to get her emotions in check, when she realizes her cute seatmate has asked her a question.

"What?" she responds blankly.

He leans a little closer to her, probably thinking she's hard of hearing, and repeats, "Are you heading home or is Atlanta home?"

The sadness lifts and then dissipates, and she makes a mental note that talking to good-looking men may be the best remedy yet to keep from sinking into the void.

"New Jersey is home," she says sheepishly. "How about you?"

"Atlanta's home for me for now, but I may be moving up to New Jersey," he says. "Can I ask you a couple of questions, since you're from there?"

They fill the next thirty minutes talking about New Jersey and the pros and cons of the Northeast. Pros include the coast, the fall foliage, the hills and mountains, and winter, if you like skiing. Cons would also be winter if you don't like the cold, cost of living, and taxes.

He seems seriously interested in New Jersey and in her responses to his questions. Most of them involve topics like schools in the area and taxes in the different towns. Marta can share some information on schools, as Steve's sister and brother both live in nearby Chatham and Bedminster and have children. She has learned a bit over the past ten years from listening to their conversations about the different school systems and public versus private. On taxes, she has to plead complete ignorance, as Steve handles all of that and she has absorbed zero tax information over the same ten-year period.

Finally, the cabin doors close, and they start taxiing for takeoff. Marta realizes she has been doing a lot of the talking, so she decides to turn the tables with a question that's sure to get him talking: "How old are your kids?"

Mr. Cutie immediately becomes animated and tells her about each of his kids—two boys and a girl—and their various activities and interests. He goes on about how athletics are important, but it is a hard thing to balance. It isn't like it was when he was growing up, when you could do a bunch of different sports. His son Jamie is eleven and already feels the pressure to commit to only one, and that just seems wrong. AAU baseball is his current favorite, but that could change in a couple of years. He's really good at golf and swimming, too, so it seems a shame to drop them now to focus on baseball year-round.

While he talks, Marta surreptitiously studies his face. It's hard to do that sitting side by side, but she manages. He has a broad face with a strong jaw. If she had to guess his nationality, she would say Slavic—angular face and nice white teeth. She momentarily loses herself in thought as another face pops into her head. She wordlessly breathes *Kevin*. Then she peers into Mr. Cutie's eyes and sees him smiling at her. She realizes there is silence and figures he has asked her another question that she has once again completely missed.

She blushes. *He must think I'm an idiot.* "What?" she asks quickly.

"I was just asking if I can get out to use the restroom," he explains with a quirk to his lips.

"Y-yes, sure," Marta stammers. And she quickly moves to stand up, only to be yanked unceremoniously back down into her seat by her seat belt, eliciting an involuntary *oomph!*

"Oh, oops!" she squeaks out as she unbuckles and stands. *God, could I act any more witless?* she thinks as he squeezes by her and makes his way down the aisle. *And wow, he definitely is six feet tall. And long and lean.*

She quickly stops staring, as she doesn't want anyone else on the plane to catch her ogling. She sits back and waits for his return. A tingle runs up her back and she wonders for the hundredth time what Kevin is doing right now.

When her seatmate does come back, they immediately fall back to chatting—this time about flying, and the many annoyances associated with it.

"One of the key benefits over driving is at least you can sleep on the plane," he says.

Marta thinks he may be hinting that he wants to go to sleep— but no, he doesn't look sleepy.

"I don't know what my problem is," she says, "but it doesn't matter how tired I am, I cannot fall asleep on a plane. Which is a real nuisance, because I would love to be able to catch up on my sleep."

She tells him about a colleague, Paul, with whom she traveled recently. Paul insisted he knew exactly what to do when their plane was delayed by an hour. He immediately called the travel agent and rebooked their flights to a different airline. Marta tried politely to question his thinking, as it seemed like a lot of effort to avoid an hour delay. They ended up having to practically sprint to their new gate and rush onto the new flight, where they promptly wound up sitting on the tarmac for three hours. "I am sure I saw our original United flight take off two hours before the new flight did," she concludes.

Mr. Cutie chuckles, and Marta continues in an exasperated voice, "That wasn't the worst of it. Paul was sitting four rows in front of me, and he fell asleep immediately while we sat on the tarmac. My only recourse was to shoot daggers at his lolling head and dream up various creative ways I'd kill him once we got off the plane."

Mr. Cutie laughs out loud. "Diabolical!"

Marta leans over and whispers quietly, "To this day, whenever I see Paul at work, I immediately see the picture of him with his head lolling back on the seat, eyes shut, mouth slightly open, fast asleep. And I want to inflict physical harm."

"We are entering our final descent into Newark International Airport, please prepare for landing," a flight attendant announces loudly over the tinny speakers.

Marta raises her head slowly, looking around to get her bearings—and finds herself staring into a pair of twinkling blue eyes.

"And I thought you said you couldn't sleep on planes," Mr. Cutie says.

She immediately realizes she somehow fell asleep on the plane, and it seems that her head actually may have been resting on his shoulder. *Goddammit.* It was the awful sleep she got last night.

Her hand flies to her mouth in horror and she gasps, "Oh my! Oh God! I really can't believe this. I am so sorry. Sorry I slept on you. I can't believe it; I really never do that."

He chuckles. "Well, you must have been really tired."

She stares at him with wide eyes. "What? Oh God, was I snoring?"

The last part comes out as a squeak, and she realizes she is holding in a deep breath. He shakes his head no, then goes back to reading his book.

She tries to get a hold of herself, but sleeping has messed her all up and she can't think straight or breathe right. She blushes every time she thinks of her head on his shoulder. She keeps having to shake her head to clear the image of Kevin sitting on the rocks at Rec Park that's filling her mind: she is leaning her head on his shoulder and is looking up in his blue eyes. It is so vivid and clear she thinks she can smell the freshly mown grass from the nearby field.

The plane screeches to a halt in its normal fashion, one minute hurtling through space and the next coasting sedately into the waiting gate area.

While they wait to deplane, Mr. Cutie reaches out his hand and says, "Hi. I'm Jason, by the way."

Marta blushes again and mumbles, "Oh, hi. I'm Marta."

Around them, everyone is standing and retrieving their belongings from the overhead bins. Marta tries to stand up and once again forgets to unbuckle her seat belt and is yanked back into her seat. Red-faced, she stammers, "Oops again."

She figures Jason must think she is a novice flyer who was just pretending to be a seasoned flyer—which makes her extremely uncomfortable. She doesn't like anything to disrupt her professional and capable persona.

She and Mr. Cutie—*Jason*—wait for the doors to open. She is painfully conscious of how close he is to her as they wait but tries not to think about it.

After grabbing her carry-on, before she starts to move up the aisle, she turns slightly toward him and murmurs, "It was nice chatting with you." She can't quite meet his eyes, but she thinks she sounds unfazed.

"Yep, same here," he replies cheerily.

She jets away the first chance she gets.

As Marta's park-and-ride van pulls up to the curb, she boards and glances back at the sidewalk.

It's as if he is a magnet. Her eyes lock on to him just as he walks through the automatic doors. Grinning, he tips his head in her direction, and then walks briskly toward the van.

Dear lord, will this ever end? She pulls herself together and gives herself a stern talking-to that mainly consists of *don't be an idiot.*

He boards the van and sits across from her. With a small laugh, he says, "Hi again."

She smiles thinly and replies, "Hi." She nods toward his seat. "Probably a good idea, just in case I doze off again."

He flashes a smile and says, "Exactly."

They move to the next terminal and a group of people gets on, which helps break up the awkward silence that has wrapped around them in the dark of the van. People talk about the weather and ask the van driver how the roads are for driving.

As they get off at the garage and collect their things from the back of the van, Marta wonders what he is doing at the park-and-ride, since he isn't from around here and really should be at the rental car place. But she doesn't want to ask, as maybe she is missing something obvious. Or maybe he is lying about the whole visiting thing altogether and would be embarrassed if she called him out on it.

After she finishes paying, she realizes Jason is behind her once again. She turns and says, "Well, nice to meet you. Hope you have a nice visit."

Jason grins, and their eyes meet for a moment. Marta hesitates slightly, then turns to the door and walks to her car.

On her drive home, she spins a leisurely daydream where he reaches out his hand as she is turning to leave, and she reaches out hers, and when they touch, they connect on a level that is not of this world. They end up talking on a deep and personal level, right there at the park-and-ride, and realize that what they are experiencing is destiny and can't be denied.

Too soon, she pulls into her driveway and back to reality. But for the next several days, her daydream is always right there for her . . . making her wonder for the hundredth time if her daydreams about Kevin—or this guy Jason, or any other compelling stranger she's met over the years—are wrong.

CHAPTER 9: We Meet Again

2003—Newark, New Jersey

Two weeks later, Marta is rushing into a planning meeting for a new product launch. She walks quickly into the large, glass-lined conference room. Work is one area where her daydreams are kept at bay, as she enjoys her work and also needs to focus on it 100 percent in order to do it well.

She is comfortable and confident in her job, and that confidence is real—no longer an act—and she is thankful for that. She doesn't think anything of this meeting, as it is common for her to be part of a new product development and launch team. She's worked her way up the ladder, so to speak, and while she is not an engineer, which is king at Sorella, she is well respected for her marketing and business knowledge within their dental group.

Just inside the door, she glances around the table, expecting the usual suspects. Tracy gives her an eyebrow raise and a quick quirk of her lips. Marta responds with a questioning look, furrowing her brow—and then her eyes shift to the other end of the table, and her gaze meets a pair of very familiar blue eyes. She stops abruptly; her mouth opens and shuts again. Someone at the table quips, "Marta speechless; quick, take a picture, this has to be a first."

She is well-known for being talkative and sociable, as Tracy has definitely rubbed off on her through these years. She is no longer that shy little girl she once was—at least, not on the outside. Yet she stands frozen. It isn't the plane ride that flashes through her head right now; instead, she sees snapshots of the daydreams she created from that day, and her cheeks flush a bright red. Everyone, including Jason, is staring at her.

Propelling herself forward, she grabs the one remaining open chair and slides into it. Looking down, she mutters, not quite under her breath, "Oh shit." Looking up, her face burning, she says—more clearly this time—"Sorry about that."

Business meetings really aren't the place for profanity, especially when the profanity is out of left field. She stares down at her offending sweater dress and boots. This is the first time she has worn her favorite outfit to the office. She chose it today, knowing she was attending this multifunctional meeting and wanting to give herself a boost of confidence.

If there was a chance Jason wouldn't have recognized her, that possibility has been eliminated by her wearing the exact same outfit he first saw her in. She gets a cringey feeling in her stomach, and it takes her back to childhood. Wearing the exact same outfit, even if it is two weeks later, reminds her of being called out by the mean girls in school when she didn't have enough shirts to vary her outfits enough for their liking. God, how quickly all the defenses she has carefully been building up over the years go up in smoke. The voice in her head says snidely, *You haven't really changed. You are still that little girl that doesn't fit in.*

Blushing, she glances in Jason's direction and struggles to recover some of her equilibrium. "Hi, Jason."

Jason offers a slight nod and says, "Hi, Marta," just as Doug, the head of Dental Equipment Engineering, clears his throat and stands up.

Marta takes a deep breath, trying to focus on Doug and her breathing.

"I'd like to introduce the newest member of Sorella's dental engineering team, Jason Turner," Doug says to the room. "Jason comes from Talyor Electric Dental Division, and he will be the engineering team lead for the launch of the new laser evac system."

Marta sits back, dumbfounded, struggling to remember if they talked about their respective jobs on the plane. They covered a lot of ground before she fell asleep, but she can't remember anything specific about Talyor or Sorella. She would have remembered if Talyor came up. She knows enough people in the industry that she would have asked Jason if he knew any of the same people. Sorella and Talyor are always poaching each other's employees.

The meeting moves forward in a bit of a blur. Fortunately, Marta isn't required to add much to the discussion, so she sits mute through most of it. She learns she is going to be working closely with Jason on the rollout, so she is going to have to get her head around this.

After the meeting breaks up, Marta makes a beeline back to her office, where she tries to think clearly about the situation. She can't believe this is a coincidence. She closes her eyes and tries to tune in to any possible signals from the cosmos. The only other times she's tried something like that before is when she rubbed the Breathe stone in high school, hoping it would conjure up Kevin. While her imagination has always opened secret doors for her, she's never thought of those doors as something she could ever truly walk through; she's always considered them no more than a minor distraction from reality. But maybe there is a higher consciousness out there, putting Jason in her path. And all she needs to do is open that door.

That thought jolts her into realizing she needs to come to terms with how she used the "sleep incident" as a launchpad for her daydreams these past two weeks. Jason is no longer a figment of her imagination. He is real, he is present, and he's going to be in her immediate future. She needs to figure this thing out. She also needs to be smart, as this is work, and she keeps her daydreams at bay during work. This has become a messy conundrum, but she is good at compartmentalizing things. She needs to get things back in their right places and then she will be okay. Feeling a bit more in control, she leans back in her chair and begins browsing through a few emails that need responses. She's composing an answer to one when the phone rings. She looks at her phone; the ID shows "Jason Turner."

Her hand hesitates just slightly before she picks it up and answers with an overly confident, "Hello."

"Hi, Marta, it's Jason. I wanted to let you know our plane trip from Atlanta must have been a lucky talisman, because it was during that trip Doug offered me this job, and I'm really excited about it. I think our chance meeting and the whole thing bodes well, don't you?"

Boy, he is disarming. She laughs genuinely and responds lightly, "Yes, of course. I totally see how my yakking your ear off and then falling unconscious on your shoulder would appear to be a lucky charm to anyone."

Jason laughs. "So, tell me about what you do at Sorella. I can't believe we didn't realize we were in the same business when we were chatting."

"Well, when I'm not falling asleep on strangers, I pretty much run Sorella's marketing department."

He laughs again. "I figured that was the case. Can I stop by your office, and you can fill me in?"

"Yes, come on by." Marta hurriedly glances around her office. The high standards for order and neatness that Steve requires at home certainly don't extend to her workplace. As she contemplates the haphazard mess, she thinks perhaps she has gone a tad too far in the opposite direction. Her office is horrible, with stacks of paper everywhere—precarious towers of files that look as if they could be toppled by a slight breeze. Marta knows enough engineers to realize this office will not be viewed positively by most. But she rationalizes, *I'm not out to impress Jason; he isn't my boss—at least, not yet.*

She doesn't know where to begin, but she does straighten a few files so Jason's entry doesn't potentially start an avalanche, and she clears off her other chair so there's a spot for him to sit. When she's done, she reckons she has enough time to run to the bathroom to check things out, make sure her makeup is still in place, and doesn't have food in her teeth.

As she walks toward the ladies' room, she tries to figure out how best to deal with the outfit situation. She could ignore it—pretend she didn't notice—or she could address it head-on and make some joke about it. Both options have potential downsides.

Humor is her typical response in embarrassing situations; a little deflection goes a long way, she has learned. She gives her head a shake and hopes something comes to mind when the time comes. She somehow doubts it, as she feels less than on-point suddenly—as she did on the plane when she was a bit off-kilter. That small girl with all her worries is still in her head, despite how hard she's worked to get rid of her. She never, ever disappears entirely.

The same self-conscious thoughts are still running through Marta's head when Jason knocks on her open door.

She exclaims a bit too brightly, "Hi again! Please have a seat."

Glancing around, he quips, "Okay! Which pile is the chair?"

Not sensing any underlying edge of disapproval, she chuckles and points to the one open chair.

As he settles into it, she leans back in her chair.

Grinning at each other, Marta asks, "Okay, where should we start?"

He cocks his head, clearly thinking about it, and in the moment of silence she glances down at his hands, which are resting casually on his thighs. She remembers a very similar pose from the plane.

"Well," he asks, "how long have you been at Sorella, and what do you really do?"

She's surprised by the question, and it must show, because he quickly says, "Or we can just talk about the new product launch."

She recovers and says, "No, no, that's fine . . ."

She pauses and begins to talk about her tenure at Sorella, trying to cover only the stuff that might be helpful for him to hear. He asks some insightful questions, and she gives him the shortest answers she can, but even so, when she finally looks at her watch, she sees that it's almost three o'clock.

Jumping up, she exclaims, "Oh, I need to sit in on a webinar that a new marketing associate is presenting, to help if needed. I can't believe I rambled on for an hour. I really have to run."

Getting up quickly, Jason straightens his pants. "Okay, well, thanks very much. I'm outta here." In a mischievous tone, he adds, "By the way, nice boots."

She looks up just in time to see his grin, and then he is gone. She forgot all about addressing her fashion blunder. She is not sure whether to be relieved or embarrassed, but she doesn't have time to dwell on it. She rushes into the conference room next to her office and tries to concentrate for the next hour—with limited success.

CHAPTER 10: Limbo

2003—Newark, New Jersey

Entering the large conference room on the tenth floor, Marta is carefully dressed in her second-favorite outfit. She isn't sure when it will be safe to wear the sweater dress again. She is early today, which is not like her. But she has shown too many flaws already. No need to add any more, just in case Jason isn't as easy-going as he appears.

Jason gives her a quick smile when he sees her. He is sitting, and he awkwardly stands and then self-consciously sits down again. She's not sure if he was going to shake her hand or what.

"How's your first week been?" she asks.

"Just fine," he says. "I at least know where the bathrooms are now."

Leaning forward, she impulsively asks, "Hey, do you want to go to lunch today?" She freezes in surprise at her own words. She rarely does things this spontaneously. She forces herself to continue, briskly, "I thought we could go down to the cafeteria after this meeting, if it goes until noon."

He nods. "Sure, good idea."

The meeting progresses routinely. Marta watches Jason closely. He has a great way of leading the meeting without being at all over-bearing or annoying. His direction is barely noticeable, unless you are paying close attention to such things. His skill is something that can't be taught. Either you have that type of group-dynamic intelligence, or you don't.

She sits back and enjoys being part of it.

The meeting wraps up a bit before noon. Marta slowly gathers her things.

When most of their colleagues have exited the room, Jason turns and quietly suggests, "How about I put my stuff back in my office and meet you down on the second floor?"

Nodding, she forces a tight smile and walks out, wondering if he is watching her. She has a strange sensation in the pit of her stomach, but she quickly gets a handle on herself and gives herself a stern talking-to: *I am married and have no, no, no interest in a workplace affair. Tacky, tacky, tacky.*

She's seen her share of office affairs over the years; they never end well.

Stepping out of the elevator on the second floor, she sees Jason leaning against the wall. Looking somewhat uncomfortable, he grins immediately when he sees her. While his hair is thinning, it is still golden-blond, and with the sun coming through the window behind him, it looks as if he has a halo. But it is his easy smile, and the way it makes his eyes crinkle, that makes him so charming and attractive.

She shakes her head to expel these thoughts. She needs to ask Tracy what she thinks of Jason; Marta is getting all mixed up in her memories of Kevin when she's around Jason; maybe she's seeing things that aren't really there.

She tries to act relaxed and nonchalant as they walk into the busy café, even though she has a tense feeling in her gut. They pick up sandwiches and find a table by the large floor-length windows overlooking the rooftop garden of the building next to Sorella, where people are sitting on benches and strolling around the pretty vegetation.

They settle into a table and make small talk for a while. Then Marta asks him about his pending move up here.

She thinks she sees a pained look cross his face as he replies hesitantly, "Well, for now, I'm settling into the corporate apartment that they have, and it certainly is nice enough. I'm not sure when the rest of the family is going to come up."

"Are the kids having a hard time with moving?" she asks. "I know when I was growing up, moving was my greatest fear. I don't know why, as it was completely unfounded. My parents are still in the same house I grew up in. Moving was never in the cards. But when you're young, it seems like a scary possibility."

Jason stares at her and seems to decide something. "No," he says, "the kids are fine with it. They even seem excited. But my wife, Janice, is having second thoughts." He rushes on, "Her family is in Atlanta and so are all her friends, so now she's not sure it's such a great idea. Originally, she was all for it—you know, more money, better job. But she is realizing now what it means for her, and she isn't sure it's worth it."

Marta bites her tongue to keep from saying, *A little late now.* She doesn't want to sound cold, as she is sure Jason has already thought that himself and is trying to be nice. Instead, she asks, "Does she work, too?"

He shakes his head no. "When the kids were born, we decided one of us would stay home, and Janice was happy to be a stay-at-home mom. She never liked her job at the bank and jumped at the chance to give all that up. She really enjoys being a mom and is good at it, but now that the kids are reaching the preteen age, it has become a bit more thankless. I think she sees it's only going to get harder, for a while at least. You know, you move from being the greatest thing in your kids' lives to being an untouchable."

He laughs, so Marta does, too.

He continues, "You become an idiot overnight, and it's tough.

Tougher for Janice, as she really needs to be appreciated. So, she isn't dealing with it very well." He ducks his head. "Boy, I'm rambling."

Marta quickly responds, "No, not at all. That's a lot of issues and decisions to be facing—a new job and all the pressures of moving, *plus* kids."

"You don't have any?" Jason asks.

Marta shakes her head no and wonders how he came to that conclusion. But she doesn't want to ask, and she doesn't want to get into her story. He can surmise what he will about her obvious reticence on the topic. Once you have been married for more than five years and are in your thirties, people stop asking about kids and start assuming there is an issue.

There is a bit of an awkward lull until Jane walks by and asks Marta a question about a meeting later that afternoon. Marta introduces her to Jason. After that, they finish their sandwiches quickly and head back to the elevator.

They say a quick goodbye before Jason gets off on his floor.

"See you next week," he says casually as he steps through the open doors.

As Marta continues up to her office, she wonders, *Does he mean next week for lunch or next week for our joint meeting?*

The following Tuesday, Marta again arrives early to the meeting, though this time it's because she's resolved to remove any possibility of lunch after the meeting from the outset. Even harmless lunches cause speculation, and she knows that if she were on the other side watching them have lunch every Tuesday, *she* would assume the worst.

Jason is the only one there and is placing an update to the project plan in front of each chair.

Oh-so-casually, she says, "Hey, I was thinking we could have lunch again this week, but it turns out I have an errand to run, so maybe a raincheck."

Did she imagine the look of relief that just flitted across Jason's face?

"Oh, okay," he says quickly. "I really need to run out as well. Got to drop off a Redbox DVD before I end up owning the thing."

She looks up in genuine surprise. "Wow, that's funny, I'm returning a Redbox movie, too—*Lost in Translation*. What are you returning?"

"Oh, it's *Elf*. You know, that kids movie."

"Well, if we both are going out, I could return yours . . . or we can do it together, or . . . um, whatever." *God, I sound like a teenager.*

Just then Don and Rick walk in, and Jason mouths, "Sure, we can go."

She wonders if he is as paranoid as she is. She thinks it would be better if that were the case. Wouldn't it be funny if he had planned his errand excuse just like she had? And it somehow turned out to be the exact same one?

As she sits waiting for others to file in, she wishes she was better at yogic breathing—something to help quiet her mind and make sure her lungs don't forget to breathe, as they are inclined to do.

Another week passes, and Marta is a little less out of sorts at work. She feels almost calm as she heads to the Tuesday standing meeting.

She isn't late, but she's not early either, and all but one seat at the table is already taken when she walks into the room.

As she pulls out the chair, her eye catches Jason's. Suddenly, she has this feeling of karma, or destiny, as she has never experienced before. She sees a clear picture of her and Jason having an affair, and it seems definitive. *This from a girl that through college had a bumper sticker that said, "My Karma Ate My Dogma"?* she thinks wonderingly.

She sits with an *oomph* and her folder drops to the floor. Abruptly she is back to being not quite in sync with her body, with a second's delay messing up her coordination. She is sure she isn't breathing. As she bends to pick up some of the loose papers, she once again sees a clear picture: she and Jason sneaking moments together.

Fortunately, Bill and Ned on either side of her do most of the picking up, as her hands seem to be just hovering over the papers.

Marta has had her daydreams for as long as she can remember. They've helped her cope with a mean and tedious childhood; with losing Kevin; with acclimating to college life and finally escaping her dad's approach to life and fathering. They've allowed her to float through the times when things have been too heavy. But until now, they've never been a prelude to an actual possibility. Yes, they've sometimes bordered on the erotic, but they have always been harmless—they have never had any potential to be real. Until now. It's like finding out one day that your cat can talk—has *always* been able to talk—you've just never really listened before.

Her hand reaches out automatically to Ned for the papers, and she stops and stares at it. She keeps thinking, *I must concentrate on this meeting.* But her mind keeps wandering. She is both horrified and thrilled at the possibility, and that changes her perception of herself.

The meeting goes on and on. She keeps her head down. The couple of times that she does glance up or a question is directed at her, she catches Jason's questioning gaze.

She feels everyone can see the difference in her. They know that she has crossed an invisible line. She is mortified when her mind conjures up a mental image of her sitting there with a red *A* on her forehead.

As the meeting finally starts wrapping up, she rejoins the real world just long enough to gather her stuff and dart out of the conference room.

Back at her desk, Marta holds her head in her hands.

What am I thinking? Is it just because he looks like Kevin?

Is the vision she had a passing fantasy, or is it destiny, showing her a glimpse of a future that she can't change? *Hard to know, and even harder to know which one is preferable.*

It is almost easier to think that it is destiny, and she doesn't actually have to do anything—all she has to do is sit back and let it happen. But she knows you can always change destiny. Free will trumps everything; she can fight what the fates preordain if she wants to.

Marta isn't religious, but she does carry with her some puritanical thoughts on fidelity and such—holdovers from her religious upbringing. And bumper sticker jokes aside, karma *is* real; she fully believes that if you do something wrong to someone on purpose, the bad karma you put out there will come back to you in some way, some day.

She needs to focus on the task at hand. She leans back and considers her options. Things no longer feel as definitive as they did in the conference room when she met Jason's eyes. She decides she isn't going to plunge into any decision. There is no reason to rush anything, even if it is fate that is showing the way. Fate can be extremely patient.

Her mind finally clearer, she gets back to work.

That night at dinner she enthusiastically asks Steve, "So how is the Jackson building coming along? Any issues?"

Steve looks up in surprise. "No snags yet, but I'm just in the middle of the design. Still need to present it to the client, so lots of opportunity for it to hit a major snag. You never know when or what. How are things going with your new project? A newfangled drill or something, right?"

Marta's laugh echoes in the quiet dining room. To her ears, it sounds both fake and guilty. She meets Steve's eyes, then quickly glances away. Her eyes dart over to the kitchen and then back to the table with their chicken cordon bleu dinner remains.

She shrugs. "It's fine. Nothing special, really."

They finish dinner in silence, and both quickly and efficiently clear the dishes and take their normal positions in the kitchen, with Steve loading the dishwasher and Marta washing the pots and pans.

As she scrubs a particularly stubborn spot from the chicken pan, she suddenly stops moving. As the warm, soapy water sloshes quietly in her dishpan, she is transported back to her childhood.

She remembers her mother standing at their worn enamel sink after dinner, doing the dishes. She wonders what she thought about when she was standing there all those years. Did she have yearnings or regrets or dreams?

Marta breaks away from her musings; she knows even if her mother were still alive, Marta could never ask her such a thing. She glances at Steve and wonders if he is truly happy. She is not sure she could ever ask him, either. Maybe he doesn't know what true happiness is. It seems possible the same was true for her mother.

The next day, Marta's phone rings and she automatically picks it up without looking up from the quarterly sales numbers spreadsheet she's reviewing.

"Hello, Marta Johnson."

"Hi, this is Jason," Jason says tentatively. "I just wanted to check on you. You didn't seem yourself at yesterday's meeting."

She doesn't say anything for a beat. Then she gathers herself and responds, "Oh, thanks. No, I am just a bit off. I don't know, maybe it's the flu or something. I guess I don't feel right." Not really a lie. Marta finds it is always best to try to keep as close to the truth as possible.

"Oh, great," he says, sounding relieved. "I mean, sorry to hear that. Something is going around."

Marta laughs. "I'm sure I'll feel better soon. It's probably nothing."

Jason doesn't respond and the silence stretches. It isn't uncomfortable, but as her mind considers this, she realizes it *should* be uncomfortable, and she jumps in with, "Well, I've got to run to my three o'clock. I'll see you next week, okay?" She softens her tone at the end of the sentence, and she can hear how uncharacteristically tentative she sounds as she trails off.

"Yeah! Sure, next week," Jason answers, and the phone clicks.

✧ ✧ ✧

For the next few days, Marta has the same dream every night.

She is running on a sandy beach, scantily clad; waves break in the background. Suddenly, she starts slowly sinking deeper and deeper into the sand. When it is at her ankles, her pace becomes a slow-motion run and then a crawl. Soon she's unable to lift her foot out, and then it is up to her knees. She can see and feel the beauty of the setting and the people who are enjoying this lovely beach day. They are lying on blankets and playing in the waves, and no one notices her. She is now moving downward instead of forward and can feel the panic rising in her chest as the sand reaches her thighs, making a sucking sound as it pulls her down. She tries to get someone's attention as she continues to slide deeper into the oozing sand—tries to scream—but no sound emerges from her open mouth.

Waking from this dream on the third night, she is drenched in sweat. Her legs feel like lead, and her lungs are about to explode. She looks over at Steve, sure that she must have been thrashing around in her sleep. His back is toward her, and his soft, rhythmic breathing tells her he is sound asleep.

Her dog, Chippy, whimpers softly and licks her hand, worried. She starts loosening up slowly, wiggling her toes to make sure she can move them. Then she moves on to her legs and her arms. She continues to inhale and holds it for eight counts before letting it out slowly. She scratches Chippy behind his ears to reassure him that she's okay, and he returns to his bed on the floor.

She starts to relax but knows sleep is a long way off.

This dream has recurred throughout her life. In the past, when she had it, she would launch into some daydream that would relax her and put her back into la-la land. But now it feels wrong to conjure up a daydream about Jason or even Kevin, as they are getting too intertwined. Marta tries to substitute some of her other well-worn favorites from the past, but they don't quite work as effectively as they used to.

Marta finally creates a new daydream of Kevin. It takes a while to mold, but once she has worked out the kinks, it proves to be an effective antidote to her nightmare.

She is a guest speaker at a dental convention. She doesn't realize it, but Kevin is in attendance. He recognizes her as he sits in the audience. After she ends her speech, a couple of people come up to ask questions. Kevin hangs back. She does notice this tall, blond, good-looking guy who seems to be interested in what she is saying but isn't plying her with questions. When most of the others drift away, he puts out a strong hand for her to shake and says, "Marta, it's me, Kevin." The connection is immediate and fairy tale–like. They talk as old friends, and the chemistry is palpable. As they talk, Marta revels in their attachment, which seems to transcend even sexual attraction.

This brief fantasy helps her conjure up the feeling of that higher-level connection she's been yearning for. It's as soothing as a warm embrace. Before she knows it, she's drifting back off to sleep.

CHAPTER 11: Company Outing

2003—Newark, New Jersey

It is early May and a gorgeous day, which is perfect because today is Sorella's annual golf outing. Jason, Tracy, Ned, and Marta are a foursome, and they are having a great time. The outing is nine holes of golf, and the teams start right after lunch.

It is close to 2:00 p.m. when the beverage cart wheels over to the group on the fourth hole. They all order beers, and Marta sits back in the cart cheering with Tracy, feeling happy. The birds are chirping. The grass is a beautiful green. The sun's rays seem to have a rejuvenating power.

She glances over to see why they aren't moving toward the fairway, as they have all hit their tee shots. She sees Jason still talking to the beverage cart girl. Marta noticed her before, as she is rather eye-catching, but now she realizes the girl has completely turned on her charms and is directing them straight at Jason. An instant dislike arises in Marta, though she knows the girl is just doing her job and making sure she gets what tips she can.

Jason leans against the pole of the cart, the sun shining off his gorgeous hair—it appears almost sparkly—and smiling at the girl.

The green-eyed monster takes over, and that is all Marta needs to climb out of the limbo she has been in. She has been holding back, and Jason is too much of a gentleman to push or assume something without a clear green light. She suddenly feels alive. She knows he is interested. She is tired of doing the right thing, worrying about everything, and never daring to do the things she wants to do. She has kept herself squashed down for too long. Today she would break some pickle jars as she promised she would way back when, but like so many promises she thought would be easy to keep, she hasn't kept this one, either.

She knows that after golf there will be more drinks, a cookout, and raffles, so there is plenty of time. She promised herself that she would keep sparkling when she was fourteen, and again when she walked across the stage at graduation. She sees now that life can work against your best intentions, and you need to fight it. Opportunities should not be squandered. And Jason was an opportunity.

After the last hole, Jason and Marta return their carts together, and as they are walking back to the pavilion, her arm bumps against his. She feels the contact as though it's a spark. She tries to remember if this is the first time they have ever touched. It feels like it is.

She swallows. "Well, you played well."

He arches an eyebrow. "I wasn't sure how I'd play after such a long break. I normally only take off a month or two down in Atlanta. I'm glad to see I haven't lost my touch."

Holding his gaze just a second longer than normal, she stands just a shade closer than she typically would. She again touches his arm briefly, and he immediately responds to those simple changes. She hopes her clues are subtle, imperceptible to anyone else who might be watching, and it is only because Jason is tuned in to her frequency that he is able to pick up on them.

She is surprised at just how easy it is to communicate the message that she is interested. She wonders, if she was the type that went looking for some extracurricular activity, is this all she would have to do in order to create untold opportunities to cheat? Maybe there is a secret frequency, and once you tune in to it you're welcomed into a secret society that you never knew existed until you became part of it.

Jason brings her back from her musings when he clears his throat and says, "You had a great shot off the tee on eight. It really sailed."

She hoots. "It only looked good in comparison to all my other tee shots. That one was at least passable." She shifts a bit closer and whispers, "It didn't help my game that the beverage cart seemed to follow us around the whole course. Any idea why that was?"

Jason smirks and says, "Hmm, I didn't notice. Was there even a beverage cart out there today?"

Marta barks out a laugh.

After the barbecue and a few drinks with the group, Marta glances up at the night sky. Clouds are covering the sky and the wind has picked up a bit. The skies will open up soon; it's time to leave.

She goes around to the couple of tables of employees and says her goodbyes.

When she gets to the table where Jason is sitting, she announces to the group, "Just wanted to say a quick goodbye. Great day out there."

Jason responds easily, "Hey, I'm heading out, too. Just let me grab my stuff. The parking lot looks pretty dark."

She shrugs. "Sure."

Tracy darts Marta a knowing look but says nothing.

She and Jason walk in silence toward the parking lot. Walking in the semidarkness seems kind of surreal, as if they were in a different time or place—on a separate plane from everyone else. She feels a bit dizzy, and the parking lot suddenly becomes unrecognizable. She bumps her arm against Jason's just to get the physical sensation of being here on earth instead of on some strange alien planet where everything is gray and filmy.

The bump seems to clear her head a bit, and she tries to get her bearings. She has no idea what Jason is experiencing, but she is feeling very weird.

At that moment, Jason says slowly, "Umm, I'm just thinking about . . . well, I don't know how to say this, so I'm just going to say it. I'm sure you know I've been attracted to you since the first time I saw you on the plane. I'm still struggling with this, but I'm throwing caution to the wind."

The weird feeling dissipates immediately. Marta is surprised at both his statement and his candor. She likes the fact he is conflicted, as it puts them both in the same boat. She's thought that maybe they would have sex one time and then never talk about it again. But his words indicate something else. In one way this makes her happy, but in another, she thinks it complicates things too much. It would be simpler if they just did it one time and then came to their senses and never did it again.

She realizes she is taking way too long to respond. She is not good at thinking on her feet, and she's not sure what the right answer is. Normally it would be a quip of some sort to dispel some of the tension that is building, but nothing comes to mind.

Her eyes must show her confusion and hesitancy, because Jason suddenly stops walking midstride.

As soon as they stop walking, she plunges in and, with matching candor, says, "Look, I am really unsure about all this. I know it sounds cliché, but I really have never done anything like this before." Her face flushes red.

Jason again surprises her. "Marta, I don't want to push you or have you feel any pressure. I really like you, and whatever happens or doesn't happen is fine. I really would like to be your friend, regardless of what happens. If we think this thing may ruin our friendship, then we shouldn't do it."

I hope his wife knows what a nice guy she has, she thinks, and then immediately chides herself, *What am I doing thinking of Jason's wife at a time like this? Am I trying to sabotage this whole thing?*

She glances away, as she is sure he can see the indecision clouding her eyes. But then she turns back and leans toward him, and as she does, she feels a kind of uber-awareness spring up between them.

She wants to see what happens if they move closer, so she leans in even more—and the feeling seems to intensify. It is a heightened sensitivity that makes her skin feel alive.

"I just need to maybe think about this a bit more, get used to it a bit," she whispers. "I don't want to do something rash just because I'm attracted to you."

He murmurs, "Not a problem." Then he leans in even closer.

She freezes up, completely rigid. He brushes his lip against her cheekbone, so lightly that she can barely feel it. She thinks he may have inhaled as he did. She tries not to show her panic, but she senses that her eyes are as big as saucers, and she can't make her body relax one bit.

Jason lifts one eyebrow and chuckles quietly. "I'm not going to bite. I just have had that urge for so long and I couldn't pass up this opportunity . . . under the stars, in the dark. You just saying you were attracted to me. That was all the encouragement I needed to do something stupid. I'm sorry, I shouldn't have."

She immediately reaches out and touches him lightly. "No, it's me. I got panicked for a minute. I don't know why, but I'm not overly trusting. It's just me. I worry about everything. I should just let go, but I don't think I can, even though I want to."

He steps away. "I really mean what I said. It is totally up to you. I don't want to do anything if it causes you stress or issues that you aren't ready for. See you tomorrow, 'kay?"

Suddenly feeling a little silly, she says, too loudly, "Yep! See you tomorrow."

"Take care, Marta," she hears as she opens her car door.

Everything suddenly seems better. Much simpler than it was this morning or even ten minutes ago. She is sure she is on the proverbial slippery slope. But how can this be wrong when it feels so right?

This could be my adult Kevin opportunity, she thinks. *A chance to experience what Kevin and I missed out on and to move past my fourteen-year-old dream that I've held on to for too long. Soulmates are probably not even a real thing. People can spend so much of their life waiting for miracles to happen, they forget life is happening every day and you need to be present for it, not live with your head in the clouds.*

She needs to talk to Tracy. Tracy is the only one she can share this with. They have supported each other through nightmarish bosses, difficult projects, and certainly through personal highs and lows. And she won't judge Marta for this.

As she drives out of the parking lot, she remembers the first time Tracy and Steve met. Tracy told her afterward that Steve was not at all like she had pictured. She said she pictured some old-school hippie sort that could make sushi or curry because he had traveled the world. Or a distracted professor sort that was so well-read he could talk about any topic. Marta laughed and assured her that while Steve was none of those things, he was a good guy and a good provider—and while he might not seem funny, he had a good sense of humor. Tracy rolled her eyes when Marta said that, and Marta could feel herself getting defensive about Steve. He was a good guy.

To this day, Tracy always seems slightly disappointed whenever she sees Steve.

Marching into Tracy's office the next day, Marta collapses into the chair in front of her desk. Tracy regards her then with a gleam in her eye demands, "Okay—dish! I want to hear all about it."

Marta tries to tamp down her friend's unbridled enthusiasm. "Nothing happened," she insists. "I'm trying to figure out stuff. I don't know. It seems kind of stupid now in the harsh light of the day."

Tracy's enthusiasm bubbles over. "Okay, so you do like him? What did you guys talk about? Do you know anything about his wife? I bet she is a witch."

"I'm glad you've got my back, but really, this is big," Marta says soberly. "I'm not sure even what I'm asking. I feel like I'm back in junior high."

"I know it's a big deal for you," Tracy says, toning down her excitement. "I can't imagine what is going on in that head of yours. I'm picturing your pros and cons list, right?"

Laughing, Marta feels better. When Tracy isn't schmoozing her customers, her approach to life is "no holds barred." She ruffles feathers wherever she goes. People either hate her or love her. She pushes back just to push back, and most people don't like that. It makes them want to take her down a peg. But that is exactly what Marta loves about Tracy: she is a fighter and a nonconformist.

That said, Marta isn't sure her friend is a great sounding board for helping her make this particular decision.

Marta knows that deep down she has the same little worried Romanian inside her head she always has, and Tracy doesn't. That is a difference that reaches down into her core. Marta has never shared anything with Tracy about her past—about Kevin. Her friend is not one for whimsy, karma, or soulmates. She is one for action.

Tracy is watching her closely. "I see those wheels turning. What are you worried about now?"

"Well, in addition to everything, I'm worried about his wife. I don't think I can be the other woman, the homewrecker. That isn't me. Is it?"

"I think she is a witch, so she probably deserves it . . ." But even Tracy doesn't sound completely sure of herself on this point. She pauses for a beat and then says confidently, "You're overthinking this. You aren't going to marry the guy. Just have some fun. You deserve some fun, don't ya?"

Back at her desk, Marta can't find a way to rationalize an affair, no matter how hard she tries. Even if Janice *is* a complete witch and deserves every awful thing that happens to her, there are kids involved, and they certainly don't deserve it. Marta can't see placing her need to have fun over a family.

She waffles back and forth. Maybe she could justify her actions if she fell madly in love with Jason. Then the only solution would be to run off into the sunset together. But she knows that's not the case. No matter how attracted she is to Jason, she is not madly in love with him.

The two of them continue talking and flirting, keeping their spouses on a nebulous periphery, for the next several weeks. Sorella's company picnic is coming up on June 3, and the day before the picnic, Jason announces, "My wife and kids are visiting from Atlanta to start house hunting, and they are, of course, coming to the picnic."

Marta tilts her head and grins. "Oh, that's nice. Your kids will love the picnic. It's a lot of fun."

Jason smiles thinly in her direction and continues down the hall.

She immediately worries that she reacted oddly to his news. She is in some sort of denial stage; it's a mind trick that helps with the guilt. She is controlling things so well by this point that she can keep thoughts of Steve and Janice walled off in a different realm from the one where she and Jason exist—so much so that the fact that she is going to finally meet Jason's family doesn't seem to be registering. The mind is clever in its ability to rationalize and compartmentalize most anything.

She does feel a measure of relief knowing she doesn't have to worry about Steve coming to the picnic. He stopped coming to any Sorella functions a few years ago. She knows seeing all the families with the kids and the babies year after year was too much for him. Also, she suspects he realized at the early events he attended that she hadn't broken off her connection with Tracy when he asked her to after all, and this was his way of showing his disapproval.

June 3 is sunny and gorgeous. Arriving at the picnic, Marta immediately sees Jason with his family at the food pavilion. She watches them for a moment and then decides to take the bull by the horns.

Tracy is standing just off to her right, watching carefully. She seems more concerned than Marta is about the potential problems associated with meeting the family. Marta knows her well enough to realize that she is standing close by for moral support.

Jason and his family are just getting settled in the second row of picnic tables. The grill is sizzling and popping and there is a steady buzz of people greeting each other and introducing real family to work family, with the prerequisite exclamations over how big kids have grown in the year, and so on.

Marta approaches the table and quickly introduces herself, beckoning Tracy over as she does.

Tracy promptly comes over. "Howdy," she says with a wave. "I'm Tracy."

Marta and she both turn to the kids and ask in unison, "How do you like the picnic?"

Carl, the oldest one, answers enthusiastically, "It's great. Do you know the cotton candy is free?"

Marta grins in response. "I've always heard that. Pretty cool, huh?"

Tracy sits down comfortably next to Janice and asks, a bit too loudly, "How do you like New Jersey?"

"It is prettier than I expected," Janice says.

Jason adds quickly, "Tracy works in the marketing department, and Marta is the person I'm working with on the product launch of the new dental sensor."

Janice smiles brightly.

The younger girl, Cloe, asks, "Do you know when the pony rides start?"

"There's a bulletin board around that corner that has all the events and activities planned for the afternoon," Marta tells her. "You need to check it out, because the pony rides last only an hour or so. I've seen many kids miss out, and boy are they disappointed."

All three kids jump up in unison. Janice tries to grab the closest one, saying firmly, "Hold on, everyone, only after you finish your lunch . . ." But it's too late; all three are gone.

Marta stares at Janice, horrified. "Sorry, I didn't realize that would incite a mini riot."

Janice laughs, but Marta sees a flicker of annoyance flash across her face.

"Oh, that's okay. It's impossible to get them to finish a meal these days. I just don't get it. *I* have to fight to stop eating, and I have to fight *them* to start."

Marta smiles sympathetically. She is annoyed by women who talk about food and diets and exercise constantly, but Janice doesn't launch into a monologue about the latest Paleo diet craze or how SoulCycle changed her life—she's just being open. *I could like her under different circumstances*, she thinks.

After a few more minutes of chitchat, Marta flashes her eyes in Tracy's direction. Tracy automatically stands and says, "Marta, let's get some wine before Patty over there drinks it all. Hey, really nice to meet you."

"Good luck house hunting," Marta adds. "You'll love New Jersey, I'm sure. Bye."

She makes sure her eyes don't linger one nanosecond extra on Jason. She calmly strolls away and heads to the wine line with Tracy. They each get a plastic cup of white wine and stand together, silently sipping their drinks. Tracy seems to sense that talking is not a good idea right now, and Marta is truly grateful.

Now that Jason's wife and kids have names and faces, it is impossible to ignore what she has until now only been toying with. She will not be the other woman. She can't be.

Just like that, her decision is made. Standing against a wall at the Sorella family picnic, she pulls herself away from the cliff she was ready to jump off. Their fling is over before it can begin. All that flirting wasn't really anything. It was meaningless. Marta wouldn't have done anything, and neither would Jason. Neither Janice nor Steve deserves such a thing.

Tracy nods. She seems to know her friend has come to her senses.

Am I really such an open book? Marta wonders. Judging by the look Tracy's giving her, she is.

✧ ✧ ✧

The world adjusts back to its normal rotation surprisingly easily now that Marta has made her decision. She realizes she has been in limbo. Everything she's done in the last few months is now a hazy memory, like a dream. She is no longer constantly weighing pros and cons just under the surface while working or doing the dishes. She feels free. She has shut that door, and she knows there is no reopening it.

She and Jason do meet one more time to talk, however—mainly so Marta can give him an honest account of her thoughts and feelings. He certainly deserves that; he has shown her the beauty of honesty in a relationship, and that is something she wants to take away from this and give back to him.

They meet for coffee on a Saturday.

"I realized how delusional I was being when I met your wife and kids," Marta tells him. "I can't be the other woman. It just isn't who I am." She explains how she was able to keep all that mess away from their little bubble before, but after the picnic, she couldn't. She reiterates the fact that she is really attracted to him (she may even say "super-attracted," which is not the phrase she would have scripted for herself, but she can't take it back and it probably is the most accurate description, anyway).

Jason is resigned and sweet about the whole thing.

"I knew I was doing something wrong, but I've never had such a strong connection with anyone else," he says. "I just wanted to find out what it was. But, Marta, you're right. It would have been wrong. I've said all along being friends could be just as important as being more than friends, and I really hope we can remain that: friends."

While the picture he's painting sounds good, Marta isn't sure they can really be friends. *We can be work associates, but not friends,* she thinks. *Being friends would be keeping a door open, and at some future weak moment, one of us could try to walk through it.* But she says none of this; she says only, "I hope so, too," and works hard not to frown.

✧　✧　✧

Marta doesn't have to worry about the possibility of friendship with Jason for too long. Two months after the picnic, he leaves Sorella and goes back to his old company. His wife and kids never moved to New Jersey, and he ultimately had to choose his job or his family. He made the right decision, and Marta is glad their relationship didn't get in the middle of that.

Still, despite her relief, she is walking through her days sad and somewhat deflated. Now, when she looks into the future, it isn't as exciting as it was. It is like finishing a wonderful book and being brought back to reality—which, compared to the splendor of the story, which held all sorts of possibilities, seems rather bleak. She asks herself again, *Is this life? A little colorless, a little mundane? Am I being fair to Steve and to myself if I don't feel any excitement when I picture our future?*

In the bright glare of day, she asks and answers these questions one way: *Do I have the job I dreamed I would have when I was young? No, but who does? Is my husband the man I dreamed of when I was young? No, but whose is? Did my dream of having kids become reality? No, but that happens. Happiness is a childish dream.*

However, in the deepest, darkest part of the night, when she stares at the ceiling trying to get back to sleep, she responds to these questions differently—acknowledges that her life is lacking something. *Maybe Jason is a wake-up call or a sign from above that I'm not as happy about my life as I should be. Maybe I don't want to completely forget the dreams I had when I was young,* she admits to herself. *It's not too late to shake my life up a bit and maybe go after some of them.*

Thinking this, she is reminded of the silly poster she had on her wall when she was a teenager. It said, "Shoot for the moon, so you at least land in the stars." *God, life is hard to figure out.*

CHAPTER 12: The Convention

2003—Las Vegas, Nevada

Cholan puts on a white long-sleeve shirt that is neither a dress shirt nor a tunic. He ties a cotton tie tightly around his waist and rubs his hand against the rough fabric and pauses. His wife, Sofie, orders them from a Himalayan crafter, and the shirts meet his needs perfectly. Easy to get on and off, comfortable, and evocative of the mysteries of the East.

He walks out of his hotel room and down the hall with the slight limp he's had since childhood. He is filled with hopeful anticipation. Someone's world could be changed tonight.

Sitting at a large banquet table, Marta is relaxing after several days of meetings and seminars. Another successful dental convention for Sorella. She only has this closing dinner left, and then she's done with only a flight back to Newark tomorrow morning still to come.

Lifting her icy mojito glass, she nods to Tracy, who is sitting across from her, and smiles. Tracy gives her a wiseass grin and tilts her head at her own glass, which is empty save a few melting ice cubes in the bottom. Marta shakes her head no.

Tracy, forever trying to loosen her up, has really been pushing that agenda since the Jason situation. It has been three months, and Marta continues to wonder what it all means, though she hasn't admitted that to Tracy. Despite sometimes feeling the need to do something crazy and Tracyesque, she knows getting another drink is not the answer to her issues. But what is?

Glancing at the stage, she notes the two empty chairs on it, as well as the maroon velvet curtains encircling the back and sides.

The dentist sitting next to her interrupts her perusal. "I really liked your new evac demonstration. I've got to say, it is pretty nifty."

Marta turns toward him and pushes her hair away from her face. Her shield of hair isn't necessary tonight. She smiles brightly and straightens her crisp white sheath dress. The expensive feel of the material and the perfect fit gives her a boost of confidence.

"I agree," she says. "I think it will make things much easier for your patients and hygienists. That is our hope."

"What do you make of this evening's entertainment?" he asks. "Sounds a bit exotic for a bunch of dentists."

Picking up the piece of paper on the table, Marta scans it. Instead of the normal keynote speaker, the agenda lists "Channeling to the Past with Cholan Kumera." She sits straighter in her chair. Her senses sharpen. "I don't know, but I'm intrigued!" She gazes to the stage expectantly.

Seconds later, the small man in a white linen shirt that is tied at his waist walks onstage, and as he does the hairs on her arms rise and she is hit with a surge of energy. Staring, she notes he has scarring around his face and neck that make his brown skin ripple when he turns his head to gaze down into the audience. When his alert brown eyes dart in her direction, Marta feels suddenly vulnerable and quickly averts her gaze. A perfect picture of Kevin pops into her head. He is leaning back against his couch at his house, and as the faint sounds of Don McLean echo from the stereo, he kisses her softly. Marta touches her hand to her lips and glances around the table blushing furiously. *My God, that was so real.*

✧ ✧ ✧

Cholan takes a sip of water and pauses. The smell of rosemary drifts up to him, mixing with the perfume worn by the women in the room. Staring above the audience's heads, he sees whorls rising off them and getting caught in the swirling, ventilated air and begin to take shape. Shaking his head, he blinks hard, and the image disappears. *A few ghosts are here tonight.*

In a softly accented voice, he begins, "Hello, American Dental Association members, so pleased to be with you tonight. My name is Cholan." He bows his head. "This is not an extravagant show but rather an intimate exploration of time and space that will allow some of you to glimpse a world that, until tonight, you could only dream of. A few of you in this room may possess the ability, with my help, to channel back to some point in your past and see what happens if you make a different decision—and how that decision can change your life's outcomes. These fortunate few will be able to actually *experience* these other outcomes. While science is still working to fully explain how and why some people can do this, we do know that it entails quantum physics and theories of alternate universes. Has anyone heard of Schrödinger's cat paradox?"

About half the audience nods their head and the other half look confused. Cholan continues, "No worries for those that haven't heard of it. I only found out about it when I went to MIT." Cholan laughs softly. "I must clarify. I went to Boston after I attended Sacramento State and visited MIT, as I don't have a mind for such things. But that is where I met Edwin. Edwin, come on out here." Cholan motions toward the left side of the stage and a bespectacled man emerges from the shadow. He takes quick steps toward the center of the stage and stops, standing awkwardly. He is dressed in dress pants and a neat button-down shirt. He looks as if he should be wearing a bow tie, but he isn't.

Nodding, Cholan turns back to the audience, "Now, Edwin did go to MIT, and he can explain all this cat business better than I can."

Without smiling, Edwin begins pacing the stage back and forth. He turns and states, "The premise Schrödinger put forth was a simple theoretical experiment to explain a very complex theory, or really to disprove a complex quantum mechanics theory of the day. The premise is there is a cat in a box, with a radioactive atom. If the atom decays, it will emit a radioactivity isotope that reacts and causes a flask of poison to shatter, and the cat is dead. But if instead of that path or channel, if the atom doesn't decay, the cat is alive. There is now a channel where in one world the cat is alive and in the other the cat is dead. Suffice it to say, the point of the experiment demonstrates that every event is a decision or branch point, where different channels of the universe are equally real but separate." Edwin stops his pacing and takes a breath. He nods curtly to Cholan and walks back to the shadow.

"Yes, yes, thank you, Edwin. Most illuminating." Cholan winks at the audience. "Now with a group as learned as this, I am sure you follow that better than I, and I have heard it thousands of times. Well, we are going to find the few of you that can bridge that divide to investigate the box, and if the cat is dead, we will try to find the channel or universe where the cat is alive. Sounds fun, right?" Cholan peers around expectantly, but there is only silence from the audience.

"I promise, no dead cats or even live cats. But we will follow your channel to find something much more interesting that is out there in the multiverse."

Glancing quickly around the tables, Cholan sees that a few still appear confused, but most are nodding their heads, and some of them are even smiling.

Cholan is pleased by the soft murmur that has begun to fill the room. Multiple universes always get people's attention. He hopes this group of dentists will be open to the universe and all its mysteries. The audience or at least some must be engaged for this to work. He can feel a swell of positivity emanating through the room. He's sure he hasn't lost anyone yet.

"Now, I am not a scientist," he continues. "I am a channeler and knew nothing of Schrödinger's cat paradox Edwin just explained. I was born in Sri Lanka and lived an idyllic life up until I was ten years old, when I was caught in a devastating forest fire and was severely burned. For many days afterward, I suffered greatly, crumpled on a dirty mattress inside our hut. Right now, I bet you are wondering, *How does a small boy with third-degree burns survive in a rustic hut high up on Mount Pidurutalagala?* Well, let me tell you about channeling . . ."

1964—Sri Lanka

When young Cholan tires of counting the saplings or watching his mother make dinner or sweep the hut, he turns inward. Since the fire, something has opened in his mind. He can move to a different place and time, reexperience his life. At age ten, he doesn't fully understand this ability, and for the most part he must simply fight for his life every day. He is lucky to be alive. That is what many of the villagers share with his parents when they stop over, bearing small gifts of food or a talisman to help with his recovery. Dozens of others did not race their brother on a cool, crisp day through that fire but instead saw the walls of flames surrounding them, felt the hopelessness of their situation, and succumbed.

Cholan's skin adheres to his bedding if he doesn't shift around frequently enough, but moving causes such excruciating pain that he resists until his mother or Phurbu comes over and, with as careful a touch as possible, tugs him into another position. He can't help but scream in agony when they do, and he often passes out from the pain. This happens several times a day. Even sips of milk tea cause searing pain down his throat, but Phurbu insists, knowing fluids are critical if Cholan is to survive these first tenuous days.

Fortunately, the burns in his throat, lungs, and mouth heal the quickest, and after the first couple of weeks he can eat and talk almost normally.

Yet as the days turn to weeks and the weeks into months, he comes to wish he had not made it out. He thinks he would have preferred to be one of the many who died immediately.

His village has few painkillers and antibiotics, but many herbal remedies passed down from generation to generation. He hates the sap from the jade plant that Phurbu applies to his burns. "The salve is killing me, Phurbu," he insists.

He doesn't know that none of these ancient remedies are a match for the seriousness of his situation. His parents are beside themselves as they see the endless pain their son is in; it's clear that his oozing, blistered skin is a constant reminder of his battle with death. Occasionally, he sees in their eyes that they, too, think he would have been better off dying in the flames.

Phurbu, the only local Ayurvedic doctor in the mountain villages, tries everything he knows. His awful teas are nothing like the delicious, sweet milk tea Cholan's mother gives him, but his smelly ointments do help somewhat.

But it is Phurbu the channeler, not Phurbu the doctor, who ends up saving Cholan.

At some point in his convalescence, Cholan whispers the story of his mental race with Sonam the day of the fire to Phurbu and shares his ability to reexperience the past.

"Your mind is strong, Cholan," Phurbu tells him. "It saved you that day, and it can save you now. Your body is in pain now, but it is your spirit that we must tend to—because once the spirit is gone, no salves or teas will save you. The loss of spirit is worse than any infection."

From that point on, Phurbu works with Cholan to give him some peace from the constant pain. Sitting at his bedside, bent over in a hunch, he whispers, "I can't do much more for your body, but you know how to daydream. Let's daydream together."

Cholan's eyes are the only body parts that don't ache with the never-ending pain. He gazes into Phurbu's all-knowing eyes and listens to his feathery voice.

"Just imagine last summer," the old man says. "Picture you and me walking through the high meadow like we did that day, searching for herbs and berries. Remember I showed you what feverfew looks like, and the magical ginseng?"

Phurbu clasps Cholan's hands in his. Cholan feels a tingle that starts in his fingers and works up his arms and into his head, giving his brain a nudge. The strange feeling rolls over him as his mind moves ever so slightly out of his body. He is no longer fully connected to the mattress or the rough cloth; a dislocation happens, and his eyes are suddenly seeing trees.

In his low, musical voice, Phurbu murmurs, "Picture the trees, picture the sky . . . is it day or night?"

> *Cholan can see the grass and the meadow as clearly as if he is standing there. The sky is a brilliant blue. The rough hut fades further and he can both feel and see the high meadow that he and Phurbu scoured for his herbs last summer. He turns his head to look around and his neck moves easily. Phurbu is beside him with a bucket. They are looking for the pretty white-and-yellow flowers of the feverfew plant. The wind gently caresses the trees. Cholan holds his breath as he takes the beauty in. He hears some birds chirping, and he is not watching from up above, he is actually walking and seeing things as they were that day.*

As Cholan slowly comes back to the hut and the constant pain, he has a smile on his face for the first time since the fire.

"I didn't feel any pain," he whispers. "It is magic."

Phurbu's eyes crinkle as he breaks into a toothy grin. "Ah, little Cholan, I think you have the gift. Mother Goddess knows your mind was often in a different place much of the time before the fire. It makes perfect sense that you are open to living in a different realm for a bit."

"But how does it happen?" Cholan asks.

"Well, you just traveled up a channel from your past," Phurbu explains. "It is more than remembering something from the past; it is going back to that time and place and existing in that channel. When I do this, I can go up a different channel. Imagine it like a river that forks and flows two ways. I can go up the other branch for a bit, just to take a look—to see what life might have been."

Cholan whispers hesitantly, "Can I do that?"

Phurbu looks pleased. "I have never met anyone that could do such things other than me and my father before me, who taught me and told me it was a gift. But clearly you have a gift, and we can see how strong of a gift it is."

Cholan is very excited—not only by the idea of revisiting different moments of his past life to blot out the pain, but also by the possibility of trying out another channel and seeing a different life than the one he has.

"When we traveled back along your river of memories just now, did you notice a decision fork? A place where the river—the memory—could flow in a new direction if you had made a different decision? That is a magic key."

Cholan thinks back, but he isn't sure. "I don't know," he says, disappointed.

"We will keep trying," Phurbu says reassuringly. "You will learn."

Phurbu continues to take Cholan back to his past, as this gives him the respite his body and mind desperately need. Each time, Cholan searches for forks, but life in a small remote village in the '60s doesn't change much day to day, or even year to year. At just ten years old, there have been limited opportunities for him to make a big decision that could change the course of his life, even a little.

But one day, as he is wandering in the forest in his past, pain-free life, Cholan suddenly realizes that he is back on the day of the fire.

Sonam is there, and when he turns to Cholan and smiles his crooked grin, Cholan knows it is that same day, because Sonam has the swollen lip from his fall earlier that day. Cholan is suddenly keenly aware as Sonam says, "I think the bread is ready. I'm heading back. Are you coming?"

Cholan starts to say no, but he can feel the duality of this channel. He feels the fork more than sees it. He tries to say yes, but he can't form the word. It feels like being in a nightmare—desperately wanting to scream and nothing coming out.

Pulling himself back from his channel, Cholan stares into Phurbu's smiling eyes—and he suddenly understands. Phurbu has known all along that the fire is his one mighty fork. He just wanted Cholan to find it himself.

Joy bubbles up in his chest. He has found his other channel, something new and exciting that can keep him away from the pain; it's thrilling. His face breaks into a big grin, but that causes his burned lips to crack, and he immediately winces in pain.

Phurbu rubs more of his jade aloe ointment on Cholan's bleeding lips and murmurs, "Maybe we try tomorrow. I will help you cross over into the alternative channel. I may need to push you, but we can do it together."

Cholan nods, not wanting to risk moving his lips again. He has something to look forward to, and that is all he can ask for. A small glimmer of hope starts to burn in his chest.

The next day, they go to work. With Phurbu's help, Cholan can speak that elusive word:

"Yes," he tells his brother, and he eventually moves his feet to walk with Sonam out of the forest and back to the village.

Phurbu's spirit is a force Cholan is aware of. He isn't there in any physical form—he is an amorphous being— yet he is able to push Cholan's body away from its real channel and guide him down this possible one.

Over the next couple of months, they travel farther and farther up his alternative channel.

Cholan is in the riverbed with the others during the fire. He chokes and smells the awful burning, but his skin is unscathed and no small, burning Cholan tree suddenly emerges from the forest. In the days that follow, his life is in the village and the woods and not on the mattress. He is still the daydreaming boy who sometimes forgets what errand he is on.

These escapes from reality let his mind heal itself and then return refreshed and ready to continue the battle. His life in his channel isn't that different from what it was like before the fire, but he feels he is cheating fate by experiencing what it is to live whole and unscathed. Each time he comes back from these channeling excursions, he thinks he can feel the slightest degree of lessening pain.

Cholan learns that his healing is a figment of his imagination when he hears Phurbu—through the thin, thrush walls of his family's home—tell his parents that his situation is worsening.

"His skin isn't healing," he says. "There isn't enough healthy skin for the healing process to take hold."

These facts are plain to Cholan as well. His skin is melting into itself. His arm is becoming permanently attached to his side. One leg is bent at the knee, no longer able to straighten. Though he could move it during the first several months, it is now stiffening into a permanent bend. And the weirdest issue is his jaw and face, which are sinking into his chest. He can no longer eat the food he was able to eat after his mouth and lips healed. His mother now has to mix his food with goat's milk or water, and even that causes him to choke and cough as he tries to get it down. His throat is being pulled down, little by little, as the skin has no resiliency to fight against gravity and is oozing down his chest.

His parents, brother and sister, and Phurbu are now the only people he sees, as the risk of infection is great. They no longer react to his condition or his looks with anything but compassion. But even without mirrors, Cholan knows he looks a fright and is becoming more like the lumpy mattress he lies upon than the vibrant boy he was. His ears always stuck out, and it is Sonam who jokes, as only brothers can, "Well, little brother, at least you don't have ears that stick out anymore, since you no longer have ears."

Cholan knows that even if he survives, he will never be the same.

CHAPTER 13: Saved

2003—Las Vegas, Nevada

Cholan sees that most of the audience have put down their forks and are listening intently. He has them hooked. Sweeping his hair away from one of his damaged ears, he announces dramatically, "The fire did take care of that ten-year-old's worry, eh? When I asked the gods to fix my Dumbo ears so the kids would stop teasing me, I did not mean for them to wipe them right off my head. The moral of that story is that you must be careful what you wish for!"

The audience is quiet, and Cholan can feel they are holding their breath, but when he starts to chuckle, they exhale as one single mass and many join in with him laughing.

"Now you understand that channeling was able to take me away from my enormous misery during those hard months on the mattress," he goes on, "but it could not really save me. It took my father, some bad luck, and some very good luck to do that."

1964—Sri Lanka

His parents are having another whispered argument when they think Cholan is asleep.

"We must try to get a doctor from Columbo, or at least some western medicine," Cholan's father says quietly. "Phurbu is right. He is getting worse. You see it. We need to do something, and this is the only option. His only hope."

Cholan's mother says flatly, "Even if you do travel to Columbo, four days there and four days back—it won't work, will it?"

"It must," his father says.

The next day, Cholan's father, Suren, gathers everyone in the village together and pleads, "We must help my son—his plight is desperate. I am going to Columbo to get medicine or help."

The villagers nod their heads in agreement, though he can see that many, like Cholan's mother, think it is a fool's errand.

Despite their reservations, each family returns to their hut and brings back rupees or food to help with the journey, and the next day Suren starts walking westward, weighed down with containers of milk tea, flatbread, and goat cheese. It is November, after the monsoon season, so at least fair weather should be his companion during his treacherous journey.

Few villagers have ever left their village for their province's capital of Kandy, let alone Columbo, which is even farther away. Those who have—usually young men who find the life of their village not exciting enough—occasionally return for visits and share stories and items from the big city. But Suren has never been one to want more than what his village could offer, and he knows little of the wider world.

He travels first through the mountains he knows and loves. The road is rough and makes tight switchbacks as he comes down the mountain. After that, he enters the less familiar territory of the jungle; he fears the big cats most. On his third day, he reaches paved roads with carts pulled by every type of beast of burden. He sees people on bikes and even a few in cars, which he marvels at.

Passing through Kandy, he continues toward Columbo. He makes it to the outskirts of Columbo, a hundred miles from his small mountain village—his heart soars and then feels a pain so intense he staggers. Grabbing his head, he tries to stay upright and then his world turns black.

Suren awakes in a white, brightly lit room that he immediately realizes is in a hospital. His joy is quickly snuffed out when he realizes that his feet are bare and the small amount of money he hid in his shoe for his desperate mission must be gone. It saddens him to think there are people in the world going around randomly hitting people in the head, hoping they carry something of value in their shoe. If he had realized his money was gone when he lay bleeding on the street, he would have given up all hope and succumbed to death right there on the cobblestone road. But fortunately, as he will later tell, he was knocked out cold and didn't have enough sense to give up hope and die as he should have.

Suren's gifts do not include daydreaming or imagining other life channels; instead, he maintains a realistic grasp on what can be changed and what cannot. His little bit of money meant that he might get someone to listen to his tale, and perhaps even manage to buy some medication or hire someone to make the journey back to help his young son. Without money, he knows all is lost.

Despite growing up in a sheltered village in a community that helps others without question, he understands the outside world is different. Lying on the clean, white sheets of the hospital bed, all hope drains out of him, just as he imagines his blood drained out of him on the streets of Columbo. But somehow, he can't give up completely. His son hasn't given up through all those torturous months of pain, and Suren, while very practical, also understands that Vishnu provides. What better place to find help than a hospital? An omen is an omen.

So, he waits patiently, letting the twenty stitches along the back of his head begin to fuse his flesh back together. The nurses check on him regularly and bring him meals that are almost enjoyable. But Cholan is never far from his mind.

✧   ✧   ✧

On the third day of Suren's stay, a young American doctor enters his room. The doctor looks younger than most eighteen-year-olds look back in the village. Suren immediately begins speaking frantically in Tamil and gesturing wildly, sharing his story. The doctor leaves quickly and returns with a middle-aged Tamil nurse. The nurse begins to translate his emotional plea.

The young doctor stands and listens without much expression on his face as Suren describes the forest fire, the miracle of Cholan's survival, Cholan's months of tortured convalescence, and how he no longer seems to be healing.

As he is explaining his son's pain and anguish, the young doctor interjects, "What type of pain medication does the boy have?"

The nurse translates and Suren responds, "No pain medication, only mind travel."

With a quick motion of his hand, the young doctor quickly leaves the room. Cholan's father hopes the gesture means to wait, but he isn't sure because that doesn't make much sense, as he clearly isn't going anywhere.

The young doctor returns with an older American doctor.

The nurse smiles encouragingly and says, "Please begin again."

This doctor asks a hundred questions throughout the story—about the herbs in the teas and ointments, and how Cholan is managing what must be excruciating pain. Suren struggles to answer the questions as best he can, and the nurse does her best to translate. He explains the native plants and teas Phurbu uses, but the real interest the older doctor has is in the channeling process he's describing.

"Phurbu takes my son's mind somewhere else, and my son doesn't feel the pain during those trips," Suren repeats. "His body stays in the cot, but his mind goes to the past—and to a different past, too."

The doctors exchange interested glances and then shift their line of questioning. They begin by asking where, exactly, their village is and how many days' travel it takes to get there.

Suren can't believe his luck. "It is four days' walk if you walk very quickly—and we will," he says eagerly.

The young doctor seems to be the one working out the logistics. "How long if we have a car?"

Cholan's father shakes his head. "I don't know, no car has ever come. I think maybe two days, because we would have to walk for the last part of the trip no matter what."

When the nurse is done translating his words, the doctors look at each other and nod.

"We will start planning the trip," the younger doctor says, "but you need to rest and get better first."

Cholan learns later that the younger doctor is Dr. Smith, a general physician who is part of the Doctors Without Borders program. The older doctor is Dr. Liam Cavato, a neurologist. He's been in Sri Lanka for six months and has a special interest in pain management through hypnosis and other mind-controlling methods practiced in the Far East. Both have come to the Far East hoping to learn something they can take back to the United States and apply. So far, they have succeeded only in getting the sick and dying of Sri Lanka some of the basic medicines the West takes for granted. The fact that a local doctor is able to control a boy's mind to eliminate what is one of the most excruciating pains imaginable is exactly what they have been hoping for. It is for this reason that they agree to accompany Suren back to his remote village.

The doctors spend the next several days trying to figure out the best way to get to Cholan's remote village. Suren is most impatient but does not want to take the chance of offending the doctors, so he only pushes slightly. He wishes there was some way to let the village know of the impending visit, but there isn't.

The physicians rent a small car, and with Suren and the nurse riding in the back seat, they travel swiftly for the first hundred miles. Suren will describe the ride afterward as both terrifying and thrilling. When they can drive no further, they hire a cart and donkey from a local village that carries the four of them the rest of the way.

The day Suren arrives back to the village is a day no one will ever forget. The fact that he is back, and back with two American doctors, is unbelievable. No one imagined this outcome in their wildest dreams. Suren is so proud; he grins from ear to ear the whole first day.

The doctors immediately enter the hut and set about examining Cholan.

It will be a year before Cholan will learn the doctors' language, but that first day, their body language says it all. He can tell immediately that they are gravely concerned by his condition and think his prognosis is quite dismal. They huddle and discuss his condition for hours in their own tongue. When his father or mother turns to the nurse for help, the doctors sternly shake their heads, not allowing the nurse to translate any of it. The nurse stands silent and stoic in the corner, appearing as dismayed as the doctors.

The first question she is allowed to translate is, "Where is the doctor? Can he come to demonstrate the mind traveling?"

Phurbu appears the next moment. Cholan didn't realize until now that the whole village is gathered just outside their hut's door.

Phurbu explains channeling to the nurse, and she, in turn, works intently to translate his explanation to English. Phurbu can see the confusion on the doctors' faces as they struggle to understand the nurse's translation.

Finally turning to the nurse, Phurbu says, "It is hard to describe something that can only be experienced. Maybe I show you?"

When the nurse translates, the doctors respond enthusiastically.

"Yes," the younger one exclaims, "please show us!"

Phurbu and Cholan have traveled the path together so many times now that doing it with an audience doesn't cause them a moment's hesitation. They travel back to his one alternative channel: the day of the fire, when he made the choice to stay behind in the woods.

When they come back, Phurbu explains and the nurse translates, "Each time we travel up this alternative channel, we can stay a bit longer before the pull of Cholan's life snaps him back to his real channel. Most forks or channels are minor ones that rather quickly lead you back to your actual life channel. But Cholan's fork goes on and on, with no end in sight." He gestures to the doctors. "If you think about all the choices you face every day, rarely does one cause your world to be vastly different from what it is. If I choose to eat a banana for breakfast this morning, I can come back to that point in time when I channel in my past and instead pick the oatmeal. A few things may be different in the alternative channel, but very soon I will be back in my actual channel without even having to be snapped back. Both channels just flow back together into one. The trick to channeling for long periods of time and seeing a different life is to find a decision point that makes a serious and severe difference in your life."

The doctors hang on his every word.

"Is it dangerous?"

"Well, I have never had an issue, but my father did tell me to always be careful, as you can get lost in your channel, and if he wasn't around to unstick me, he wasn't sure what might happen. But I am not sure if any of that is true, or if he was just trying to keep me on my toes. I have never been lost in my channels; nor has Cholan."

Phurbu's rudimentary explanation to the two American doctors does help the doctors begin to understand. And witnessing Cholan's transformation after channeling makes them understand the power of it.

They ask Phurbu and Cholan to channel a second time, only this time they hook Cholan up to all sorts of equipment—gingerly, careful to find the few unscathed patches of skin to attach them to.

Their shiny instruments measure blood pressure, pulse, and heart rate. The readings they produce show Cholan's blood pressure drop, his slowed heart rate, and his breathing shift to a trancelike state. They understand, as his parents understood intuitively, that something is affecting his body's perception of pain in a powerful and positive way, and this is what they have been seeking.

Cholan hopes that with or without channeling, the American doctors would not leave him to melt into his cot, but he understands the harsh realities of the world and understands they very well might. Fortunately, he never traveled that possible fork in his river. Throughout his many years of friendship with both men, he never dared ask them that question. Some things are best left unknown.

Seemingly with no effort at all, the doctors do the impossible. Cholan is taken by car to Columbo City Hospital. His future is about to change dramatically.

Cholan barely registers much of the trip down the mountain and on to Columbo, as he is floating on a haze of painkillers—an experience that is like channeling in some ways but very different in others. Even in his hazy state, he knows he's traveled into a different world, but all he is focused on is seeing and experiencing life without mind-numbing pain. He doesn't even mind the strange plastic suit he has to wear. A nurse in the hospital explains that the suit is to keep the germs away from the open wounds on his skin. He doesn't share with her or the other nurses that he has lain on a dirty mattress for months, as they seem very obsessed with cleaning his skin and keeping it clean.

He doesn't mind their ministrations as much as he minded Phurbu's because of the delicious pain medication that flows into his arm through a little needle and string. He tastes it as it runs through his body. It tastes like the peppermint his mother grows in her garden—just a hint, and then it gets into his head and makes him all fuzzy.

Once he is in stable condition at the City Hospital, he is transported to a large army airbase, to be flown to America on a Doctors Without Borders charter flight. He is, of course, accompanied by Dr. Smith and Dr. Liam, as Cholan comes to call him, because *Cavato* is too difficult to pronounce. Fortunately, *Smith* is pronounceable in most languages.

The flight is a majestic, life-changing experience for Cholan. The airplane is the largest thing he has ever seen. The smooth, cold metal of the body is something he can't comprehend. Everything he has touched in his life up until this point has been rough and jagged: his blankets, his clothes, the walls to the hut, the roads, his parents' hands. The plane is smooth and hard but feels almost soft under his hand. It reminds him of the smooth rocks he and Sonam find in the river to see who can skip the farthest.

As he lies on a soft cot, he grazes his fingers against the smooth metal. He imagines he is now inside one of those river rocks and has somehow shrunk down to fit inside it. When the plane takes off and hurtles through the air, he imagines Sonam is hurling the rock with him inside it across the cool water of the stream near their village.

His mind plays such tricks on him for most of the trip. He knows it is because of the sharp metal stick in his arm, which is hooked to a bag that Dr. Liam says has the medicine that takes away the pain. Cholan's head is fuzzy, but not fuzzy enough to completely forget that he is leaving his home. The farther he travels from his parents, brother, sister, and Phurbu, the bigger the hole in his heart gets. The knowledge that he may never again feel the loving embrace of his family causes a pain in his chest that the medicine doesn't take away.

Phurbu is torn with indecision about coming with Cholan to the strange land. The doctors desperately want him to be part of their mind study, and he did come all the way to Columbo with them, going right to the edge of that decision fork of flying to America. But in the end, he stayed.

"I have not seen all the world," he confided in Cholan before he left, "but I know it. And I know this journey would change me in ways I don't want to be changed. Besides"—he winked at Cholan—"now I will have this fork, so I will be able to experience some of what you will experience in America. It will be like I am with you!"

He accompanied Cholan and the doctors to the tarmac. The last time Cholan saw Phurbu, he was waving as they boarded the plane and took off, becoming a smaller and smaller speck down on earth.

Cholan arrives at LAX in December 1964. When he sees all the city lights from the plane, he worries that everyone has thousands of tiny fires. *If all these fires are burning, the smoke will be worse than it was in my village*, he thinks. His aversion to smoke is even stronger than before now that he knows what it is like to be a stick of kindling.

As the plane descends toward the earth, the sheer size of the buildings he sees jars his view of the world.

I am even smaller than I thought I was, he realizes. *This is a large and strange world. If I do survive the burns, how will I survive here?*

CHAPTER 14: An Ideal Candidate

2003—Las Vegas, Nevada

S miling at all the upturned eyes watching him, Cholan says, "Yes, I arrived in a very strange world, indeed. Thankfully, it was only Los Angeles and not," he spins around with his arms outstretched, "Las Vegas."

The audience rocks with laughter.

"All right, let's get down to the evening's agenda: we are going to see if a few of you are like the boy with his head in the clouds and possess the ability to channel."

Cholan pauses and scans the faces before him, hoping his initial feeling holds and there are a few good candidates among this group.

"We will take you back to reexperience a moment in your life— not just to remember it but to re-*live* it. Not everyone can do this. But if you can, we also will see if you have a decision fork that will allow you to peek into an alternative version of your life. Hopefully not something as life-altering as the fire was for me—but one never knows. So, enough about the concept, let's get to work. Please, everyone, if you are interested in trying this, start by raising your hand."

✧ ✧ ✧

Leaning her elbow on the table so she can keep her hand slightly raised, Marta is feeling something between eagerness and unease.

"I will ask a series of questions," the speaker says. "If your answer to them is yes, please keep your hand up. If your answer is no, put your hand down. First question: who here daydreamed quite a bit as a youngster?"

Marta keeps her hand up, as do most others in the audience. Her lips part in the barest of smiles, thinking of all the daydreams she has spun about Kevin.

The speaker's next questions are interesting and catch most of the audience's attention: "Who has vivid sexual fantasies? Or who has read or may still read romance novels?"

The audience, either from embarrassment or actual elimination, is left with only a smattering of hands still up.

"Who still has vivid daydreams about people, places, or things they think may go beyond the normal scope of daydreams? They either pop into your head unbidden or happen in odd places, like work meetings or family gatherings?"

Marta keeps her hand up. Glancing around, she notes she is one of only a handful with their hands still raised. She is very tempted to tuck her hand back in her lap; the voice of worry reminds her that blending in is the safest path. But she concentrates on her soft linen sleeve as it falls away from her wrist and the light jangling of the gold bangles she's wearing. This gives her a surge of confidence and the ability to fight against the voice. She wants to be the relaxed, confident, even sophisticated persona she has cultivated over the years. Tonight, it feels important to ignore the shy, nervous girl inside her.

Sitting up straight and keeping her hand up, Marta tells herself, *Keep your hand up, you know this is you.*

There are only five people left with their hands raised. The speaker beckons with a dramatic sweep of his arm and commands, "Would all of you with your hands still raised come up to the stage? Let's see who may be able to peek at their life from a different path and share it with us."

Marta stands up. Looking back at her empty chair, she wonders why she is moving forward. Normally her inner voice would keep her rooted to her chair. But a feeling of destiny propels her toward the stage.

"Go, girl!" Tracy barks.

Marta chuckles.

The group is ushered up the stairs and led off to the left of the stage. Marta finds herself behind the curtain, just out of sight of the rest of the audience. She inhales deeply and smells a mustiness that reminds her of standing in the wings of her elementary school stage during her fourth-grade dance recital.

Fourth grade was a good grade, as Kevin was in her class. That is how she categorizes the various grades—not by favorite teachers but by Kevin's proximity. She remembers wearing a black bodysuit and tights. Nancy, her dance partner, was on the other side, and they were waiting for the signal from Mrs. Streeter to do a leap and then a forward roll onto the stage. Marta's stomach was tightly clenched, and she thought she might faint, but when Nancy gave her a big grin from across the stage, she forced her feet to push off into their first leap. She did the routine. She did it for Kevin, who was in the audience. She wanted him to notice her and hoped being brave and strong would do the trick. It didn't. Marta shakes off the image of that young girl in the black leotard—leaping for her life, feeling so scared and alone.

Smiling at the other four people in the group, Marta recognizes Jeff and Lauren from Sorella. A sliver of apprehension work its way up her spine. She doesn't want to reveal deep secrets to these people. She likes them, but she suddenly is afraid the channeler will reveal who she really is to her coworkers—her worst nightmare.

She takes a deep breath and refocuses her attention. Her panic subsides a bit when Edwin approaches the mismatched group. He holds a clipboard in his hands. He starts asking the group some questions: name, age, where are they from? She notes that he looks very serious. He is older than she, but she can't tell by how much. He doesn't have wrinkles or any other telltale signs of age, other than being slightly balding, he just *seems* older.

After a short wait, Edwin calls her name. Marta follows him to a small alcove farther back from the stage, where there are two folding chairs. They sit. She immediately doesn't like him. She can hear Cholan continuing to elaborate on his story for the benefit of those still in the audience, and she wishes she were among them, with another mojito and perhaps some dessert. She figures she will dispense with this charade as quickly as possible, not because of her inner voice but because she's suddenly feeling very unsteady.

"As you know, I am Edwin. I want to follow up with a few questions."

She shrugs her agreement.

He asks similar questions to what the channeler asked the group. He seems satisfied with her answers and taps his pen on his cheek as he reviews what he has written.

Torn: she's terrified of revealing too much in front of her colleagues but can't deny that the possibility of channeling is intriguing.

Leaning toward her, Edwin peers directly into her eyes and carefully says, "Is there any single situation or event in your past that, if you could, you would want to go back to and change? A different decision you'd want to make?"

Marta inhales sharply—and pauses.

Edwin seems to know immediately that her answer is yes and that she is hesitant to share. Without waiting for her to answer, he marks something on his clipboard. "Many people want to change something that occurred in the past," he says. "Sometimes they get so fixated on it that they really aren't able to grow or move beyond it. Cholan can let you see what coulda, woulda, shoulda happened. Not just let you *see* what your life would have been like, but also to *feel* what it actually would have felt like."

He goes on to talk about *It's a Wonderful Life*, which is one of Marta's favorite movies.

As he speaks, it dawns on Marta that she's been worried about the wrong thing. *The channeler isn't going to unveil the worried, backward girl to my peers, he is going to reveal the crushing pain of my first love! On display will be what happens when two people who may be soulmates are yanked apart by fate or some other equally capricious god. My secret heart will be divulged to my peers—but even worse, to me.*

". . . Cholan can do what the angel did," Edwin goes on, not noticing Marta's distress. "Not show you what life would be like if you had never existed, but rather what it would be like if you had done something different. You get to be part of the different life or channel just for a bit . . . hopefully. You get to see if you made the right decision or not. You may find you regret your decision even more, if you find that you had a 'happy' channel that you missed out on. Or you may find you made the right decision, and your life either didn't really change much based on that decision or would be different but for the worse. This could allow you to move past a regret you've held on to for years."

Marta wavers and then realizes she is holding her breath, which is always a clear sign that she is worried or, as in this case, stressed. She slowly lets the air out of her lungs and thinks, *Breathe.* She frowns. And the memory of that day flashes through her head. Her mother knows what happened, because she was there, but even she has no idea how the phone call has haunted Marta. It feels like yesterday it is so vivid.

The decision to share one of her deeper stories with this short, bothersome man is a tough one. After toying with the idea, she decides, *No way.*

Again, Edwin seems to discern her decision, because he hurriedly interjects, "You can decide if you want to go onstage with an actual opportunity to visit this other channel, or you have the option for a consult in our Boston offices, which costs $250. That would be a much more private setting. Of course, we don't even know if your situation or regret is a viable one, do we?"

Marta imagines that without the perceptive, officious little man before her, this Cholan guy would surely have some nights when his stage was empty. She is uncomfortable with Edwin. She senses that he is able to see into her soul. There are too many hidden insecurities, worries, hopes, and dreams tucked deep inside her, and this man is the last person she wants shining a light into those deep recesses.

She again weighs her options, focusing on breathing every time she feels her lungs not cooperating. She thinks she can keep her experience to herself. No way can Edwin really read her mind or see into her soul. She really likes the idea of being one of the special handful that was chosen from the group. Also, giving up this opportunity would be like wasting $250, because now that she knows about channeling, she will have to try it either way. Scheduling a private counseling session and paying when she could get it for free goes against her nature and the way she was raised. She hasn't run far enough away from that small farm to justify throwing away that kind of money.

Also, she can practically hear Kevin urging her to do this.

Taking a deep breath, she chews her lip. Since eighth grade, she has tried to keep her promise to Kevin to take chances in her life and not listen to the worried girl inside. Now, it is his voice that whispers in her ear to be brave and to breathe. She does just that: takes a deep breath and lets it out. She rubs her thumb against her finger, imagining she has Kevin's special rock in her hand right now. The experience she wants to channel comes from a raw, bruised place in her heart she wants to protect. But she also realizes she doesn't need to share anything more than just a single incident. She doesn't have to include that when Kevin walked out of her life more than twenty years ago, she never got over it. All that can be kept safely locked away. Right?

I hope I can pull this off.

Edwin leans forward eagerly. "So, what is your decision?"

She moves her head up and down, still not 100 percent sure. Nevertheless, she begins to tell her story, bewildered by the fact that she's sharing it for the first time with a complete stranger.

"I had a boyfriend named Kevin when I was fourteen. He moved away the summer before high school. We sent letters to each other for many years. We were both sure that one day we would meet again, and ultimately, get married."

Edwin jots notes on his clipboard.

"When I was twenty-three and had just gotten engaged to my husband, Steve, Kevin called my parents' house. I wasn't living there anymore, but I was visiting the day he called. My father answered the phone. I didn't realize until a bit into their conversation who the caller was. When I did, I couldn't move—it was like I was frozen. My father ended up telling Kevin that I no longer lived there, I was about to get married, and he shouldn't bother calling ever again. By the time I snapped out of it and tried to make a move to grab the phone from my father's hand, it was too late. He had hung up."

Marta stops talking at this point, takes another deep breath, and holds it. She pictures her dad walking calmly over to the fruit bowl in the kitchen to get himself an apple and leaning on the counter with what she can only describe as a smug, satisfied look on his face. He wasn't a mean man, but he wasn't one given to whimsy or fancy—and in his mind, when one is engaged to someone else, old boyfriends are the very definition of whimsy or fancy.

"I've always regretted not having enough nerve to run over and grab the phone from my father so I could talk to Kevin," she continues calmly. "No one ever crossed my dad, so I'm not even sure I actually would have taken the phone if I'd had the chance, but maybe . . ." She stares anxiously at Edwin.

It doesn't seem so bad now that she has shared it in this summarized version. She's left out the fact that her mother walked into the room shortly after her dad hung up and asked, "Who was on the phone?"

"Kevin!" Marta choked out. "My old boyfriend."

Her mother took one look at her stricken face and asked, "Did you talk to him?" When Marta shook her head, her mom turned to her father in exasperation and exclaimed, "Oh, Ernest, how could you?"—at which her father just walked out of the room.

Marta's mother came over and wrapped her arms around her. Marta sat there, immobile, her emotions running the gamut from euphoria that Kevin had called to horrid regret that she hadn't wrenched that phone from her father's callused hands.

Edwin interrupts her memory and utters excitedly, "Hmm, this is definitely workable! It works best when your alternative channel requires you to take action. You know, to move. Cholan can get people to move easier than he can to get them to stop doing something. We studied this extensively at MIT back in the early days. We applied Newton's second law and found some merit that moving an object using an external force is easier than figuring out exactly how much force is needed to stop an object's momentum and bring it to stillness."

Marta stares at Edwin with her mouth open and consternation knitting her brows together.

"Oh dear, too much detail. I forget myself. I will tell you Cholan's theory instead. It is much simpler. You know his story and the channel that saved his life. In that channel, he needs to walk out of the forest with his brother instead of staying behind. Cholan figures because he has practiced moving so many thousands of times, it is easier for him to do that in other people's channels."

Marta smiles wanly. "That I kind of follow."

Edwin claps his hands and announces quickly, "But now we must prepare—and I also need you to fill out a questionnaire and then sign this waiver."

"A waiver?"

He shrugs. "We have everyone sign one, as we never know what could happen. We may be messing with different universes, as Cholan mentioned. Of course, we have never lost someone or had anything bad happen." He lets out a quiet laugh. "Yet." He holds out the paper. "More a formality, I think."

Marta looks at him questioningly, but he falls silent, pursing his lips. She takes the proffered form, responds to some medical questions—all negatively, she's always had excellent health—and scrawls her signature at the bottom.

Edwin begins to explain what will happen onstage and what it will feel like if Marta is able to channel. "I myself have never channeled, but this is what others have shared with me," he adds as he finishes.

Marta stares at him. It's hard to believe he could have worked with Cholan for all this time and never been tempted to experience this himself. "Never? How co—"

"This will feel like a very realistic dream," he cuts her short. "The kind you wake from and don't realize it was a dream because it seemed so real. This dream will include real experiences from your life, including people and places you know well. Cholan will be helping you push out of the actual channel of your life and carve a new channel, which can be difficult. You will feel some electrical pulses of sorts, and it may get hard to breathe. You may feel discomfort as this occurs and experience a physical sensation of being pushed or pulled. You should fight against that feeling for as long as possible. Eventually, it will overpower you, and then you will feel a jump or dislocation in time as you come back to your actual channel. Then, very suddenly, you will be back here, in the present."

Marta shakes her head. She is listening, but nothing Edwin is saying makes any real sense.

"Cholan will be with you the whole time. You won't be able to see him, but you should be able to feel a presence guiding you. Go with him."

Marta nods. That is a comfort and a relief.

"You will awake on the stage, and that is the transition people have the most difficulty with. Sometimes there are emotions that need to be dealt with. Sometimes tears."

There is a look in his eyes right now that makes her feel he is trying to convey something more to her.

"Sometimes the visit or trip is a very personal and profound experience; other times it can be disappointing," he continues. "No matter, you will have only a short time to gather yourself before we start discussing with the group what happened, and then you will answer any questions. I will have told them the basics of your journey. You will be gone for only a short period of time, but in the alternative channel it could be hours and even days. Throughout, just remember to breathe."

A memory of Kevin telling her the same thing when she was fourteen pops into her head. She takes it as a sign that this is the right thing to do. Edwin has clearly noticed her habit of holding her breath. He may not be very likable, but he's possibly the most perceptive man she's ever met.

Edwin attaches a small microphone to the collar of her dress.

CHAPTER 15: The Alternate

2003—Las Vegas, Nevada

Just behind the curtain, Marta stands beside Edwin, who still has his clipboard. They both watch Cholan. Marta glances at the tables directly in front of the stage and can see faces listening raptly to the channeler's mesmerizing voice. It trips and flows like a river. Sometimes it is a whisper, and other times it rises loudly before falling again. His accent adds mystery to his words. You need to listen carefully to understand him. Marta wonders if perhaps he is hypnotizing everyone in the room with his voice.

"...this phenomenon has been studied by some of the brightest minds at MIT," he's telling them. "No one is sure, but my MIT friends think it is another multiverse we are pushing through to. Let's find out where we will be going tonight."

Cholan glances over toward them, Edwin gives her a nudge, and they both step out into the bright lights. Marta blinks and realizes she is again holding her breath. Her steps falter slightly as she focuses on exhaling and inhaling slowly and steadily. She can feel the panic rising in her chest. Her vision narrows to what is directly in front of her, and everything else turns black. Her feet won't move forward. She freezes, and her breathing stalls. It is like the dreams she's had so many times: wanting to run, but her legs won't move, needing to scream, but unable to make a sound. Panic chokes her.

Edwin turns toward her, and he must see the panic in her eyes, because he slowly walks her back off the stage. Sitting her gently down in a chair, he flips the page on his clipboard, smiling at a woman who is standing nearby. "I will be right back," he murmurs. "Sit and breathe." Then he removes her microphone, clips it to the other woman's blouse, and walks her out to the bright lights.

Marta watches Edwin hand his notes to Cholan, who quickly scans them.

He turns to the audience. "This is a classic one. Revisiting high school. Many of us have regrets about how we navigated through those problematic four years; a select few of us can go back and see what might have been. Lily, why don't you tell the audience where we are going to try to go?"

Marta puts her head between her knees, inhales and exhales, and blocks out Lily's hope-tinged voice. She focuses only on her breath, now that she is away from the gaping hole she was going to plummet into and is able to breathe again. Her heart is slowing. But then she looks out at the stage and the bright lights, the panic starts to rise once again. She shifts her eyes back to the floor and senses more than sees the lights onstage growing dim. She hears Cholan's voice say softly, "Lily, you are back at cheerleader tryouts, you remember the time, you are back at tryouts, you remember the time . . ."

Marta closes her eyes, but her body feels strangely connected to what is happening onstage.

Cholan takes a hold of Lily's hands. "Ready?"

Lily inclines her head.

"Picture the auditorium—smell the odor of sweat, the bright lights. You are dressed in your gym shorts and sneakers, ready to try out for cheerleading. You're nervous, but know you can do this. You've already decided to try out. That was the hard part."

Cholan finds himself sitting next to Lily on hard bleachers, listening to the squeak of sneakers on the gym floor. He watches Lily rise when her name is called. She is trembling but performs the simple cheer routine all the newbies have learned well. Her execution is flawless, in fact, and shows a natural grace from her years of ballet. She returns to the bleacher with a big grin on her face. A girl next to her, who has ignored her up to this point, leans over and blurts, "Wow, that was the best so far." Lily's grin widens and suddenly the pretty sweetness in her face, so easily overlooked, shines brightly. Cholan feels a surge of confidence course through her. He watches a few other girls talk to her—and just like that, her high school world is tipped on its side. They stay in the channel, watching her circle of friends shift and widen, and they experience a few sophomore boys talking to her as they walk down the hallway between class. They're in an alternative channel— one created by her decision to throw caution to the wind and try out for the cheerleading squad. Then, suddenly, there is a compression and a pull, and Cholan enfolds her.

Cholan and Lily sit in the comfortable chairs on the stage and they both blink open their eyes. The lights are dim now. People are still eating their dessert, as only five minutes has passed for all of them.

Cholan sits quietly as Lily gathers herself. Sometimes the dichotomy can be difficult to handle. But not so this time. Lily is beaming and seems to still be basking in the glow of social acceptance she just experienced. Edwin walks onto the stage with two cups of water.

Cholan smiles encouragingly. "Let's share what just happened to us."

Cholan and Lily tell their story from both of their perspectives. After telling about the experience, Lily rises and turns toward the group and states, "I was so dumb not to try out. It's painful to think how different my life would have been. But I'm still being stupid now, as I'm revisiting these regrets. Well, no more. I'm going to try new things and see what the world has to offer," she announces confidently. "I missed out on changing my life by being too scared, and I'm not going to let that happen ever again."

There is a smattering of applause from the audience.

Cholan stands, too. He sweeps his arms out to encompass the room as he exclaims, "Lily discovered something in channeling that few discover, and it could very well change her life. Of course, now she must make sure it does. One needs to learn from one's past and use that to guide their life going forward. Opportunities like this one do not come along very often, and their message can't be overlooked."

Cholan lowers his voice, as if just speaking to Lily. "It is now up to you and only you." He raises his voice and adds, "This is why I do what I do." He pauses, "As a ten-year-old, I assumed it was the fire god Agni in the forest that day, seeking vengeance for a wrong in a past life. But now, when I think about my journey and my life, I realize it wasn't Agni in the forest that day. Certainly, Agni may have started the inferno, but it was Vishnu who was guiding and protecting me and setting me on this path. It was a painful path, one that I would not have survived without channeling and of course my father and those American doctors. But if all that leads me to a stage in Las Vegas, helping Lily move beyond a life of regret and wondering, that is my calling—my purpose."

Lily stands even taller and more confidently as Cholan finishes his pronouncement. She carries herself with a purpose she didn't have when she walked onstage. Her smile is enigmatic, as if she alone now understands the mysteries of the universe.

Marta watches all this unfold from the side of the stage, and her heart tightens in her chest. She ponders the past, present, and future. *What does this all mean?* The lump in her chest swells, and she worries she may be sick. She had a rare opportunity right in front of her, and she couldn't muster up the courage to grab it—just like when she wasn't able to get up from the chair when her father picked up the phone. How unbelievable; she was about to finally rewrite that part of her life, and instead she just heaped another regret on top of the original one.

The regret that she has kept suppressed for close to fifteen years comes hurtling out of its cage all at once. She is losing her grip on all her carefully constructed controls. She digs her nails into her fist, thinking, *I should have been on that stage instead of sitting on the sidelines, living in my head. I promised myself and Kevin long ago that I wouldn't do that. And I haven't kept that promise. Instead, I'm living in my daydreams, but that isn't really living.*

CHAPTER 16: Unsettled

2003—Las Vegas, Nevada

Cholan returns to his hotel room, to the same four walls that gave him no peace in the afternoon and will not, he knows, give him respite tonight, either. He is even more unsettled now than he was earlier, despite thinking the night's demonstration was a moderate success. The unease has moved from his neck down to his shoulder blades. He heats up a pot of water, and while he lets his tea steep, he gets into his dressing gown.

Fidgeting around until he is somewhat comfortable on the bed, his teacup balanced on his leg, Cholan mulls over his emotions and searches for an explanation. He closes his eyes, and the woman with the brown hair and hazel eyes pops into his head. The one who couldn't walk out onto the stage. He remembers sensing her struggle to overcome her anxiety, almost a panic. He recognized that she needed him; he almost got up to coax her forward. But he has never done such a thing before, so he stayed sitting on the stage, observing the battle she was waging. He felt certain in that moment that she wouldn't turn back—but he was wrong. He remembers how her hands clenched into fists and her sad eyes filled with unshed tears.

He sips his tea. He read Edwin's notes afterward and found her story and decision fork compelling. It stirred in him what he lost when he came to America. He lost his family and his homeland; Marta lost her first love. He can at least channel back to visit his past, but she has no such path. Cholan accepts this strange connection with Marta, but he has never experienced a reaction like this before—not to someone he hasn't already channeled with. *What a mystery.*

He leans back against the silk-covered headboard. Everything about the room is designed to evoke tranquility: the colors are a muted gray, the wide windows are covered with gauzy, willowy curtains in a soothing ecru. But none of it is working. Even the delicate cup balanced on his lap, full of his own brewed mixture of teas, isn't doing anything to calm his nerves.

He is inclined to visit his well-traveled alternative channel— tempted to go back to the day of the fire, where he leaves the forest with his brother instead of staying back. But his mind leads him instead to the unexpected and very infrequently traveled path of his actual memory channel. He nods his head, as if his body needs to physically agree with the idea to revisit his actual past. His mind takes a slight step inward and slides smoothly through time back to when he was ten and first came to America—the part of his story he didn't share with the audience.

1964—Los Angeles, California

A shiny ambulance takes Cholan to the Los Angeles County Hospital. He watches through the ambulance window as an unfamiliar world flashes by, one so strange that he feels he's just landed on the moon. He thinks all the United States must be like LA, only once he travels and sees more of America in the years to come will he realize that if he had landed in Kansas or some other Midwestern city, he might not be quite so overwhelmed right now.

Cholan is wheeled into the hospital, and that is where he stays for the next several months. He plunges into his new life alone, save for Dr. Liam and Dr. Smith. These two doctors have brought him to this baffling future, but they also are the only link he has to his past. They met his parents and saw his village, and, more importantly, they encourage him to talk about his life before America. Cholan begins to realize that the hole in his heart—the place in Sri Lanka where he once lived with his family in their village—may never heal.

Sitting in his clean hospital bed, he closes his eyes as he lifts off the silver cover from his dinner tray. He prays that today will be a plate of rice and curry with a crisp round of roti to dip with. He lifts and inhales and drops the cover back down without looking at it. He knows it is not curry. But his stomach grumbles, so he picks up the silver dome again and sets it off to the side. He sees a square of some meat and some long green pods and a round roll.

He picks up a fork and tries again to master how to eat with this inflexible tool. He has given up eating with his hands, as the horror it provokes in those around him has made it clear this is some sort of unforgivable sin in this new world; he needs no grasp of English to understand that it will not be tolerated.

Dr. Liam is a neurologist with a special certificate connected to pain medicine and therapies. Cholan decides promptly that he wants to be a doctor of pain medicine, too. More than the many surgeries he's undergone, pain medicine saved his life. Dr. Liam will explain to him when he has mastered enough English to understand him, "I study what we call 'mind over matter.' I have studied many cases like yours, where the medical prognosis was hopeless, yet the patient has recovered, using prayer, positive attitude, or sheer will to defy the grimmest of odds."

Dr. Liam will tell him that science and logic would say Cholan should have died during any one of those first five months. That the initial third-degree burns didn't stop his heart is perhaps a miracle, but the real miracle is that pain from the burns didn't sap all his will to live, resulting in his body taking the easy way out—death. "You obviously have a strong constitution, Cholan," he'll explain, "but it was channeling that allowed your body and mind to take respite from the constant, unbearable pain, and that is what allowed you to beat the scientific odds. That is what we must understand so we can share it with the world."

For now, though, Cholan understands none of this, and his only view of the outside world comes through a miracle box called television. On this magic box, he watches several different shows. His favorites include *The Andy Griffith Show*, as it is the closest thing he can find to his old, simple life, and the direct opposite of that, *The Lawrence Welk Show*, which broadcasts the glamour and sparkle of show business, along with wonderful, toe-tapping music that his body feels through the airwaves. At first, he just watches the images, but slowly, as only a young mind can do, he begins to understand English words and begins to piece together the stories being told.

The shows make his difficult hospital stay more bearable. While he now has access to the best medication and his pain is greatly controlled, he also undergoes excruciating surgeries to repair his melting skin, coupled with exhausting rehabilitation to strengthen his atrophied body.

The grafts from the little bit of his healthy skin and from actual pig skin begin to take hold. Cholan's leg is released from the position it was locked in, his jaw and neck are cut away from his chest, and the new skin doesn't sink due to gravity.

The doctors are kind, but they tell him he won't ever completely recover. The scars, and likely other issues as well, will last his lifetime. For Cholan, it is still a miracle that after months of seeing no progress while in his village, in America he is beginning to heal.

Within a month, Cholan starts to walk and is allowed to wander the hospital. His bad leg drags, but sometimes he forgets about that, especially once the nurses and other helpers get used to his scars and limp and no longer look twice at him as he walks by on his daily rounds. He is also getting used to the food; not only has he stopped praying for rice and curry, he actually looks forward to spaghetti and meatballs now.

One day he limps by the nurses' station in the pediatric wing and Gabby holds up her hand to stop him. She grins and says, "Dog."

Cholan cocks his head and repeats, "Dog."

Gabby holds up a stuffed animal. It is brown and white, with big floppy ears and a tail. He grins widely. She points to it and he replies quickly, "Dog, dog."

He remembers a similar animal he saw on TV, and now he has a word for it. He continues walking, murmuring "dog" under his breath.

From this day onward, Gabby gives him a new English word to learn, accompanied by a visual, each day. On Fridays, she lines up the four items for the week and gives him a test. If he gets all four, she either gives him a candy bar or gum. If he doesn't get all of them, she gives him a picture book. He really doesn't mind getting the picture books, as they almost always have beautiful pictures with just a few words, and he is getting good at sounding out most of them.

He thinks Gabby should have been a teacher, although she is a great nurse.

Cholan continues his daily rounds and heads to the pediatric unit. It is mostly filled with babies, and they don't hold much interest for him, except for one. Baby David, who has a heart problem, has been in here for months, just like Cholan.

He looks around until he finds Crystal. She helps the nurses with the babies and is another one of his favorites. She beckons him over. He sits in the rocking chair, and she brings over Baby David and lays him in Cholan's arms. David has scars on his chest and some on his head; he is Cholan's brother of the Scar Tribe.

"We are brave warriors and have fought a great battle that we must continue to fight every day," Cholan whispers, speaking Tamil so no one else will know what he is saying. He knows David understands. The baby stares at him with deep, all-knowing eyes, as he has seen too much already. It doesn't matter that David's hair is patchy or that his chest is sunken in. All that matters is that he is alive. Cholan may never be able to wear sandals again, since his toes have fused together, but he is alive, too. When he tells this to Baby David, it helps him understand this truth for himself.

Holding that warm, little body close reminds Cholan of his mother and how much he misses her arms. This memory makes him both happy and sad.

It is David and channeling that save him during these first couple of lonely months, when he cannot communicate with or understand the people around him or the world he has been thrust into.

Every day, Cholan channels back to before the fire, when his mother hugs him and holds him. Or he goes back to his favorite channel, the day of the fire, so he can see everyone he misses so dearly.

He can't stay in the channel as long as he could when he was with Phurbu, but each day he gets a little better at channeling. Dr. Liam is thrilled that Cholan can channel by himself and encourages him to stay in practice, even though it is no longer required for pain management. When he channels, the doctor hooks him up to sophisticated monitoring devices, working to capture the unexplainable and unseeable.

In January, Cholan moves to the rehabilitation wing of the hospital. He can now wear his own clothes, and he discovers that he has grown out of the few items he brought from Sri Lanka. Dr. Liam buys him many of the clothes and personal items that every young American boy needs, and Cholan grows to need them as well: a clock radio; jeans, which he thinks are exceedingly uncomfortable but over time grows to love; and sneakers, which feel uncomfortably constricting in comparison to the loose sandals to which he's accustomed. But even sneakers grow on him, especially since sandals aren't in the cards for him anymore.

Cholan adapts; or, if he is being honest with himself, he changes. While he never will forget his old life and his loving upbringing, he comes to know that he will never go back to his old life—and doesn't want to. *I can make this world better through my gifts*, he rationalizes at first. But eventually, he acknowledges the truth: he is a child, and the American Dream is persuasive. Who wouldn't want a new face and body, as well as the trappings of the English language, radios, TV, and yes, uncomfortable but also very cool sneakers?

2003—Las Vegas, Nevada

Cholan finally eases into a fitful night's sleep that includes dreaming of Baby David crying for him but he is not able to reach him. He wakes just as light begins to break through the dark, and he feels more settled despite the dreams. He senses things will be all right. He just needs to be patient, and all will be revealed when the gods determine it should be. Worry won't change what fate has already drawn up.

After an equally terrible night's sleep, Marta wakes and for a moment doesn't remember last night. Then the memory comes rushing back, and her heart sinks. Why couldn't she force herself to get out of her head and channel? She wanted it so badly, but she panicked. It feels just like when she was unable to get up when Kevin called her house.

She lies in bed, unable to face the day and her life. She retreats inside her head and lets the memories play—she remembers Kevin's and her hopes and their dreams.

She finally drags herself out of bed, and the regrets from last night push away her long-ago memories of her first love.

She squares her shoulders and tamps down those thoughts. *Dreams and channels aren't reality and don't exist in any tangible way,* she lectures herself. *Life is hard and painful, not dreamy and perfect. Stop wallowing and just get working.*

She goes through the motions of packing and getting ready to leave. Action, any action, seems to help her broken spirit.

Marta arrives at the airport with little time to spare—again. Dragging her gray bag behind her and dodging the more leisurely travelers, she tries to thread past a family of four lugging enough stuff to outfit a small daycare, when she bumps into a small man she didn't see.

She raises her hand in apology and mumbles, "I'm so sorry."

Warm brown eyes crinkle at her and she stops in her tracks. "Cholan?"

"Edwin, look, it is Marta," he says, nudging his companion. "I was so hoping to see you again. I never thought it would be so soon. How nice when things work out." He grins and raises his eyes to the sky, as if acknowledging the hands that are guiding all things. He murmurs, "I'll go and come back"—a traditional Sri Lankan greeting.

Marta nervously glances at her watch and then takes a deep breath and all the tension releases from her body. She sets her bag down in front of her and beams at both Cholan and Edwin.

"Hi," she says simply. Suddenly, making her flight is no longer as important as it was moments ago.

Edwin again seems to read her clearly. "Marta, I am sure you have a flight to catch, as do we. We were just talking about you and how much we would like you to come to our Boston office for a private session. It would be on us. You should have gotten a free one last night, and if you come to Boston, you still can."

"Oh!" Her heart skips with excitement. "Really?"

"Yes, yes, that would be best and is only right," Cholan insists.

Edwin reaches out and hands her a business card. "Call the office and we will get to it. No guarantees, but your channel sounded like an excellent one. Kevin, right?"

"Yes, Kevin," she replies. Her eyes mist and her heart, which hasn't experienced anything close to the raw pain she experienced the summer Kevin left, feels suddenly open and exposed, as if the barriers she has been carefully constructing her whole life are no longer in place. She feels lighter, freer, suddenly and she takes a deep inhale, but her thoughts never stay silent for long. *I hope my heart doesn't get completely destroyed . . .*

CHAPTER 17: Memories

2003—Newark, New Jersey

The first thing Marta does when she gets home is search for her childhood treasure box. Eventually she finds it on the top shelf of the clothes closet, under some blankets. This is the shoebox she decorated with colored pencil drawings in middle school that holds the memories of her childhood and has accompanied her, along with the *American Pie* album, on every move she has made since leaving her parents' small, hardscrabble house in Brunswick.

The LP is where it normally is, on the top of her stack of vinyls. She places it carefully on the record player and the music begins swirling and awakening the memories.

Sitting down on the floor with her back against the wall, Marta slowly opens the box. She breathes the air that escapes, imagining it is coming directly from long ago. She takes out a packet of letters that are held together by an elastic band that looks ready to give way. She reaches in and takes out *The Black Stallion* book, with its library card glued onto the back page. Under that she finds her journal from her Harriet the Spy phase. She places them down, side by side. The last item she takes out is the rock with the word *Breathe* etched faintly on its smooth surface. She rolls the rock in her hand, remembering all the years she carried it in her pocket, rubbing and rubbing it, hoping against hope that it would conjure up Kevin.

Setting the rock on top of the novel, she picks up her old journal from third grade. It has pink paper, and she remembers writing with her black pen all her observations and thoughts those many decades ago. Her writing saved her, giving her a way to express her thoughts and feelings without anyone else's influence. Not her father who always pushed her into things she wasn't sure were right. As her fingers move over the page, she feels the lifeline those pen strokes on the page provided her. These journals are the real Marta. Scared, nervous, trying to be brave. *What happened to my dream of becoming a teacher and writer? Just not brave enough.*

Flipping open the journal, she reads an entry.

October 12, 1973

Oh I would die for a blue sweater just like Michelle wore today. I wish I dared to ask her where she got it. It looked so soft. If I just had one more sweater, I wouldn't have to wash my orange one in the sink anymore, and instead could wait for washday. Oh well, one day, I will have a shirt for every day of the week, maybe even a few more.

Goal—be rich enough to have different outfits for each day of the week.

Marta smiles wistfully at the nine-year-old she once was. She now has more clothes than she could wear in a month. *Hmm, what would that worried observer of things think of her life now?*

She flips to another page.

August 5, 1976

I watched Nadia Comaneci on TV today, and she looked and acted so much like me. She won a gold medal but wasn't even happy about that and instead was already worried about her next routine. Papa thought she was the greatest, but I didn't. I don't want to turn into her. I don't mean turn into an Olympic gymnast; I mean never get to enjoy things. I worry about everything, but how do I stop and smell the flowers? How do I stop worrying? I honestly don't know. It seems easier to worry.

Goal—don't become Nadia.

Marta remembers thinking that Kevin was going to save her from becoming too much like the poor Romanian gymnast. Even though Marta looked like her, she didn't want to become like her. *But I did become more like Nadia after Kevin moved away.*

Now she wonders if her inability to channel in Las Vegas means she has become too much like Nadia with too many voices and routines in her life to find even a little happiness. Sitting up straighter, she shakes off the melancholy. *There are always second chances. Hopefully.*

Digging deeper in the box, she finds a trifold program from the fourth-grade recital she remembered when she was behind the stage in Las Vegas. She once again remembers the dance she did that year—the one she thought might just get her noticed by Kevin.

Was I braver back in fourth grade than I was in Las Vegas? How can that be? I've worked so hard on becoming stronger, braver.

Marta picks up *The Black Stallion* and holds it reverently, staring into the horse's dark, liquid eyes. She loved that horse with an intensity that made her ache. She could practically feel the Black's skin against her cheek. If not for him, fifth grade would have been dismal, as Kevin was not in her class.

The next book that helped her along her journey came in sixth grade, when she read *Are You There God? It's Me, Margaret*. Margaret saved Marta in so many ways. She made everything that Marta was thinking and feeling okay. Marta never had anyone she could really talk to, but Margaret spoke for her and to her—telling her it was natural to worry, everyone did, but also that everything would turn out okay, so she shouldn't worry too much. When Marta had learned that Judy Blume lived in New Jersey, she memorized her book photo, hoping she would bump into her one day, so she could tell her how much her book meant to her. She never did.

Sixth grade was also when Marta was shown a path that was different from her parents. She began to see the light at the end of the tunnel—began to feel she had some control over her situation, wasn't tethered to her family's small farm with its never-ending cycle of work. She had her daydreams, her books, and now her plan to lift herself out through college. Her daydreams began to expand, and she saw herself solving and overcoming all her problems. Even the puzzle of how to get closer to Kevin seemed like a solvable problem. She just *had* to make it happen. They were meant for each other.

Smiling wryly, Marta pulls one of the letters from the stack at random and reads it.

Hi Marta,

Just started junior year and I always think about you when I start a new school year. I imagine that you might show up like you did in eighth grade. I know you have told me a thousand times that you were in school for all those prior grades, but in my mind, you suddenly appeared as if by magic that first time in the nurse's office. Thank God we both broke our wrists. I know I would have noticed you in homeroom. But what if we didn't connect? As I said, it was the casts that had magic in them. We talked about this, right? You do believe in magic? I do.

   I almost have $800 to buy that pickup truck. So, get ready with that pink carnation when we meet again.
Love,
Kevin

Marta remembers sometimes Kevin would hold her and stare deep into her eyes and say he truly believed she must have been wearing an invisibility cloak for those first eight years. Maybe their casts *were* magic.

   She folds the letter back up, puts it carefully away, and pulls out another one.

Hi Marta,
I'm trying to figure out if I even want to go to junior prom. Are you going to yours? I just don't really have any interest or need. My friends keep bugging me about missing an opportunity that I will never get back, but I am not so sure. I have you as a girlfriend, so going out there to find a stand-in just doesn't seem to be worth the effort. No girl compares to you up here or anywhere. What are you going to do? Don't let my crazy thoughts influence you at all. You should go for sure, and I would love to see pictures of you in a fancy dress. I can hear you right now: "It is a waste to spend money on a prom dress." But you could wear it again, maybe for senior

prom. Right? That wouldn't be too wasteful. Or your mom can sew real good. Maybe she could change it up a bit for senior prom, so no one will even know it's the same dress. I know girls are weird about wearing the same dress again. I think I am rambling because I really don't know anything about this stuff. Just go and have fun and send me a letter and a picture when you do. I really want to see and hear all about it.

Love you always,

Kevin

Marta went to her junior prom but didn't have much fun. Kevin was right about proms, and she never attended another one. *I wish we had had some sort of eighth grade dance.* She imagines herself and Kevin as the king and queen of the night, both sparkling in their love, surrounded by good friends. The DJ plays "American Pie," and they dance so close that the world just fades away.

She closes her eyes. She pictures them in the meadow in Rec Park, saying goodbye: Kevin giving her the etched stone, and she clinging to him as their world truly does come to an end. Kevin had chased away the frightened, little Romanian gymnast, and in her place had emerged a girl who laughed at the sun, danced in the meadow, and sparkled with happiness—who never forgot to breathe and inhale life, who knew she was entitled to live with joy. But where is that girl now?

Joy is a scary prospect. She remembers the musty backstage of the Bellagio and the fear of that black hole, which represented all her fears rolled into one gaping, frightening thing. She sees that now: fear that Kevin won't be everything she has built up in her head—or, worse, that he won't want her anymore. *Or am I actually most afraid that he will be exactly like I remember and he will want me, and then I'll need to make irrevocable changes to my life?*

Marta packs her memories back into the treasure box and tucks it away on the shelf. Despite all she has gone on to achieve since she and Kevin parted, she knows something died in her that day in Rec Park, and she mourns it still. Could channeling bring her back to what she lost?

I need to find Kevin, and the channeler is the answer to that. I will face my fears and take the leap. After all, it may not be a gaping hole—it may be my chance to fly.

CHAPTER 18: Marta Tries Again

2003—Boston, Massachusetts

The next day at work, Marta calls the number on the card Edwin handed her at the airport.

The receptionist, with a strong Boston accent, asks, "So, how did you hear about us?"

"I almost channeled with him a few days ago in Las Vegas, at the dental convention," Marta explains.

"Oh!" the receptionist immediately responds. "How nice. So, Edwin already vetted you? I'll make sure we pull your chart so you can start right where you left off."

"Yes," Marta says, encouraged. "Edwin thought I had a good chance to channel, and I feel ready to try again."

"The earliest appointment is on September 26, in a week," she says. "That should work, since you have already gone through Edwin's protocol and that means I don't have to mail you any of the usual paperwork." She laughs lightly.

September 26. Kevin's birthday. *How strange*, Marta thinks.

She hesitates a moment, then she replies briskly, "Yes, September 26 is fine."

✧ ✧ ✧

Marta makes the four-hour drive to Boston one week later. Cholan's office is located in an old, mill-style building that has been renovated into trendy business offices and suites, just over the bridge in Boston. It is one of those areas that is slowly taking root in a previously run-down section of the city. She can almost feel the funky vibe as she walks through the neighborhood.

Anticipating her appointment with trepidation, she's on pins and needles. One minute she's worried she won't be able to get over the black hole again. Then, the next, she's worried she won't be able to channel or that it won't be amazing. Next, she worries it *will* be amazing. Then Steve pops into her head and she senses either way she is heading toward a major regret—but she knows she can't stop herself.

She breathes in and out, thinking, *One thing at a time. I need to channel first, then I will worry about what it may mean after. I may not even be able to do it.*

She steps into a nice but rather conservative, and decidedly small, waiting area. It fills her with a feeling of peace and serenity that emanates from the dark oak paneling and the framed pictures of forests and mountains that must be Sri Lanka. Even the carved teakwood tables and chairs have the look of what she imagines Sri Lankan furniture would have. The combined effect gives her an immediate connection to that ten-year-old boy and his lonely journey. Her heart catches, she feels the young boy in everything about the office, and she wonders if something like feng shui is at work.

She wonders if she is imagining all this, and perhaps the decorations are actually all from Target.

Growing up, her mother often told her she felt too much. Marta always wondered what that meant, but suddenly she understands. She can't imagine others have stepped into this office and felt the pain that's squeezing her heart at a boy's hard and forlorn journey.

She swallows hard and says to the smiling receptionist, "Marta Johnson. I have a two o'clock appointment."

"Hello," the receptionist chirps. She hands Marta a form to fill out. "Standard waiver form."

Remembering the one she signed in Las Vegas, this one appears identical, so she signs and returns it immediately.

Stepping through a paneled door, Edwin gives her a kind smile and an outstretched hand. She stands up in surprise; she wasn't anticipating that Edwin would be part of the process in Boston, too; she somehow assumed that he was only for the roadshow. Now she realizes he probably plays just as an important role in these private sessions as he does in the public ones.

Marta can't believe she initially disliked this little man. Now, she gets a rush of emotion at the sight of him. She gushes, "Oh, Edwin. I'm so glad to see you again. I never really got a chance to thank you before. I know I disappointed you in Las Vegas, but I don't think I was ready yet to do this. You were so nice and understanding."

Edwin blushes. His gift is perhaps not as flashy or sought-after as the channeler's. He is clearly pleased with her heartfelt words of thanks. He inclines his head. "This setting may be better . . . umm, safer for you. You said it was a black hole you saw?"

Marta nods. "Yes, but it feels different already today. I was very much on edge in Las Vegas, but I feel better here. Like you said, safer."

"Since we already know you have a good fork and the prerequisite traits to channel, we are going to move right into the session with Cholan," he murmurs, and inclines his head toward the door behind him.

He leads her through the door and down a short hallway, at the end of which he opens a large, dark door. They enter a bright office with old, multipaned mill windows stretching from the high ceiling to the floor. Marta can't quite see through them, but she assumes they overlook the Charles River. The room is light and airy but has a calming feel. Marta figures it must be that feng shui effect again, or maybe it is the music playing softly in the background, which sounds faintly like church bells ringing. The walls are the lightest of greens, and there is a hint of incense or candles burning somewhere, a spicy citrus smell that invigorates rather than nauseates. As she peeks around, she sees Cholan rise from his desk, arms outstretched.

"Marta," he says in his singsong voice, "it is so good to have you here. I can't tell you how happy I am to see you again. Here is better, anyway. Las Vegas—who needs all that?" He waves his hand around the room with its earth tones and comfortable chairs.

He clasps her arms lightly with both hands and then steps back to look at her, as if she is a long-lost relative and he is comparing her to a picture in his mind when she was much younger.

Marta blushes, looking down. She is not used to such a close and frank inspection. She feels his penetrating gaze peeling off some of her protective layers, and she has the urge to wrap her arms around her body to shield him from going too deep. She hadn't really thought about this part of the experience; she was focused solely on the actual channeling and forgot there would be a process to get to it.

Cholan, appearing satisfied, gently says, "Please, take a seat. We talk a bit, yes?"

Marta nods and sits.

Edwin produces a clipboard that she would swear was nowhere in sight when she first entered. She imagines he can conjure up his clipboard on demand. He sits down with his pen poised.

Cholan states very matter-of-factly, "So you have a good channel . . . Edwin thought so. A phone call from Kevin."

Marta thinks there might be a question there but isn't sure. She is glad she doesn't have to go through the details again. Edwin proves to be as thorough as he appears to be, and she realizes the paper attached to the clipboard is covered with notations already. He isn't going to write anything down; he is just referring to notes from their discussion in Las Vegas.

Cholan mutters—more to himself than anyone else—"Yes, yes, that is a good one. Let us give it a try." He gets up with a quick motion, and Marta wonders again at his age. He seems old, but that may be due to the scarring around his mouth and his slow walk. He could be closer to her own age.

"Come this way, Marta," he beckons her. "Let's do it."

Marta gets up and, following Cholan closely, notes the spring in his uneven step. They walk through a nondescript door at the back of the office. It closes silently behind them.

They are now in a dimly lit room with one window covered by a Venetian blind. There are three comfy-looking chairs that look like overstuffed recliners. Cholan motions her to sit. Marta hesitantly picks the one in the middle. Edwin makes a note on his clipboard before he and Cholan settle into the other two.

"Now, we are just going to relax, and I want you to describe your house and what you were doing when Kevin called," Cholan says quietly.

Marta nods and begins: "I was at my parents' house, sitting on the green recliner, and then the phone rang."

"Okay. You picture that, now close your eyes. Is the sun shining? What does it smell like? Oh, yes. You remember . . ." He reaches for her hands, and she feels a jolt of electricity that softens as it spreads up her arm.

His voice trails away. Marta feels his voice flow over and around her. She relaxes slowly. Her mind takes over her body, which is very unusual. She never can relax on demand. She's tried things like meditation and yoga over the years to help her live in the present a bit more and spend less time in her head. Her mind was resistant, but not so with Cholan.

Suddenly, time stutters and every nerve ending in her body explodes. She sits bolt upright, trying to get her bearings, as she realizes she isn't in the office any longer but is instead in her parents' house before it was renovated. For a moment her brain is bifurcated, as it is somehow watching this from a slight distance with the knowledge that what she's seeing isn't real—but that consciousness starts to fade almost immediately, and she surrenders to the experience.

She can feel a calming presence and knows someone is near, but she can't see him. She knows it is someone she can trust, someone who is supposed to be there, but she doesn't know who it is. Her breathing calms and she unclenches her hands. Just as she is getting her bearings—the phone rings.

She tries to get up to answer it but can't get herself to move. Her father comes into the room and picks up the phone with a deep "Hello." She feels the presence beside her pushing her to get up. She tries with all her might to stand. Finally, she raises herself up and rather unsteadily moves across the floor. Someone has her hand and is keeping her upright.

"Marta?" her father says. "Now who would be calling Marta?"

Marta approaches him from behind just as he says, "Well, Kevin, Marta doesn't live here anymore, and in fact is getting married in a few months."

"Dad," Marta croaks, "give me the phone." It sounds more like a plea than a command, but it surprises her dad enough that when she slowly reaches for the phone, he just hands it to her.

She puts the phone to her ear and shakily says, "Hi, this is Marta."

There is a pause on the other end, and then she hears, "Marta, this is Kevin—remember me?"

Marta slowly sinks to the ground just as her mother rushes in from the other room asking, "Ernest, who was on the phone?" She sees Marta sitting on the floor with the phone to her ear and gives her a quick smile before turning to her father and herding him into the other room.

Marta quickly turns her attention to the phone and the question still hanging in the air. "Hi, Kevin, of course I remember you. I can't believe you called. This is just great," she gushes.

Kevin rushes on, saying that he's been meaning to call for years and finally decided today was the day. They fill each other in on what they've been up to for the past several years and laugh about the last time they saw each other.

"Boy, was that awkward," Marta says. "I couldn't think of anything to say. It was so much easier to share stuff in letters. I was completely tongue-tied."

They both laugh and agree it was too much for a couple of seventeen-year-old kids to handle.

"I think I had too much other stuff on my mind back then," Kevin says, "and it seemed too hard to spend time working on the long-distance relationship. I thought my future was right around the corner. But I've always regretted that I didn't keep writing to you."

Now it seems, at twenty-three, the awkwardness is over. They have both done some exploring and are coming back to find each other.

Thirty minutes flies by. The call is interrupted when Marta's father reenters the room, signaling that he needs to use the phone. He never lets Marta or her sister talk for longer than ten minutes, so Marta knows her mother must have held him hostage for the last twenty minutes. She makes a mental note to thank her mother, as she is sure it took nothing less than a Herculean effort.

Marta interrupts Kevin midsentence. "Kevin, I need to go, but give me your phone number and I'll call you back tonight, when I get back to my apartment."

He agrees immediately and gives her the number.

She writes it down. "Got it."

"So, you'll call me tonight?" he asks eagerly.

"Yes, definitely. We need to figure out a plan to meet, this time without our parents." Marta laughs, picturing their parents trying to make small talk in her driveway while she and Kevin ambled in silent discomfort around the yard.

Kevin laughs right along with her, and she feels sure he's holding the same image in his own mind.

After hanging up, Marta continues to sit on the floor until her father nudges her with his foot to get out of the way. He picks up the phone, continuing with his "I have to make a call" charade. He grumbles something about "getting married," and she gets up swiftly and walks away.

Sheer and utter happiness is the only way she can describe the feeling. It's as if she has a secret gift that no one else can see, and it's the most wonderful, special thing in the world. She moves in a warm glow.

Suddenly, she starts to feel deep pressure within her chest and can't quite catch her breath. She pushes back against it as she calls out, "Bye, Mom," and nods to her father, who ignores her.

She runs to her old Honda Civic and drives back to her apartment with the piece of paper with Kevin's number on it clenched in her hand. Time is trying to catch her and she doesn't want that to happen. Because she feels pure elation! This is what they mean about being on cloud nine. Marta has never experienced anything like it.

It takes five minutes to drive to her apartment, and she stares into space for the rest of the afternoon. The internal discomfort is there but isn't really bothering her. At 5:01 p.m., when the phone rates are low, she dials Kevin's number.

He picks up immediately, and they continue their conversation without a pause. It is amazingly easy. No uncomfortable hesitations or worry about what to say next. Everything just flows effortlessly.

"Do you remember our song?" she asks him.

"Do I remember it! I got it to be our class song for high school graduation. Everyone thought it was so cool. Don McLean's 'American Pie.' Our song."

"Wow, I wish I had thought of that. That is really cool." Marta shakes her head in wonder. "You essentially introduced me to real music during our time together. I remember going over your house during that year, and your parents letting you play music on the record player in your living room. I thought your parents were amazing." She grins at the memory. "I remember lying back on your couch, holding the album cover with the thumb that had the American flag painted on it. I looked at the album and then at you, and the music just moved over me. It feels like it was just yesterday. My favorite line is 'I was a lonely teenage broncin' buck with a pink carnation and a pickup truck.'"

"Love it," Kevin murmurs.

"I had no idea what the song was about back then, but, boy, did it speak to me. I bought the album the week you left for Vermont, and it has moved with me to college and everywhere. I've listened to 'American Pie' thousands of times. At some point it became clear to me what the song was saying—it's a long goodbye song."

She sings quietly,

We started singing bye, bye, Miss American Pie.
Drove my Chevy to the levee but the levee was dry
Them good ole boys were drinking whiskey 'n' rye
And singin', "This'll be the day that I die,
This'll be the day that I die."

Kevin hums along, then says, "Remember my crazy parents and how shocked you were when they came in and did a little dance together, right in front of us, on the living room floor?" He chuckles. "What song was it that got them all goofy?"

"I'll never forget that. It was a Bob Marley song. They came in singing 'No Woman, No Cry.' I bought that album, *too, and every time that song comes on, I picture you sitting on the couch, laughing, as you watch your parents dance."*

More memories rise to the surface, and they talk about all of them. They start making a plan to see each other—and suddenly the pull within her chest tightens. Or maybe it strengthens? It's hard to explain, but the discomfort becomes pronounced.

She breathlessly asks, "How about if this weekend we meet in Newport? That's maybe halfway." She doesn't mention that she will have to cancel dinner with Steve's parents in order to make that happen.

Kevin doesn't raise any such mundane issues on his end, either. He quickly replies, "Great idea. Let's do it. What time can you get there?"

Marta smiles softly into the phone, even though she can't catch her breath.

He laughs. "Breathe, Marta, breathe."

She laughs too, and a whoosh of air rushes out of her worried lungs. They agree to meet at 4:00 p.m. on Saturday at the carousel.

She whispers, "I can't believe this."

He murmurs, "Me neither."

They hang up.

Suddenly, she isn't alone in the apartment. A comforting presence nudges her—similar to how it nudged her to pick up the phone at her parents' house, but this is a bit more insistent. Almost against her will, Marta closes her eyes.

Immediately, a ripple courses through her body and she feels the world tilt. She hasn't actually moved her legs, but can feel she's moving away from the spot she was just standing in. It is as if the world is shifting around her.

Marta opens her eyes and the first thing she sees is light filtering through Venetian blinds. Her eyes adjust, and she remembers where she is. Time restarts.

Cholan is sitting on the same chair he was in when she left but is now holding her hand. He has beads of perspiration on his forehead and upper lip.

Edwin comes forward with a cloth and two cups of water. He gives Cholan the cloth and one of the cups of water, and then turns to her.

"Drink this and spend a few moments gathering your thoughts," he says earnestly. "Judging by the amount of time you both were away, it must have been very interesting, but I know it can be very emotional as well."

Cholan sips his water and beams at Marta. "Well, that was good, yes?"

Grinning from ear to ear, she lets out a contented sigh. "Yes."

"Edwin, what was the time?" he asks Edwin.

"Close to the top—forty-seven minutes. I think that is fourth or fifth place."

Marta turns to Edwin and asks, confused, "Fourth or fifth place?"

Cholan explains, "We keep track. The longer in the channel, the better, and subsequent sessions normally keep getting longer."

Marta shakes her head, confused. "We spent forty-seven minutes in my channel?"

It didn't feel like forty-seven minutes, but she isn't sure if it felt much longer or much shorter. He could have said two minutes or two hundred minutes and she would still think it didn't seem right.

Edwin shrugs. "We don't know if time is different in this realm or if your mind is simply able to skip or fast-forward to meaningful parts. Most people can stay in a channel for just a few minutes by our clocks but experience several hours of time in their divergent channel." He arches an eyebrow. "Who knows? Time and space are funny that way."

He glances over at Cholan as if to see if he wants to add something, but as soon as his eyes land on the channeler, he jumps up and nods curtly to Marta. "We'd like to review some details with you, if you don't mind, to better document things so that we can compare your experience to Cholan's experience."

Marta realizes that Cholan has his eyes closed and seems very small and tired. She quickly rises and awkwardly bows to him, then she blushes and straightens up, trying to appear nonplussed but sure Edwin can see right through her awkwardness.

"Thank you very much," she blurts out. "This was, uh, amazing."

Cholan opens his eyes and smiles gently. "No. Thank you, Marta. You must know your channel is very special."

She is not sure if he is referring to the forty-seven minutes or the actual channel. His eyes close again.

Edwin's office is stuffed with books and papers; they are heaped on the floor and on every possible shelf. There is no feng shui going on here, but Marta is more comfortable amid the mess. It looks a lot like her office.

Edwin clears a few books off a stiff-backed chair that looks as if it were picked up from a tag sale, then weaves to the other side of his cluttered desk. He sits down, waving at her to also take a seat.

Marta picks her way to the chair, hoping its weight limit goes beyond the five or six books that it was holding until a few seconds ago. She sits gingerly and glances up when Edwin clears his throat.

"Now," he says, "tell me what happened."

Marta recounts the channel as best she can while Edwin writes furiously on his clipboard.

After she explains the whole thing, he says simply, "That is a good story."

Smiling wistfully, she says, "Yes."

When they are done, he ushers her to the door. She walks out of the funky office building with a spring in her step. She is holding on tight to sheer joy. It is total and eludes description. She didn't share this utter happiness and joy when she recounted her channel to Edwin—partly because she knew she wouldn't do it justice, partly because this bliss is something she wants to keep to herself.

She feels a lightness in spirit. All her normal worries and nagging doubts that are a part of her daily existence are gone—just like that. It is what she imagines the Dalai Lama or the pope may experience when they are meditating or praying. She has a pang of guilt at her audacity in comparing her channel to such holy experiences, but she quickly pushes that aside; she knows she *did* have some sort of spiritual experience. Perhaps not a holy one, but something quite extraordinary nonetheless.

Once in her car, the word *nirvana* pops into her head. She has a silly grin on her face that she can't seem to control. As she starts her drive home, she doesn't listen to the radio or the book she has on audio. She just drives and relives the channel over and over. She is living in the present right now—not planning or thinking or worrying about the future. If she found a secret meadow this instant, she would get out and dance. She giggles and thinks, *I could get addicted to this*—but she is sure Cholan and Edwin wouldn't let that happen, even if she tried to throw her life savings at them and spend the rest of her days channeling.

Coming down to earth slowly, she thinks of Lily and her pronouncement about living her life differently. Marta knows she, too, must make a change. The spirit of the girl she was in eighth grade has been reawakened. The question now is, what should she do with her? There is no clear direction, other than the certainty that she can't continue with her present life.

Marta had big dreams at one time, and she was so sure she was brave enough to achieve them; they were right there in her grasp. But those dreams somehow got turned inside out as she started navigating life. Her dreams changed to refuge and security, ensuring she didn't live large. Safety is the direct opposite of passion. You can hold yourself too carefully. Joy can be experienced only if you are willing to take a chance.

Marta fell into her job. She fell into her marriage. She loves Steve, but he is not her soulmate. She knows she just met her soulmate . . . again. Her connection with Kevin was intense, and the rightness of everything about it—she can't explain it away. Her whole being feels alive and connected to something larger than herself. Her first love, it turns out, *was* her soulmate, and that isn't some sort of mind game that the passing of time can trick you with. She is not just in love with the idea of her first love; she is in love with her first love—and nothing will change that.

She has let the world and its various forces push her down the path of least resistance for too long. The cautious voice she thought she had successfully squashed in her adult life is controlling things more than she ever realized.

It hits her halfway home: she must find Kevin, the real Kevin, even though the thought of doing that scares her silly. The black hole is there and feels very real. But it also makes her realize she is truly alive for the first time in a long time. Life is not meant to be safe or easy. Her father's insistence that life is hard is truer than she cares to admit. Maybe her life has been too easy because she made it that way. Life is not meant to flow past you and around you like you are a pebble at the bottom of a swift river. You need to be more like the large boulder—thrusting yourself above the surface, gulping in air, seeing the sun. Yes, that also means getting hit by all the flotsam the river may serve up—but that is better than lying down at the bottom and never feeling the strong current of what life could be.

She knows what she must do. She has got to throw the proverbial pickle jar out the window and let it smash into tiny bits.

In the weeks that follow, Marta finds herself spontaneously transported back to her other possible life at odd moments. During these spells, Marta knows where she is—back at her childhood home—but she isn't sure exactly when. She feels she is around twenty-three years old. But how does someone actually feel that?

She knows that she leaves her present channel during these excursions, but she doesn't know how to control these jumps. It's like falling asleep in the middle of class and suddenly waking with a start to realize everyone is staring at you. From these semi-channels, Marta comes to in a state of sheer panic and glances around anxiously, only to find she is sitting at her desk or standing at the stove, spoon in hand. Her heart slowly stops pounding and her fingers unclench. *Breathe*, she thinks, and then her lungs release the air they have been holding in.

CHAPTER 19: Kevin's Birthday

2003—Burlington, Vermont

Sitting dejectedly in his favorite booth in the Snowy Oyster in Burlington, Kevin is waiting for his perpetually tardy brother. It is September 26, his fortieth birthday. He can't believe turning forty is bothering him as much as it is. He's become someone he doesn't recognize lately. Last week he went to a Harley dealership to look at a bike. He doesn't even really want one, but he's feeling this urge to do something dramatic, and buying a Harley, particularly on his teacher's salary, seems like a solidly dramatic gesture.

Time is slipping away. He's missing the kids' time and attention. Kelly doesn't seem to notice or care that when Megan turned sixteen, she stopped being the kid that hung on your every word. *Well,* my *every word,* he realizes. Megan and Kelly have been at odds basically ever since Megan could talk. Their relationship has long been a constant battle, with Kelly trying to control and manage Megan's life and Megan rebelling against the constraints.

Shaking his head, Kevin remembers coming into Megan's room when she was two or three and finding Kelly in tears. Kelly was trying to get Megan dressed in a pair of pink overalls, and Megan had other plans. The toddler possessed a definite fashion sense even before she could form a complete sentence, and she fought and kicked like a banshee when you tried to force her into something she didn't like. Kevin walked in just as Kelly was giving up the fight. She sat on the ground, looking winded and wounded. Megan was standing over her, triumphant.

As soon as Megan saw Kevin, she ran to him, and he scooped her up and swung her legs up over his head. Megan's knight in shining armor had arrived to witness her victory.

As Kelly sat dejected on the floor, holding on to the offensive overalls, Megan pointed to her bureau. Kevin brought her over and they opened the drawer. Megan wiggled out of his arms and stared intently into the drawer until she located her favorite denim dress with embroidered flowers on it. Kevin helped her get into it, followed by a pair of white tights.

This was the start of Megan's dress phase, which would last until fifth grade. Megan never wore a pair of overalls again and Kevin isn't sure Kelly ever forgave her.

Kevin's musings are interrupted when his brother slides into the other side of the booth and apologetically utters, "Sorry, things were crazy at the house, and I just couldn't leave Sally saddled with all three kids. Hey, happy birthday, bro."

Trying to sound as whiney as possible, Kevin says, "You'd think you could get here on time *once* a year, at least. When it's my *birthday*. Especially this one."

He playfully punches Mark's arm. Seconds later, Jill drops off their Allagash North Sky stouts, and he suddenly feels better for the first time in weeks.

Ceremoniously, the brothers clink their bottles, and each take a satisfying gulp. Then leaning forward, Mark slides an envelope across the table toward Kevin.

Kevin looks questioningly at his brother. They normally don't give each other anything besides a few hours together to catch up and hang out on their respective special days. Mark just shrugs, so Kevin slides his finger under the seal.

In the envelope is a corny, over-the-hill joke card. But Kevin pauses as he reads the message Mark has written inside:

Here is something that may let you relive the Glory Days, and I don't mean college or all the stupid pranks we pulled through high school. This is to find Marta. Good luck, and happy channeling.
Love, Mark.

Kevin unfolds a piece of paper that turns out to be an advertisement: *The Channeler, Revisit and Reimagine Your Past, $250, Boston, MA*. He glances at Mark.

"Listen," Mark quickly explains, "this guy can take you back in time to visit an actual past, supposedly—like, an alternative past, but a real one? I've paid for one session with him so you can stop mooning over Marta and see if the past was so special or if maybe it's just you making it seem so special."

Unsure what to feel, Kevin gets up and hugs his brother. "Thanks, man! This is really great . . . I think."

He turns the paper over in his hand, keenly feeling the agony of his split with Marta, which still feels fresh, all these years later. He knows he is caught in the clutches of that long-ago relationship, though he resents Mark's implication that it stopped him from living his life. It didn't. Instead, it acts more like a safety blanket—always there when he needs it. Still, he recognizes he lost something important when he moved away.

He disappears inside himself, conjuring up the smell of the grass and the sun shining down on them in their secret meadow. Their first kiss. He is lying next to Marta, exploring her mouth in the warmth of the day.

He opens his eyes when he hears a cough, expecting to see Marta's hazel eyes smiling back at him.

Instead, Jill is looking at him pointedly. "And what will the birthday boy have?" she asks, apparently for the second time.

He darts a look at his brother, chagrined. "I guess the usual. Snowy burger, medium, with fries."

"Make it two," Mark says.

Jill nods and retreats to the kitchen.

Mark lifts his eyebrows at his brother. "So, still going to act surprised when Kelly springs the cruise on you this weekend?"

Kevin forces a smile. "Yup. She really wants to go, so I'll go along with it. I guess she thinks that because I love the water and boats that I'd really love a bigger boat and more water. God, I can't even imagine being stuck on some floating hotel with four thousand other people. Yikes, I get queasy just thinking about it."

"Better you than me," Mark quips. "Maybe it will be okay."

The next day, when he is alone in the house, Kevin dials the number from the advertisement.

"Hello, I wanted to make an appointment to, uh, channel, I guess."

The receptionist responds brightly, "Oh, great. Let's see. Have you gone through any of the material online?"

"Um, no," Kevin responds in surprise. "Do I need to?"

"No need," she said smoothly. "We do like you to work through the questionnaire prior to the appointment, though, so let me mail it to you, and then I'd love for you to send it back to us before coming. Sometimes it's easier to complete it at home instead of in our office— you know, so you can take your time. Also, if it seems you aren't a likely candidate, we can possibly save you the money and the trip."

"Well, it's my brother's money, a gift, so I don't mind wasting it," he says with a wry chuckle. "But please do send it to me, as I guess I may not want to waste a drive down from Vermont."

"Great," she says. "In the meantime, let's make you an appointment, though, just in case. October 12, okay?"

After a quick look at his calendar, Kevin confirms for the twelfth. She gives him a few more instructions, and he thanks her and hangs up.

After the call, he leans back in his chair. It's not so much that he believes people can channel, it's more that he thinks his life could use a little shaking up. Just taking the step of making this appointment means he is still open to trying new things and exploring life. He feels a bit more alive already.

He can almost see his dad smiling. He always wanted his oldest son to be open to new and different things—to be willing to *try* stuff. Channeling certainly fits that category. Kevin realizes this is what Mark had in mind when he sprang for this gift. Mark isn't a believer in unicorns and fairy tales either; this gift is a way of saying to believe and not give up on life.

Kevin worries he is settling into a routine. He remembers the surprise and pain of his parents' divorce, and he wonders if maybe his parents realized they had settled and they didn't want to be the sorts to do that. They both were certainly believers that people shouldn't give up on their dreams, no matter how crazy those dreams may be. Plus, channeling seems much more appropriate than a Harley, even if it turns out to be a complete hoax.

The channeling paperwork comes in a manila envelope just a few days later. Kevin brings it to school the next day and opens it sitting at his desk at Burlington High School, after the school has emptied out and a quiet has settled in.

Laying the sheets in front of him, he starts to read and mark his answers. As he works through the first page, titled "Candidate Questionnaire," he thinks his answers may be what the channeler is looking for but can't be sure. *I'm sure there are no right or wrong answers*, he tells himself.

Next are a couple of pages titled "Decision Forks." He reads the introductory paragraph.

- *Please review your past and try to identify a meaningful time when you made a decision that may have changed the course of your life. This can include things like:*
- *not trying out for the football or cheerleading team in high school*
- *proposing to someone or not proposing to someone*
- *saying yes or no to a proposal*
- *moving away from home or back home, or any variation in between*

Even if you know what fork or path you want to try to channel back to, please list several, as sometimes a path will not be workable, and having alternatives is always a good idea.

In the page left blank for his response, Kevin writes, *Parents' Divorce.*

Kevin was in high school when his parents decided to get divorced. To him, it seemed like a random decision, as they hardly ever fought, but whatever the reason, they were firm in their belief that it was for the best. And once they made that decision, they gave him the unenviable opportunity of choosing which parent to live with. He was "old enough," according to the courts, to make his own decision. But it was an impossible decision. He loved both parents, so picking one over the other just about killed him.

Finally, Mark had said, "Just roll the fucking dice, man, because this just sucks."

Mark didn't mean for his suggestion to be taken literally, but Kevin actually did roll the dice: odd for Mom and even for Dad. He threw a five, so went to live with his mom, as did his siblings.

It turned out that this most difficult decision ultimately ended up not being such a big deal. His parents divorced amicably. He and his siblings got to see their dad pretty much whenever they wanted or needed to. Their dad continued to teach them the best places to fish and to appreciate the sun on the water in the morning. He told them to live in the moment and to try not to worry about the future. And he was a good example. Kevin's dad could forget about problems and enjoy a day on the lake better than anyone. He always appreciated the little things and made sure he pointed them out to some rather obtuse teenagers who, at the time, didn't fully understand what he was trying to say.

Then, five years after the fateful roll of the dice, his father died of a heart attack, and the option of spending time with him ended abruptly.

Now there are times, when Kevin is sitting quietly and looking at a sunset, that he feels his dad's presence and can hear him say, "Now this is living." His dad would not want Kevin to dwell on the unfairness of losing him when Kevin was just twenty-one. He would want him to continue to see and experience the world and all it has to offer. Kevin tries to do that, though he's not as good at it as his dad was. He wishes his dad were here now so he could ask him about Marta. Would he think he should focus on moving past it—or running back toward it?

On the second blank page, he writes down another "decision fork": *Proposing to Kelly.*

He lays his pen down and, with his chin on his hands, remembers meeting Kelly for the first time back in college.

CHAPTER 20: Kelly

1983–1985—Burlington, Vermont

S trolling back to his dorm after class, Kevin is a junior. He takes the stairs two at a time, and as his hand reaches toward room 312, he has a sinking feeling.

"Dammit!" he mutters. His hand reaches into his empty jean pocket. He twists the knob hopefully. It barely moves. Brian will be in his chem lab for another hour or so.

Crap. He had planned to turn over a new leaf this year. Get his shit together a bit.

He continues down the hall, thinking, *Well, no time like the present to meet the new RA.*

Knocking nonchalantly on the door marked *Kelly, RA*, he waits. A petite, brown-haired girl answers the door and shakes her head as if she already knows his issue and is disappointed in him.

Hesitantly, he says, "Hi, I'm Kev. I left my keys in my room this morning and am locked out. My roommate's in class for another hour. Can you help?" He infuses his words with all the sweet earnestness he can muster.

The RA's eyes soften. "Sure. Give me a second, I need to get my master."

Kevin peeks into her room. He knows RAs have their own rooms, so this is all hers. It is meticulously clean and smells like flowers, or spring, or something fresh. Music is playing—not classical, but it certainly isn't AC/DC. All he knows is he loves it.

His mother was not a clean freak by any means. Organization was not her strong suit, and she didn't think cleaning and keeping order were important. She proudly displayed a plaque that said, "Good moms have sticky floors, dirty ovens, and happy kids." While the nut did not fall far from the tree, Kevin still has an appreciation for organization and cleanliness—and having been to many friends' houses growing up, he knows his mom's crazy house is not the norm. Seeing Kelly's tidy dorm room, he recalls the saying, *Cleanliness is next to godliness*. As he takes in a deep breath of clean air, that saying suddenly makes a lot of sense to him.

"I'm Kelly, by the way," she introduces herself as she rejoins him. "I understand I may be seeing a lot of you this year."

Kevin grins devilishly.

Kelly blushes. "I mean, your old RA provided me with a list of potential problems on the floor, and you made the list—something about experimenting with microwaves and possible safety/ fire issues?"

Chagrined, Kevin realizes he misinterpreted her meaning. All the same, he's intrigued by her seeming forwardness.

Kelly seems much older than twenty; she has nurturing in her soul. She can help a freshman make the sometimes difficult transition from a "helicopter mom" to flying solo for the first time. She also can make undergrads of any age feel guilty with just a glance. Kevin thought that skill only developed once you became a parent, but not so with Kelly. Hers is already a finely honed art form.

He gravitates toward Kelly's mature traits. After years of dating and having sex with typical eighteen- to twenty-year-olds, he's ready to move on to the next phase, and Kelly seems like the perfect fit for that.

Soon after meeting Kelly, Kevin starts cleaning his room a bit more and limiting the microwave experiments, much to his friends' disappointment. Once Kevin and Kelly start dating, Kevin matures willingly; he knows he has to grow up a bit. He can't go through life with the messiest dorm room and expect people to take him seriously. The problem is, as soon as he starts moving away from such childishness, he loses the ability to draw the line. He will later realize that he gave up a bit too much of himself in the progression toward responsible adulthood.

They are a classic case of opposites attracting. Kevin is too easygoing for his own good, and Kelly has the drive and the focus to keep him moving in the right direction, or at least moving forward. And she does the same for herself: She routinely initiates new projects that she fixates on. Some take longer than others, but she always completes them before moving on to the next one (and there is always a next one).

In 1983, Kevin is her new project, and quite a challenging one.

A year later Kevin and Kelly move in together in the spring, and the project continues.

"It will be an absolute blast. I promise. I will plan it all out," Kevin says, giving her a winning smile.

"No way! The only way I'll agree to your crazy idea is if I get to do all the planning."

Kelly had graduated a year ago and just left her job at the museum as assistant to the curator without any real explanation. Kevin isn't pressing for one, however, as it's working out perfectly with his idea for the summer: a road trip across the United States, just the two of them, a graduation present to himself before he has to start his real life.

He lets Kelly have her way, of course, and the plan she makes is meticulous. They have a wonderful time, exploring Yellowstone, the Grand Tetons, the Grand Canyon, and a bunch of smaller tourist attractions. Kevin has to admit that they see more of the country than they ever would have if they had followed his preferred plan—"winging it"—but sometimes he wishes they could just relax and enjoy the moment instead of being constantly on the move to the next destination.

One day, they are hiking the Continental Divide in Loveland Pass. Kevin is wearing an old hat that he picked up in the Badlands, kind of an Indiana Jones–type thing. His cut-off jeans look better than they sound and are paired with his favorite Ramones T-shirt. The sun has lightened his hair and tanned his skin—well, for a fair-skinned Norwegian guy.

As the hike climbs in altitude and they leave the world behind, Kevin feels so *in the moment* he wants to burst. Kelly, walking ahead of him, looks so cute in her tan khakis and green tank top. Kevin leans forward to swat her adorable butt, catches his foot on a rock, and falls headlong with an *oomph*.

Kelly turns around and crouches over him, a worried frown on her face. "What happened?"

Kevin grins at her flirtatiously and pulls her down on top of him. He whispers in her ear as he nuzzles her neck, "I've always dreamed of making love with you on the Continental Divide. Something about the perfect symmetry of where our mighty continent splits. Come on, let's do it."

She tries to extract herself, but Kevin has a good grip on her. And her attempts to wiggle away are only increasing his interest.

"Come on, Kelly," he pleads. "Right here, right now?"

She leans slowly toward him and stops struggling. She melts into him and slowly kisses him. The sun is straight overhead, and her face is in shadow.

Kevin breathes in her aroma and relaxes his grip. As soon as he does, Kelly, with a wiggle and a twist, breaks free of his hold and stands up. She straightens her clothes and brushes off her knees, then holds out a hand like a peace offering to help him up.

He is blinded by the noonday sun and feels abandoned and cold. He does not take her hand; instead, he continues to lie on the ground until she withdraws her peace offering.

He begins to feel a little silly. He pulls himself up and mutters, "Party pooper"—which only makes him feel sillier. He strides briskly up the path, past Kelly.

"That wasn't even the right spot," she says as he walks by.

He retorts with some irritation, "Not really the point, Kell."

She continues justifying her refusal with various comments for the next thirty minutes like, "What if someone saw us?" and "It was too rocky, anyway."

Kevin stays majestic in his stony silence, his face cemented in a serious pout.

When they reach the actual divide, she continues to cajole and try to make up with him. As he stands on the divide, the wind picks up and blows across his face. The clouds are beginning to gather in angry groups. He glances down at Kelly and sees that her eyes are as troubled as the sky. His chest constricts. He hates being the cause of someone's unhappiness. He forces a smile on his face and some of his annoyance fades. He throws an arm around her shoulders, and they sit down near a small copse of trees and pull out their water bottles.

"So, I'm thinking I'll try fishing," he tells Kelly one evening at dinner. "Maybe I can become a captain of a boat. That would be cool. What do you think?"

"Have you seen *Jaws*?" She shakes her head. "There is no way I am letting you go out on a boat in the middle of the ocean. You could die."

He laughs. "That happened like, once, years ago. That won't happen if I am captain." He stares down at his plate. "I'm not sure it's even a job anymore. I just love fishing, and wouldn't it be great to do something you love? Plus, imagine how pissed your dad would be, right?"

A picture of Marta and him sitting on a rock talking about their hopes and dreams flashes through his head and he slumps in his chair. Things were so much simpler back then. Everything seemed possible. Becoming a teacher in the Peace Corps seemed so perfect then—but now, suddenly, it seems almost silly. Kelly would never uproot her life and move to Africa—and would he really want to do that, anyway?

Ultimately, Kelly and her dad band together and convince him to work at her uncle's insurance agency. He decides he will do it to get some work experience on his résumé until he can find something else, but he insists it is just a short-term gig while he figures out what he really wants to do.

He learns the ropes quickly according to Uncle Ben, and almost immediately he feels those ropes starting to bind. Everyone he meets at the agency tells him how they just kind of fell into insurance. They thought they would do it for a while until they found something better, and now these folks have been working at the agency for twenty, even thirty years.

All these people have let go of their dreams in one way or another, he realizes. Maybe it is a requirement of growing up. He feels his grip on his own dreams loosening little by little.

Marta is the only one he holds on to. He has always thought that she is out there, just waiting. She remains the dream that will never die.

One night Kelly rushes into the house and immediately blurts out, "Guess what? Lynn just got engaged. I can't believe my baby sister is going to get married."

Looking up, Kevin notices that she's watching him carefully. He straightens up. "Well, they've been dating since high school, right? It shouldn't be a surprise."

Her face darkens and she abruptly turns away. It dawns on Kevin only then that this is one of those girl things Mark warned him about just last week. "Watch out," he said. "No older sister wants to be the last one married."

He gets up and throws an arm around Kelly. "It is really great news. How wonderful for her."

She doesn't say anything just then, but soon she starts hinting that it's time for them to take that step, too. She is still a planner, just as she's always been.

Kevin has given up most of his bad habits since college, and some of his left-wing opinions have been tamped down as well. The apartment they share bears no resemblance to his dorm room. Even his autographed AC/DC poster has been relegated to a box somewhere in a small storage area in the basement.

I guess it's the right thing to do, he thinks after days and days of Kelly's not-so-gentle prodding.

Three weeks after Kelly's announcement about Lynn's engagement, Kevin meets Mark for drinks.

"I guess I'm going to ask Kelly to marry me," he shares halfway through his first beer. "There really isn't any reason not to, and this Lynn thing has got her all worked up, just like you said it would."

"That doesn't mean you *marry* someone!" Mark explodes. "Don't you dare pin this on me, I was just stating a fact. In fact, that is exactly the *wrong* reason to marry someone."

"Okay, okay, you're right," Kevin says quickly. "I didn't mean that. I do love her, and she is good for me. She focuses me and I lighten her. It works, I think."

Mark frowns. "Still not wildly romantic, but much better than your first explanation."

They move on to safer topics.

CHAPTER 21: Daisy

2003—Burlington, Vermont

I n the blank for the third "decision fork," Kevin writes one word: *Daisy*. Shame rises in him, even after all these years. Then he squares his shoulders and reminds himself that he didn't walk away from his family, from his responsibilities. He remained, and he has worked hard to redeem himself ever since; his father would be proud, not disappointed.

He forces himself to write down the words: *Almost Affair*.

1989—Burlington, Vermont

Kevin is thrilled. He is twenty-six years old and is going back to school to get a teaching certificate. Equal parts of his excitement stem from him dodging the bullet of falling in with the rest of the miserable folks in Kelly's uncle's insurance agency. The rest comes from finally acting on the dream he had when he was fourteen and in love. This feels like the first solid first step he's managed to make toward his long-ago dream and plan with Marta.

Turns out Vermont has a special program due to a shortage of teachers. If you have a college degree, you can get your teaching certificate if you complete an eight-week summer program and do some student teaching. Just a couple of short months and, voilà, you're a teacher.

He didn't share with Kelly that he is enthusiastic about the prospect of summers off. He loves the outdoors and fishing, and if he can't do something like that as a vocation, as a teacher he will at least get some good life balance and be able to spend summers pursuing his hobbies.

The day he completes the application for the program, he wonders if Marta is a teacher now. He'd like to think she is.

On a bright Saturday morning, Kevin walks into the classroom of the teaching certificate summer program at the University of Vermont's main campus. He approaches the door with a bit of trepidation. Will he be a good teacher? He feels the weight of responsibility on his shoulders now that he has a brand-new baby at home. She is a darling bundle of joy, but in her sweet and innocent way, she's demanding that Kevin step up and take life more seriously than he ever has before.

Eight people sit at desks that harken back to high school. Kevin settles into the desk closest to the door when Daisy comes rushing in, a light sheen of sweat on her forehead, and he wonders if she ran all the way there. She is, as her name conjures up, pretty in a delicate, sunny sort of way. Her brilliant smile signals someone completely unworried and carefree. She sits down with a *humph* in the desk to Kevin's right, and the stale, chalky air of the classroom is replaced by a fresh scent that he knows perfume companies would pay millions to capture in a bottle.

He turns toward the front of the room when he hears a nasal voice say, "All right, class."

Kevin immediately senses that Mr. Brown will not be instilling the joy of teaching into this crop of potential teachers; he hopes that he will at least instill a few fundamentals that are interesting and useful. The ten students in the room range in age from twenty-five (his guess for Daisy) up to fifty.

Mr. Brown writes his name on the chalkboard, which is almost too cliché, before starting off with some basic rules and the course outline. He makes it very clear that he has a large amount of information to impart in a small amount of time.

They are to work in pairs most of the time.

"You will just pair up as you are sitting," Mr. Brown says emphatically, "unless anyone has a *real*, solid reason to modify that."

They all glance around furtively, trying to see how the pairing will work. Daisy and Kevin are the only two in the back row, so it seems no matter how the first eight get paired up, they will be partners. Daisy looks like a lot of fun, but Kevin worries she's not overly studious or serious. He thinks he should try to connect with an older, more serious student, as he certainly can't be carrying the majority of the load. But when she turns and smiles at him brightly, he thinks, *Oh well, I'm sure this will work out just fine.*

She reaches out a hand and gives him a surprisingly strong handshake. "Howdy, partner. I'm Daisy."

He grins in return. "I'm Kevin."

And that is that.

They finally get their lunch break at noon, and the whole unsure group of them heads to the cafeteria. You can almost hear the audible exhale as they make their escape out of room 212. Daisy and Kevin and the other eight all sit at one long table, just like in middle school. Kevin marvels at the rest of the summer students sitting around the tables in the cafeteria. They all appear amazingly young, even though he figures he is only five or six years older than they are. None of them join room 212's table. Kevin thinks they must be the old, boring table.

The 212s chat with each other as everyone eats their lunch. A guy named Tom shares that he is trying to hold down his sales job while he takes this course; once he gets his certificate, he plans to take early retirement from Vermont Mutual. He looks stressed out already, though, and it is only day one. Kevin can't imagine what he will look like in eight weeks. The rest of the group are like Kevin: they either have an easy, mindless job or no job at all.

Daisy pipes up, "I just graduated from Paier College in Connecticut with a degree in fine arts and graphic design, but I'm back in Vermont to take care of my mother, and I've been doing mind-numbing temp work."

Priscilla interjects, "Been there, done that."

"My options are severely limited for graphic design jobs," Daisy admits, "so I figure I'll try my hand at teaching—maybe become an art teacher and at least partially fulfill my dreams."

She is matter-of-fact about this sacrifice, and Kevin thinks that will be his approach to this job choice as well. He knows while it isn't exactly what he and Marta planned all those years ago, it is close enough, and he is stepping up for more important reasons, such as providing for his child.

The hour break ends way too soon, especially for Tom, who spends most of the time responding to his pager going off and then hustling off to the pay phones to deal with some upset customers, even though it's Saturday.

The afternoon goes by a bit quicker than the morning did, and they all seem more comfortable with the whole school thing. Some of them raise their hands to answer questions, and the interaction helps them gel as a group. Mr. Brown seems to appreciate their interest in learning, and he loosens up ever so slightly. In just one day, they are that much closer to teaching, and they just learned how important an engaged class is to a teacher. Kevin wonders if that is the key—if in order to become a good teacher, you first need to become a good student. If that is the case, by week eight, they will all be bringing bushels of apples to Mr. Brown.

Shortly before four, they get their first homework assignment: change a sample class lecture on the water cycle to make it appropriate for a visual learner. This is due on Monday evening, the next class.

Each of the assigned pairs huddle together after class ends to figure out how to get it done.

Kevin turns to Daisy. "Do you want to bang this out now or on Sunday?"

Her lips quirk into a smile that makes her nose wrinkle as she ponders his question. She finally replies, "I really need to get back to my mom right now, but I would be able to meet back here at eight—or we could do it over the phone. I live pretty close to here, but if you don't, the phone is fine."

Kevin considers his options and quickly concludes, "We can meet back here at eight. But probably in the library, as I think they close up these classrooms."

Daisy grabs her stuff with a nod and says breathlessly, "See you then—bye!" before dashing out of the room.

Kevin gathers his gear more slowly before heading home. He is strangely excited about things. While not one to overanalyze, he is pretty sure he is excited in equal parts about learning about teaching, which seems much more interesting than he would have guessed and being paired with Daisy. He grins from ear to ear the whole ride home. This has not been the norm of late, but he doesn't overthink it; he's just happy to feel happy.

It's just after 5:00 p.m. when Kevin walks through the door to what can only be described as chaos. Little Megan is crying, and Kelly looks as though she is at her wits' end. Tears brimming in her eyes, she thrusts the baby into his arms, an abrupt move that momentarily shocks Megan into silence. Kelly is even more upset by the baby's sudden quiet, and tears spill down her cheeks. She turns away, looking both angry and embarrassed, and stalks off upstairs.

Smiling down at his beautiful baby girl, the rest of the world melts away. The two silently regard each other. Both look rather pleased with this turn of events. Kevin finds a clear spot in the middle of the cramped family room, and they lie down to continue to stare at each other from this new angle. She is just a precious pile of mysteriousness. She seems to know everything there is to know in the world and yet at the same time know nothing at all. They play for twenty minutes or so, which consists mainly of Megan pulling his hair. With the sun angling low through the window, his blond hair reflects the light in a way that appears to be keeping her in a trance.

Kevin finally hoists her up on his hip and murmurs, "Let's make some dinner, shall we?"

Megan coos in agreement, but when he puts her in her high-chair, she stiffens and looks as though she may fall apart.

Before she can lose it, he drags the chair from around the table and tucks it in close to the stove. Just like that, she regains her humor and gazes up at him as if he is the most amazing thing ever. He guiltily glances up the stairs, waiting to see if Kelly heard the drag of the highchair and is going to complain it is too close to the stove. Silence.

With a sigh of relief, he gets to work—chopping vegetables, then sautéeing them with left-over chicken meat. He gives Megan a pile of Cheerios on her tray, and she laughs every time he sneaks one and tosses it up in the air to try to catch it in his mouth.

Kevin is batting .500 with the Cheerios when he hears the bath water start. He cracks a smile. Even though the apartment is cramped and a mess, the future looks clear and focused for the first time in a long time.

Megan and Kevin eat dinner together, and he leaves leftovers for Kelly. Later, he creeps upstairs to make sure she hasn't fallen asleep in the bath. He finds her curled up in their bed with a towel wrapped around her hair, still in her ratty bathrobe. He really needs to get her a new robe. He decides to get one for her birthday, which is coming up in October; *Remember*, he tells himself, hoping that he will be able to retain this gift idea for the next three months. Then he covers Kelly with an extra blanket and walks back downstairs.

Like a perfectly orchestrated plan, Kevin feeds Megan her last bottle at 7 p.m. and settles her into her crib. He sits in her cozy room, looking out the window at the stars that are just beginning to peek out of the sky, and once she falls completely asleep, he heads back downstairs to clean up a little.

His efforts don't really make a dent. *What has happened to my super-organized wife?* Before Megan, he would have thought not even a superpower could mess with Kelly's organization skills, but now it's turned out that a tiny bundle that can't even walk or talk is her kryptonite.

It has been a while since he's been out at night, and he has forgotten how much he loves the darkness and the aloneness of the night. He can think much more clearly in the dark, as it feels like all the noise and turmoil are muffled by the blanket of night and only the important items remain.

He tries to remember the last time he was out after sunset. It was before Megan was born, if you don't count the runs to the convenience store for diapers or baby Tylenol. He decides he is going to start taking her out at night. He knows she will appreciate the clarity and peace it brings. Not Kelly, though, she doesn't understand his fascination with the night and long ago gave up pretending to share it.

He stands in the driveway, staring up at the sky, letting the peace wash over him, for a few more minutes. Then he gets into his car and drives the fifteen minutes to the library.

He is pleasantly surprised to find Daisy already at a table with two stacks of books piled next to her. She glances up as Kevin approaches and beams.

"I arrived a bit earlier than our appointed time, so I got a head start on things. My mom fell asleep earlier than usual, and I figure there may be times when I will have trouble making it on time and you will have to pick up the slack."

"No problem," Kevin says, and he slides into the empty chair across from her.

She looks relieved. He imagines she was worried he would be one of those uptight, controlling partners who are not very understanding when it comes to personal issues. She needn't worry about that with him.

They review what Daisy has already researched, and he realizes he may have jumped to the wrong conclusion about her. She's smart, and she seems more than willing to work hard.

Looks like I picked the right partner after all.

They finish the assignment by ten fifteen, thanks to Daisy's head start, and walk out to their cars.

Ever since Marta wrote to him about her first car—a light green, "very old" VW Bug—Kevin has gravitated toward Bugs as though they were a direct connection to Marta. So, when he pulled into the parking lot earlier and there was a spot open next to a beat-up orange Bug, he parked right next to it.

Kevin laughs when Daisy heads right to the quirky little car. "Wow, that's your car?"

Daisy looks up somewhat sheepishly but responds quickly, "Yup! She's my baby."

"I've always loved Bugs."

She snorts and shrugs. "Well, as you can see, she's in tip-top shape." She laughs a silvery kind of laugh, and her eyes crinkle up at the corners. "Since you seem to be a real aficionado, maybe I'll let you drive her sometime."

With one more nod, they get into their cars and head in different directions.

✦ ✦ ✦

Kevin pulls open the front door to a quiet, sleeping house and realizes that he once again has a slight grin on his face. The place looks tidied, which means Kelly did wake up at some point.

Putting his book bag down, he finishes loading the last couple of dishes from the sink into the dishwasher before heading upstairs to bed.

"Okay, I'm off," Kevin says a few nights later. "Megan is asleep; I'll see you in a couple of hours. I'll try to be quiet when I get home."

"Seriously, you are going to the library again?" Kelly complains. "I had no idea becoming a teacher took so much work."

"Kelly, it's not for much longer," Kevin says patiently. "I'm doing this for you—for us. You know that."

She sighs and stares down at her stained sweatshirt and sweat-pants. "Go, it's fine. Whatever."

Kevin starts to snap back. He hates it when she says "Whatever." But he bites his tongue; he doesn't want to fight. He still has hours of work to focus on, and it's hard enough to get everything done without having to spend the first half hour venting about things to Daisy. God, he wishes Kelly would go back to work at least part-time at the yarn shop. That could give her some of the adult conversation and activities she complains she misses so much.

He shakes his head, remembering the last time he suggested that to her. Boy, she was pissed. He can't seem to do anything right these days.

Slinging his book bag over his shoulder, he calls a soft "Bye" in Kelly's direction before sliding out the door.

He really can't blame her for being a little upset. He is spending a ton of time with someone called Daisy. He can only imagine the picture a girl named Daisy conjures up in Kelly's head. He has made sure not to mention anything about the sweet VW she drives, since she knows about his infatuation with Bugs.

No reason to add fuel to the fire, he thinks with a grimace.

When he returns from the library, he finds Kelly awake and reading.

"How was Daisy?" she asks snidely.

"Kelly, really. I've told you. Daisy is this poor girl taking care of her old, sick mother. She is struggling to do both and is barely able to function most of the time. So really, cut it out." He figures maybe she will feel bad for Daisy or at least picture a haggard, dowdy spinster instead of a wildflower growing strong and sweet in some meadow, as her name conjures up, if he describes her this way.

Her scowl morphs into a look of contrition. "Sorry, I don't know why I say some of the things I say."

"Just remember how sweet it will be to have summers off," he says. "You, me, and Megan can relax and hang out, fishing and swimming at the lake. Can't you picture us on the sand and in the water?"

He leans down and traces a finger along her thigh, circling, then leans down and lightly touches his lips to hers. She swats his hand away from her thigh, turns her head away from him, picks up her book, and continues to read.

Kevin gazes down at his wife and wonders, *How can I make her happy? Nothing seems to be the answer.*

A few days later Kevin talks to Mark about being rebuffed by Kelly.

"Making love becomes a low priority, at least for most of the first year for new mothers," he says sanguinely. "But it'll resurface at some point in the second year."

"A whole fucking year?" Kevin blurts out.

Mark just laughs and laughs.

He has three kids and a great wife, so Kevin knows they at least had sex twice after the first baby. His brother again reassures him that things readjust after the first year. "It will never be like it was before kids," he says with a shrug, "but you'll make it work."

"Sex shouldn't be *work*," Kevin remarks glumly.

Mark snorts. "My poor, naïve brother."

Daisy turns out to be a great partner. She and Kevin develop a very comfortable working relationship that produces some nice grades for the two of them. They have a solid A in the class and are both finding that they enjoy most of the work and are naturals at teaching—or, at least, at presenting teaching plans to their very supportive classmates.

It is on their fifteenth day of classes, which seems like a lifetime at that point, when Daisy slides into her chair next to Kevin's and stage-whispers, "This is going to be your lucky day."

Kevin tilts his head quizzically.

"My aunt is coming to visit today and is taking care of my mom tonight," she explains. "I thought you might want to take Betty for a drive."

Betty is her VW's name, and Kevin immediately nods affirmatively. It is Thursday, and suddenly it feels like an old party night from his college days.

"I just need to go home right after school to check in," he says, "but I can meet you back here in an hour."

Daisy nods. "Perfect, that will force me to work on my résumé for at least an hour."

Kevin rushes out the door and straight to the pay phone just outside to call Kelly.

"Hey—just wanted to let you know they're only giving us a quick break tonight, and then I have to come back for a lecture or something from an outside professor," he says quickly.

Kelly lets out an annoyed sigh and then gathers herself and says, almost nicely, "That's fine. Megan was really happy today. We went for a long walk, which I think tired her out."

Kevin is relieved, as he knows if Kelly had thrown any sort of hissy fit, he would have called the whole thing off. He's not feeling good about the lie to begin with. But he also feels a bit justified in taking a break from the grind. *I've earned it, haven't I?*

"I'll see you in a sec," he says, then hangs up.

When Kevin gets home, he rushes inside, takes Megan out of Kelly's arms, and swings and twirls her around.

"What can I do?" he asks. "Give her a bath?"

Megan is laughing and even Kelly is smiling as she sits down on the couch. "Yes, give her a bath; that would be great."

Kevin carries the baby upstairs and quickly runs a bath. Megan can sit up now and is just beginning to crawl, which is the cutest thing. She watches and listens to everything he says, and he continues to believe that she understands most of what he shares with her in that sweet, all-knowing baby way.

They splash and play, and Kevin is soaked by the time they are done. After handing her off to Kelly, he quickly changes into an old pair of jeans he has never worn to class; he feels that his clothes should reflect the clothes of a teacher, and these jeans definitely do not express that vibe. But tonight, he's not going to class.

He puts on a comfy T-shirt and his old Bates College sweatshirt, and he feels the weight of the world lift from his shoulders. He does need a break.

He makes grilled cheese sandwiches for both of his girls before gliding out the door, feeling as light as a balloon.

It's only when Kevin pulls into the school parking lot beside Daisy's Bug that the niggling doubts begin. *Should I park near her car?* This thought immediately makes the whole thing seem like a tryst and not a meeting of two friends.

Kevin pushes back. *I am just playing hooky from my real life for a few hours, and so is Daisy, and that is nothing either of us should be feeling guilty about.*

He continues to rationalize things as he gets out of his car. He sees Daisy, her hair in a ponytail, sitting in the passenger seat of her car. Kevin feels like he is back in high school, and they are meeting in the school parking lot to sneak off to Mansfield Hollow Dam, the local makeout spot.

He shakes his head again and leans in through the open window. "Hey. Can I really drive her?"

"Of course! You can't be a speed demon, though. My baby doesn't do well with speed, even if you wanted to."

He opens the door and slides into the driver's seat. He grins when his knees bump up against the steering wheel. "I didn't realize you were so short."

She snorts and playfully punches his arm.

He focuses on getting comfortable with the car and getting his knees out of the steering apparatus. It is a standard, which he knew it would be, and he is pretty sure he can handle that, although it's been a long time.

He starts the car and is relieved when he manages to back out of the spot smoothly. "Where to?"

Daisy shrugs. "How about Silver Lake? We can get burgers at Potts to eat up there."

Kevin nods enthusiastically. "Great idea."

As they walk across Pott's parking lot after getting their burgers and a couple of Labatts in bottles, Kevin stares at Daisy's ponytail, strangely fascinated by it. He has seen her in class with it a bunch of times, but today it seems extra bouncy, and he keeps thinking, *Girl next door.* You know, the type you hang out with when you are young and then suddenly, at fifteen, realize is no longer that annoying kid next door but is that *girl* next door.

A sudden memory of Marta flashes through his head: he sees her with a ponytail, smiling at him. Marta flashbacks don't happen very often these days, and he savors the moment. He has been too busy to have many spare moments where those memories can creep in.

He freezes for a minute as Daisy walks ahead and lets the memory take hold.

Marta standing outside a McDonald's the summer before high school, when they were inseparable. She's holding his McDonald's bag behind her back, demanding a kiss before she will relinquish it. Kevin leaning over as if to kiss her and instead grabbing her ponytail. She does a perfect pirouette, ducks her head, escaping and dancing away with the bag. Kevin gives chase, and they end up tumbling into a grassy area in a pile of flailing arms and legs. They kiss sweetly, the bag forgotten on the ground next to them.

Kevin staring into Marta's clear, hazel eyes, and with total sincerity mouths the words, I love you. This is the first time he's uttered those words, and they catch him by surprise. Marta's eyes widen and become serious. She touches his cheek, and he closes his eyes. She kisses each eyelid and wraps her arms around his head in a bear hug. Kevin can't see anything for that moment, and she whispers in his ear, "Man, so do I."

Suddenly, Kevin hears a loud beep. He jumps back to the present and realizes he is standing in the middle of the parking lot, right in the way of a car that's trying to drive through.

Daisy glances back at him questioningly, and he grins self-consciously. "Sorry, I got lost in a trip down memory lane."

He sheepishly waits for the car to pass then slow-jogs to catch up with Daisy. "Weird, that doesn't normally happen."

She shrugs and they continue walking. He's glad he doesn't have to explain anything more. He hasn't talked to many people about Marta and the importance his first love holds for him. He gets the feeling, if he isn't careful, he could blurt the whole thing out to Daisy, and she would get it—but he's not sure he wants to go there.

He shakes his head to dispel any remaining cobwebs before climbing back into the Bug.

They drive to Silver Lake and find some large, smooth rocks that are not yet fully in shadow and sit down to munch on their burgers and beers. The gulls are flying overhead, and the sun is getting low in the western sky. No one else is down by the lake, and it seems so natural when Daisy leans over and softly touches her lips to his.

Kevin reaches for her immediately, without even thinking. Suddenly, they are splayed across the rock and clutching each other for balance.

He's caught off guard, uncertain how he went from eating burgers to having Daisy's shirt balled up in his hand, but his surprise doesn't keep him from working to unclasp her bra. They quickly strip off the rest of their clothes and shift off the rock and onto a sandy spot on the ground. Daisy is wildly uninhibited. Intent on the act, she guides him with a heated focus that borders on desperation. Kevin tries to hold back and take it slower, but she clearly doesn't want that.

It has been a long time since he had sex, never mind with someone who is so eager.

Daisy suddenly moans and momentarily stiffens. Kevin feels her body convulse and release, and her body suddenly feels all soft and pliable in place of the strong, demanding force it was moments ago. He gazes down at her; her eyes remain closed, and she's wearing an enchanting smile on her face. She looks otherworldly.

He moves forward and back two more times and feels that sweet peak and release. All his stresses empty out at the same time. He leans down and lies on Daisy more fully as his arms go limp. Her eyelids flutter open, and she grins lazily, so he leans down and kisses her perfect lips. Then he rolls off her and props himself on one elbow.

They stay like this for a few more minutes, then slowly start to untangle themselves and piece back together their clothes.

As they do this, reality starts to set in. He can't remember how they got to where they are. It was totally unplanned, and the guilt hasn't taken root yet. But he knows what just occurred is bad. He can't even think about Kelly and Megan while he is trying to fix his hair and put his T-shirt back on. His brain keeps asking, *What was I thinking?* And he truly wants an answer, as he doesn't know what he was thinking, and he certainly doesn't know how it happened so fast. *God, who am I?*

The burgers lie ruined in the sand, but thankfully their beers remain unscathed. They move back to their original positions on the rock. He takes a long swig, and the bite of the beer as it eases down his throat helps ground him.

He hands Daisy her beer and looks around to see if anyone is nearby, knowing it's a little late to be checking now. The whole thing took probably five minutes max, so unless someone showed up as soon as they started and ran over close enough to see them behind the rocks, no one has any idea of what just happened. The fact that it all happened so quickly seems to diminish its significance. *Can five minutes really change your life?*

Daisy drinks deeply from her beer and looks at him with eyes that are clear and untroubled. She seems genuinely happy. Kevin doesn't want to ruin that for her by revealing his growing angst or by going on some self-flagellating tirade about ruining his life. She isn't the one with a kid and a spouse. Kevin takes another drink and lets out an almost contented sigh. Despite everything, the cool beer, the waves lapping at the shore, the stillness, and the release of his pent-up tension are calming his nerves. Mother Nature is telling him to chill.

Leaning her head against his shoulder, Daisy doesn't say anything, seeming not to want to break the peace, either. He's glad she doesn't feel the need to fill the silence. He remembers too many girls that got downright chatty after sex, when silence would have been so much his preference.

Glancing down at her, he knows instinctively that she isn't

going to be one of those sorts that start making demands or turn into some sort of *Fatal Attraction* chick. He tries to picture Daisy boiling a bunny, and he lets out a chuckle.

She cocks her head so he can see her cute, upside-down face. Smiling lazily, she asks, "What's so funny?"

Kevin can't very well bring up the boiled bunny, so he does what any guy does when he is at a loss for words. He twists her around and kisses her gently on the lips. Her eyes become translucent as a light sparks in them, and then she leans into his body—hard.

Quickly shifting away, he holds her at arm's length, laughing. "Whoa there! What are you thinking? I can't possibly do it again."

Daisy looks chagrined. "Oh, sorry. I got carried away."

He knows she is thinking he meant physically, he couldn't do it again, but he meant mentally—or philosophically, perhaps. He needs time to think without a warm, enthusiastic creature almost sitting on his lap.

They finish their beers in silence, and he rises and scoops their destroyed burgers back into their bag while Daisy sits. She seems to enjoy watching and the half smile remains on her face.

Wow, we really could have sex again if I wanted. He had forgotten what unscheduled, uninhibited sex feels like. He stops himself from reaching over to her. Instead, they start tramping back through the path to the parking lot.

When they settle back into her car, he turns toward her and blurts out, "Look, I didn't really mean for this to happen. I'm married and everything, and I really don't know what happened . . ." He stares at her pleadingly.

Daisy touches his arm and bites her lip hesitantly. He has a visceral reaction to that. He blinks and forces himself to look somewhere else, and again an unbidden memory of Marta's worried face and her biting her lip in a similar way flashes through his head.

He knows the exact day that picture in his head is from. It was the day he told Marta he was moving away. She tried hard not to appear worried as she went through life, and she often had an easy smile on her face, but when she was troubled, her reaction was to bite her lip and hold her breath.

He physically shakes his head to clear that picture and bring him back to Daisy and this current predicament.

Daisy says softly, "Kevin, listen, don't worry. It was just a fluke, and it was really me. I shouldn't have kissed you and then essentially ravished you. I didn't mean for it to happen, either. We can just forget the whole thing. This was just a crazy moment where we did something totally nuts. It was my fault. My life has been really limited of late, and while I don't regret it, I have no plans to be a homewrecker or anything close. We just had to blow off some steam, right?"

Kevin nods, still troubled but feeling better talking about it. "I need to think about this, but I will tell you—I don't regret it either. It was great." He swallows hard. "But I have a wife and kid, and I can't do anything to hurt them. Well, at least anything more to hurt them."

Daisy grins impishly and raises her right hand. "I solemnly swear not to ravish you again on the beach at Silver Lake."

Kevin chuckles. "Deal."

Turning the key in the ignition, they slowly drive back to the school parking lot.

Slipping quietly through the front door at home, Kevin is happy to be there; a wave of contentment and gratitude washes over him as he steps inside. The feeling hasn't been around much recently. He wonders if it is connected to guilt or having blown off steam or a realization of all that he has and how easy it would be to lose it.

Shrugging his shoulders, he doesn't care why he is happy; he is just happy that he is.

Walking through the family room, he finds Kelly dozing with the TV on. He leans down and kisses her cheek. Her eyes fly open quickly, but then she smiles sweetly and breathes, "Hey."

He turns off the TV, gently pulls Kelly up off the couch, and ushers her to bed.

2003—Burlington, Vermont

Kevin rereads his last entry, knowing he made the right decision back then and realizing anew what a critical turning point for his life that incident was. He definitely could have gone a different path—and if he had chosen to continue with the affair, it might have blown up his whole family.

His tryst with Daisy never happened again; in fact, it was never even mentioned between them, as if that magical night had happened in a different time or space. He knew that neither of them would ever forget it, but he pushed it into the far recesses of his mind, and he assumed Daisy did the same.

After that night, Kevin made a promise to himself: his priorities were Kelly and Megan and school, and he would never again let anything threaten that. While his family life was by no means perfect, it was what he had chosen and committed to, and that was that.

CHAPTER 22: What Might Have Been

2003—Burlington, Vermont

K evin looks down at the fourth blank page on the "Decision
Forks" and fills it in: *Calling My First Love Before I Got Married*.

He pictures himself at twenty-three, picking up his phone
and dialing information. It is May 22, 1985, and he is sitting in his
cramped, gray office cubicle . . .

"Hello, Brunswick, New Jersey . . . yes, the number for Ernest Carini."

His palms break out in a sweat as he writes down the number
the operator gives him. While he wasn't able to remember it before,
as soon as the operator said the numbers, the wheels turn, and the
memory of the number fell into place. He jots it down and slips the
paper into his pants pocket, nervously glancing around the small
office to see if anyone is wondering why he is getting a New Jersey
number when the agency's geographic reach barely goes into New
Hampshire. No one even looks up.

He decides he better collect himself and figure out what he is
going to say before he calls, although the piece of paper is burning a
hole in his pocket. He can feel his life's karma getting all out of balance just from that little paper. Normally, if something bothers him
enough for him to notice it in this way, he will deal with it sooner

rather than later, just to be rid of the uncomfortable feeling and get back to his normal, steady state.

He suddenly remembers his dad saying, "Take the chance, you only live once."

He steels himself and again picks up the phone and dials Marta's parents' number, the same number he dialed all those years ago.

His heart is pounding. He doesn't have anything planned to say.

The phone rings twice, and then a deep voice says, "Hello."

"Hello, is Marta there?" Kevin forces out of his tight throat.

"Marta?" the deep voice repeats. "Now who would be calling Marta?"

"Um. Hello, Mr. Carini. It is, um, Kevin. I was wondering if Marta is there."

There is a pause this time, and Kevin waits, clutching the heavy phone to his ear. His life is hanging in the balance, and he can hear the seconds ticking by as the fickle gods determine what his life will be.

"Kevin, Marta doesn't live here anymore. In fact, she is getting married in a few months. I don't think you need to talk to Marta. Don't you agree?"

And the phone goes dead. The gods have decided.

Glancing over the blank pages, he has filled with his scrawl, Kevin remembers something else: after the lake incident, after he rededicated himself to his family, he began having more Marta flashbacks. It was as if there were a direct connection between what happened on those rocks with Daisy and his long-ago feelings for Marta. The fact that these memories resurfaced after he was sure he had long ago forgotten them had been a bonus for him in the whole weird situation.

Thinking of Marta now, he knows which "fork" he will use to try to channel. He will see if this channeler can get Marta's father to give him Marta's number so he can talk to her and see what might have happened back then. Maybe this channeler can overpower those gods all those years ago and have them make a difficult call.

CHAPTER 23: Coincidence or Karma?

2003—Boston, Massachusetts

Neither Cholan nor Edwin made any connection to Marta's story before Kevin comes in. The details are too vague to connect the dots. Kevin seems like just another customer, and he continues to seem that way—right up until Cholan travels with him back to his old insurance office cubicle and witnesses him talking on the phone to Marta's father.

A sense of déjà vu washes over Cholan. He knows exactly what is going to happen, and he even tries to shift over to Marta's house to get her to stand and pick up the phone. But it's impossible; no matter how he strains, he hits a cold, immovable wall that he can't see but most definitely can feel. He ripples back to the present. He needs to think.

He slowly eases back to his chair next to Kevin, who is reclined on the settee. Kevin's brows are furrowed, and he has a bit of sweat on his top lip. Cholan gently nudges him, and he comes to quickly.

Wide-eyed, Kevin gazes at him and asks simply, "Why couldn't I do it? I wanted to insist he give me Marta's number, but everything just disappeared. Did I fall out?"

"I just need to collect myself and figure something out," Cholan says calmly. "We will try again. It often takes a few tries before we can break into the alternative channel."

Kevin looks relieved. Cholan rushes out to find Edwin.

After he's explained the situation to Edwin, they both come back into the room.

"Let's try again," Cholan tells Kevin. "This time, you may feel me help you pick up the phone to call again after Mr. Carini hangs up the first time. I think that will be our best option."

Kevin glances back and forth between the two. His brow is furrowed and he is about to ask more questions, but then he shrugs and his shoulders relax.

"You will need to be ready to work your magic on Marta's father," Cholan warns him. "That part is solely up to you, as I can't make Mr. Carini do anything. I can only help you act."

There is a ripple and time slips sideways.

Immediately after Marta's father hangs up on him, Cholan helps Kevin hit redial. The phone rings.

"Mr. Carini, I really need to speak to Marta," he says in a rush when the older man picks up. "It's a matter of life and death. Can I please get her number?"

There is a pause, and Kevin can hear the murmur of voices, then Kevin hears a voice through the years hitting his ear and echoing in his head. "Kevin, is that you?"

He says excitedly, "Marta, is that you? I can't believe it. Yeah, it's me."

Cholan feels the connection and the electricity flowing between the two of them. He is happy to see their love from both sides—to feel the strength of it. It makes his heart sing. This is a new discovery. Channels aren't just for one person. They may exist for everyone that is part of the channel.

✧ ✧ ✧

"Come now, this is truly amazing, you have to admit it," Cholan prods gently.

Edwin scowls even more, which Cholan didn't think was possible. They have been discussing Marta and Kevin for some time now.

"The odds against this happening are astronomical." Cholan shakes his head in wonder. "Two people, both able to channel, and they choose the *same* channel. Amazing, isn't it?"

Edwin snorts. "It's dangerous, is what it is! You have no idea what could happen, and neither do I."

"But this is karma, and when I have the ultimate sign from the gods land in my lap, I can't very well ignore it," Cholan presses. "Let's just see if we can get them to come. If they do, we can see what I can do with that. I would never do anything to harm someone, you know that."

"I wish we could call Dr. Lee and see what he would say about you messing with two channels or two people in the same channel," Edwin says. "I bet if he were still alive, he would side with me on this. Bridging universes with one person is dangerous enough, but doing it with two is sheer madness."

Cholan chuckles. "Ahh, remember those early days? We never would have met if Dr. Liam hadn't connected me with Dr. Lee at MIT to help me get started in Boston. Thank God for you and that group of crazy astrophysicists. If not for you guys, we would not be here doing what we do. I never could have converted my little, secret ability into something that could help others."

Edwin scowls. "My parents never forgave me for wasting my MIT education on this crazy adventure," he says. "Even with Dr. Lee explaining to them that we are applying the theories of quantum physics in our work, they never bought that it was anything other than voodoo science or the like."

Cholan cracks a grin. "I remember you explaining to them that we were dealing with the multiverse and bubbles of time and space created during the Big Bang. I know you understood all of that, but honestly, I really can't fathom it, either. So I don't blame your parents one bit for thinking I had cast some spell on you and forced you to give up your dreams of becoming a professor."

Edwin turns serious. "Never really my dream. But it certainly was my parents'. MIT served us well, though. It would have taken us years to ferret out the right questions to ask to find the most likely candidates if we hadn't had the chance to run all those student experiments." He smirks. "I do remember how baffled you were by all of our explanations of what was going on."

Cholan grimaces. "Talk about mumbo jumbo. Remind me—what was the name of thesis you wrote on the topic?"

Edwin radiates with enthusiasm. "Oh, I called it 'Why Does the Caged Bird Sing?' A reference to Maya Angelou, of course, but I used birds to explain how channeling was crossing over into other bubbles of time and space. It simplifies the explanation of how much more likely it is that the Big Bang created multiple universes, rather than just one . . ."

Cholan's eyes begin to glaze over.

Edwin pokes him and says sternly, "Pay attention. You can understand this. Just as Schrödinger's cat makes the duality of outcomes relatable, my thesis does the same. You see, if you are trying to teach a bird to sing, it is much more likely when you finally get the bird to sing that it will sing multiple notes and not just one. It is almost impossible to think you could teach it to sing just the one—that makes sense, right?"

Cholan nods obediently.

"Well, the same applies to the Big Bang. It's unlikely that such a momentous event created just the one world we live in; it is much more likely that multiple worlds were created at that time. And you and your channeling might be glimpsing those other universes. Like you tell the audience, bridging over to these universes. I still don't think it's possible to break into them entirely, but I think you get close. Remember the air temperature tests we did when you channeled during all those studies we did? All the drops and increases are signs of areas where those universes collided in the early stages of inflation." Edwin shakes his head as he notes Cholan doodling on his pad. "You really should try to understand what you are messing with."

Cholan gives him a rueful look.

"Just like at MIT," Edwin scolds him. "Cholan! This stuff is important. These may be entirely other universes, not just unrealized paths. Which is precisely why we shouldn't be messing with Marta and Kevin. What if we throw another universe into chaos? What if they aren't in the same one at all?"

"It will be fine," Cholan says mildly. "We are in the same one or may just peeking into a different one. Not crossing over. I feel sure of it."

Edwin snorts in disbelief.

"Contrary to your belief, I *have* absorbed some of this over these years," Cholan says a bit indignantly. "I think Dr. Lee would be all for it if he could still vote."

Shaking his head, Edwin ultimately reaches for the phone to start the process.

Despite Marta's decisiveness on the drive home from Boston after channeling, three weeks have passed and Marta still hasn't taken any action. Today, Marta steels herself, takes a deep breath, and types Kevin's name into YP.com to look up his phone number. She finds six Kevin Dixons in the state of Vermont. Her hand is shaking as she scrolls through the numbers. There is only one who is forty.

She writes down the number and stares at it, holding the phone in her hand. She hears the voice in her head low and demanding, *Don't do it. You will start something scary. You aren't brave enough.*

She looks around and suddenly all the energy she was generating throughout her body dissipates and she wilts down, placing her head on her desk, no longer able to pretend she is the brave Marta that would do something so daring.

She jolts up, practically jumping out of her skin when the phone rings loudly in her ear. For one wild moment, she thinks, *Kevin is calling.* Looking around the kitchen guiltily, her cheeks flame hot. Then taking a deep breath, she realizes she is alone, as Steve has gone for a walk with Chippy. With a brain that isn't fully functioning, she takes a deep breath and with a shaking hand puts the phone to her ear. The phone feels heavy in her palm.

"Hello?"

"Marta?"

"Yes." She knows she recognizes the voice, but in her addled state she can't place it.

"Hello. This is Edwin calling."

Now completely confused. She thinks, *Maybe there is some rule against contacting people you meet in your alternative channel?* Marta knows she signed some paperwork, but she didn't read it very thoroughly. *But how could they know I was going to call Kevin?*

Confused and feeling as though she's just been caught doing something she shouldn't, she squeaks out, "Oh, yes. Hello."

"How are you?"

Again, she thinks, *Am I in trouble?* But she's able to respond smoothly, almost lightly, "I am fine. How are you?"

"Oh, me? I'm good." He clears his throat. "Cholan wanted to see if you would come in for another complimentary channel. He is interested in testing some things, and as you know, you are a very promising candidate."

Taken aback she responds, "Oh . . . yes, of course." She pauses, "Uh, I wanted to ask you about some weird things that have been happening since I channeled. You know, just to make sure it's okay . . . well, that I'm okay."

Now all business, he asks, "Weird things?"

"Well, I've been having lapses—or . . . daydreams, or something like that. It's kinda like falling asleep in class and waking up suddenly, I don't know . . . it's like I've gone AWOL for a bit. Is that normal?"

Edwin asks a few questions; Marta answers them all to the best of her ability.

"I'll share all this with Cholan," he blurts out when she's done, his excitement palpable. "These could be mini-trips back to a channel. See? I told you that you were promising! We've never found someone that has this ability. Only Cholan, his village doctor, and the doctor's father. This is spectacular." He shifts his tone and asks brightly, "So, you are willing to come in for another excursion? If Cholan agrees that these may be mini-trips back, we can delve into your history to see if we can find out what it is that makes you so special and lucky."

She expected Edwin to tell her the episodes were common—that most people experienced them. Now she repeats Edwin's words silently: *Special and lucky.* It gives her a warm feeling in her chest. As she holds on to this feeling, she notes that now Edwin sounds strange, just a tad off—but she doesn't dwell on it, as she is trying to process the coincidence of this call while Kevin's number is staring up at her from the table.

Her mind begins to race, conjuring up a bunch of thoughts all at once. *Is Edwin's call an omen? And if so, what is it telling me? Maybe that I shouldn't be contacting Kevin at all, and instead should be satisfied with channeling. Dammit. That would suck. Maybe it's just that I need to take it slow before I take any big steps. Ugh! I wish signs were easier to read.*

As these thoughts flow into her consciousness, she decides that no matter what, she isn't willing to give up on the epiphany she had driving back from Boston. She wants to try to become a boulder in the river. *I won't give up so easily.*

Edwin interrupts her jumbled thoughts with a brusque, "Well, what date and time will be convenient for you?"

Reaching for her calendar, she stops herself, realizing that her schedule is irrelevant. This is the most important thing in her life right now; she'll make herself available.

"Next week sometime would work," she says.

"How about Wednesday at 11:15?"

Marta agrees, and after they hang up, energy surges through her. She feels invincible. The voice reminds her that she didn't do anything brave, as she didn't make the call. But she is able to silence the voice with the bubble of joy she has filling her chest. She feels she's just won the lottery, and feeling excited about her appointment, she thinks, *Maybe I'll be brave enough to call Kevin later, after another chance to meet him in my channel.*

Edwin enters Cholan's office, clears his throat, and declares stonily, "Both Marta and Kevin will be coming in on Wednesday—Kevin at ten forty-five and Marta at eleven fifteen." He shakes his head and softly closes the door.

Cholan feels lightheaded just thinking about how to proceed. Marta is very easy to shift into her channel, and maybe she can do it herself by now. She's one of the easiest subjects he's ever worked with.

Kevin, though—he was a little more difficult. Despite the confidence he claimed to have during his conversation with Edwin, Cholan is nervous. *Could this be a mistake?*

CHAPTER 24: Couple's Channeling

2003—Boston, Massachusetts

Wednesday dawns bright and clear. Cholan goes for his normal two-mile walk in the morning before heading to the office. He can feel the tension in his back and neck. They are on the brink of uncharted territory.

Unbidden, the memory of the incident that made them start with the formality of the signing of the waiver form pops into his head. It happened many years ago: he channeled with a client who had epilepsy, though he didn't know it before they started. Cholan shivers, remembering how he got lost in that channel that made no sense to him. It was a frightening world of chaos and fractures. The client was nonplussed, as maybe someone with a brain disorder was used to that type of disorientation, but Cholan will never forget having to fight his way back from a place he never wants to see again. Now they ask about medical conditions to ensure he doesn't stumble into a place he can't get back from. But is what he is doing now even more dangerous—breaking down partitions between worlds or universes.

Kevin rushes into Cholan's office waiting room. It is 10:45 a.m. exactly, and Edwin is standing in the little room when he charges through the door.

"Hello, Kevin," he greets him. "How was traffic?"

"Oh, not bad," Kevin says. "You never know with the interstate, do you?"

Edwin doesn't bother with any further small talk; he beckons Kevin to follow him down the hall. This time, rather than going into the room they used last time, they turn and enter the door just across from it. Kevin follows Edwin inside without a question.

As soon as Cholan hears the door close quietly behind them, he peeks out of his office and walks with his crooked gait toward the waiting room. The receptionist called him moments ago to let him know that Marta has arrived . . . early.

He thinks, *That was close!*

Taking a deep breath, he steels himself, and opens the door.

"Marta, so good to see you again. I am so happy to be traveling with you again." He smiles serenely at her.

Her hair is pulled back in a low ponytail today and she is wearing white sneakers, leggings, and an oversize mauve sweater. Her eyes crinkle when she smiles back at him. "Oh, me too," she blurts out. "I barely slept last night; I was so excited."

Cholan leads her into the normal channeling room, and she settles into the middle comfy chair, then looks at him expectantly.

"Give me one moment, will you, Marta? Just sit and relax. I will be right back."

"Sure."

Cholan backs out of the room, watching for any sign of suspicion on Marta's flushed face. Seeing only eager anticipation, he enters the smaller room. It has only one chair and a stool, and the windows aren't darkened as they are in the other room.

"How about those Red Sox?" Cholan asks cheerily, tapping Kevin's baseball cap.

"Yeah, almost playoff time," Kevin says. "They look good this year. Are you a fan?"

"Me?" Cholan scoffs. "No, not really, but my wife and her family live and die by the Sox, so I pick up stuff through osmosis. They do look good this year. Maybe they will finally break the curse. It has to happen one of these years." He laughs congenially. "Okay, are we ready to travel back? Remember—picture yourself. You are in your insurance cubicle. Picture the walls and the phone—we are there now." Time slows and then stutters. *"Kevin, pick up the phone . . ." he nudges.*

Cholan slows down the sequence—he hopes—then leaves the room and darts across the hall to reenter Marta's room.

She perks up when she sees him and exclaims, "I was wonder—"

"Let's go visit your parents' house on the day Kevin called, Marta," he cuts in. "Remember the feel of the chair you were sitting on. Remember the sun coming through the window."

Cholan feels the slip of time and the shudder flow through Marta, he hears the phone ringing, and pulls himself out of the channel, practically sprinting across the hall to Kevin.

When he eases into Kevin's channel, he hears Kevin talking on the phone. Cholan tries to feel his way over into Marta's space, but there is only a whirlpool of blackness in every direction and he has no idea which way is Marta. He stays with Kevin, and hears the surprise in Kevin's voice as he asks, "Marta, is that you?"

Cholan realizes Marta is channeling on her own, and she has taken the phone from her father's hand without Cholan's guidance. Cholan brings his attention fully back to Kevin, who is struggling a little. Cholan reaches his energy out to him to reassure him; he can feel the breath in Kevin's chest release as Cholan envelops him in his being. The pressure eases and Kevin settles and begins to talk. He tells Marta about college and his teaching plans. His voice sounds almost normal, but there is a little hitch at the end of each sentence, as if the words are echoing in the space.

Glitch in the matrix pops into Cholan's head and he quickly pushes the thought away. Then he feels a force hit his body like a wild elephant or a lion and it starts to try to pull his body apart. He clutches at the air wildly as if trying to collect his errant limbs. Suddenly, Cholan is catapulted into a black vortex. He spins and spins—completely disoriented, invisible waves buffeting him. It is like when he got pummeled by a huge wave when he went to the beach with Dr. Liam that left him gasping for breath. Just like back then, his nose and mouth are filled with something like the salt water from the long-ago wave. He can hear Marta and Kevin's screams reverberating in his head and knows they are somewhere in this spinning world with him, but where?

He spots a small glimmer of light or at least less darkness above him; the edges are just slightly less dark than the rest of the space he's swirling through. When he focuses on that opening, he can breathe more easily and the spinning slows—but every time he looks around for Kevin and Marta, he loses sight of the opening, and the wave of water fills his lungs, causing him to lose all control again.

Realizing he needs to focus on the opening, he stares at it and at the same time wills Kevin and Marta toward him with just his mind and not his eyes. Feeling around with his arms, he feels nothing but rushing water, only heavier, like cement with a force behind it. He is sweating and beginning to tire. He is drowning in the sea of cement.

This isn't working. Trying a different tack, he thinks of Marta's channel and the calm of Marta's house as she sits on the recliner. He can't see anything, but he feels a crack, the edges are invisible, but he senses Marta is next to him. He can barely connect with her energy field—she is hardly emitting any power on her own but has given in to the might of the vortex. He gathers himself and, with every ounce of strength he has, starts guiding her by pulling her with his mind. He keeps her enveloped in his space as he works to shift now to Kevin's channel; she goes easily.

He ripples through the waves, fighting against the current, and feels a slip back through the crack. He knows he is back in Kevin's channel. The situation with him is vastly different. Kevin is flailing and fighting, and Cholan struggles to make a connection to him. Cholan backs off and instead, from beneath him, tries to raise Kevin without connecting directly. Cholan becomes a balloon that pushes and nudges Kevin upward, all the while only guessing and hoping that this is the way out.

The three of them rise—Marta enveloped in Cholan's energy, Kevin flailing wildly but being moved by a cloud below him. Gradually, Cholan's breathing becomes one beat easier. No longer breathing through cement, he now is in water, and then quickly he is breathing as if he has a pillowcase over his face. His mind begins to clear. He is alive. His chest tightens but not due to lack of air.

What if they can't breathe at all? What if they are dead? A new anguish fills his heart. *Edwin was right. This was a terrible idea. I am truly messing with things no one fully understands. How wrong of me to take such a chance.*

They ripple together, shifting through space and time.

Cholan lifts his head weakly and finds himself in the smaller room, collapsed on a chair. His body feels as if it has run a marathon. Every muscle aches and pulls, his head is foggy, and he can't remember where he is or why. Edwin is shaking him gently and Cholan tries to touch his arm to get Edwin to stop, but it is as if his arm is disconnected from his brain: it moves slowly and responds only when he focuses all his attention on it.

Edwin holds a glass of water to Cholan's lips, and this action helps Cholan's mind reconnect with reality, as they have done this a thousand times before.

Reality begins to dawn on him as his synapses start to fire a bit faster. He was channeling with Marta and Kevin in their joint channel. They were doing it, just as he hoped. And then everything went horribly wrong.

Gasping, he stares into Edwin's eyes. "My God. Where are they?" He sits up straighter. "Marta? Kevin? What happened to them?" It all comes out a bit garbled, as his tongue is refusing to move properly and seems to be swollen.

Edwin, disapproval in his eyes, waves his hand dramatically

and says, "Shh. Kevin is here. I think they are both okay, but neither one has fully come to yet."

Getting up with Edwin's help, Cholan staggers over to Kevin's chair. He seems to be dozing lightly. Cholan reaches out and shakes his shoulder.

Kevin's eyes flutter open. He looks around disoriented. "Wow," he says slowly. "That was crazy, right?"

Cholan forces a smile and gives Edwin a glance that he hopes Edwin knows means, *Go check on Marta.*

He must understand, because he immediately eases out of the room. When Cholan hears the door click closed, he inquires calmly, "So, what happened? I think I lost you for a bit."

Kevin begins in a rush, "Well, everything felt just like before, but instead of me calling back to try to get Marta's number, this time Marta picked up the phone from her dad on my first try. Isn't that crazy? I heard her voice, and we had kinda the same conversation as I had in my first channel, just without me having to push through and dial the phone again. I was kind of surprised, but at the same time not really—that's weird, right?—and just when we were planning to call each other later, when Marta got back to her own apartment, this choking blackness swept over me." Kevin looks around hesitantly, as if waiting for the blackness to reappear. "I couldn't see or hear anything; it was like a rock was on my chest, and I didn't know if I was lying down or drifting in space, but I knew I couldn't breathe. I think I may have passed out. The next thing I knew, I woke up here with you and Edwin. Hey, where did Edwin go?"

Cholan reaches over and hands Kevin a glass of water. Ignoring his question and without looking him in the eye, he says, "Something went wrong on my end. I lost you and couldn't find you in the channel. That's never happened before."

Kevin eyes are troubled, he's clearly trying to piece things together.

"Rest now, please. I'll be back to check on you soon." Cholan rises, steps outside, and goes immediately to Marta's room.

Edwin and Marta are talking as he comes through the door, but when she sees Cholan she exclaims, "There you are! What the hell happened? That was so scary."

He repeats what he just told Kevin: he lost her in the channel, and they got into a weird spot that, thankfully, they were able to get back from.

Tilting her head, contemplating his explanation, she plainly states, "I guess this is why you have everyone sign that waiver, huh?" She sighs heavily. "I'm exhausted and have a pounding headache. I've got to go."

Cholan muffles his own sigh—of relief—and sits down.

Edwin immediately jumps up. "Yes, yes. We will call you to discuss this further if you want. We may want to ask you some more questions about your experience, but not now. You are both too drained."

Cholan starts at Edwin's words, and he sees panic cross his friend's face—he was clearly referring to Kevin and Marta, but Marta doesn't catch the slip or assumes he meant Cholan and Marta. Cholan composes himself just as she turns to him, reaching out to clasp his hand.

"Please take care and thank you. I think you saved me down there, or wherever it was I got myself into."

Cholan looks down quickly so he doesn't have to see Edwin's reproachful eyes.

Once Marta and Kevin are gone, Cholan breathes easier. He sinks into his chair and curls up to take a much-needed nap, when Edwin enters and stands over him, saying nothing.

Cholan finally states flatly, "I know. You were right. That was bad."

Nodding curtly, Edwin turns on his heel and quietly closes the door.

Thankful for the reprieve, Cholan knows that will not be the last of their conversations about this fiasco. Cholan thinks, *While I am not responsible for the fork in Marta's and Kevin's life channels, I am now involved, and Edwin and I are the only ones who can connect the dots for the two of them.* As his chin dips down to rest against his chest, *They deserve to know* runs through his head in a constant refrain.

The next morning, Cholan's mental and physical strength are back; despite the stress of yesterday, he just needed a good night's rest to bounce back.

He pokes his head into Edwin's office when he arrives. "*Ayubowan.*" He clasps his hands, and bows his head. "Look, I am very sorry. You were right and I should have listened to you."

"Yes, you should have. But what is done is done." Edwin squints at him. "What are you thinking we should do now?"

"Well, I was thinking about that. This is very unusual. I know you weren't in their channel, but they have something very special. I have never experienced anything like their connection before. It is magical."

They sit in silence. Cholan is back in their channel, feeling the pull through the phone as they talked to each other.

Edwin breaks the quiet. "I think we need to tell each of them about the other and offer to give them one another's information. They can do what they will with it. What do you think of that?"

Cholan nods. He is glad Edwin came up with this idea on his own, as it is just what he was going to suggest.

"They will both want to share their information. They truly are soulmates in every sense of the word."

Searching around his desk, Edwin withdraws two files. He flips one open and gestures for Cholan to close the door. "I will let you know how it goes."

A short while later, Cholan hears a soft rap on his door.

"Come in, come in," he calls out.

Edwin enters, looking pleased.

"Sit!" Cholan exclaims. "And tell me what happened!"

"You were right." Edwin grins. "They both wanted their contact information shared. So now the rest is up to them."

"Right, right, but what else did they say? Did you tell them about yesterday?" Cholan asks in alarm.

"No, I didn't get into that at all," Edwin says. "Best to leave *that* alone. What I told them is that after you channeled with Kevin, you realized you had been there before with someone else, and we connected the dots that Kevin was Marta's Kevin and Marta was Kevin's Marta. I told them this was very remarkable and had never happened before."

Cholan nods his head vehemently. "Good, good. Did you tell them they are soulmates or anything like that? They should know that, right?"

"No, no," Edwin shakes his head. "I think we have meddled enough. I didn't want to share anything more. We connected them. If they are soulmates, as you say, the rest will take care of itself—it won't matter if we tell them or not."

"True enough," Cholan concedes. "It will happen; there is no denying what I felt in their channels. But were they thrilled, amazed . . . what?"

Edwin shrugs. "They both were very excited, but I also felt some real trepidation, too. As you can imagine, channeling is one thing, and actually meeting is quite another. There is no guarantee that real life will be the same as the channel."

"Pshaw!" Cholan scoffs. "I have no doubt. They are meant to be. In fact . . ." He darts a mischievous look at Edwin. "How about a friendly wager?"

"Oh, excellent." Edwin's eyes shine. "Shall we be so bold as to go with the classic *Trading Places* wager?"

Cholan rubs his hands together. "Exactly what I was thinking. If they end up together, you owe me a dollar. If they don't, I owe you one."

CHAPTER 25: The Visit

2033—Boston, Massachusetts

Cholan was left to wonder and imagine Marta and Kevin's life after they connect with each other. He is confident they went on to have a wonderful life together, but Edwin is not so sure. Cholan tries to explain to him the connection he felt when channeling with the two—how closely aligned they were, how there was no other explanation other than that they were soulmates—but Edwin's doubts remained.

Cholan continues with his channeling practice. His experiments with time and space and people's channels bring happiness to some, disappointment to others. But he never again experiences a connection like Marta and Kevin's. The purity of their young love and the longing that is wrapped up in their channels is unique and special.

Thirteen years after their fateful attempt to join Marta and Kevin's channels, Edwin retires to Florida, of all places, and with his departure, Cholan decides to close his practice. Cholan has now reached the age Phurbu was back when he decided to stay in Sri Lanka and not travel to the United States. At the time, Cholan hadn't understood his decision to remain, but now—with the benefit of age, and after so many years of separation from his family—he better understands why Phurbu stayed and what he as a young boy gave up by coming to America. In all those years, he'd never returned to Sri Lanka in the flesh, but he channels back to visit his family and his village so many times over his lifetime. Through his fire channel, he visits his parents, brother, sister, Phurbu, and the village as they all were in his childhood.

For the next many years after he closed his practice, he and his wife, Sophie, live a quiet life: doing the *New York Times* crossword, sipping the strong Indian coffee Sophie special-orders for him, strolling through the streets of Boston, eating at their favorite restaurants, and visiting with nieces and nephews, brothers and sisters.

Life is as it should be—until, they are well into their seventies, and Sophie dies quietly and unexpectedly in her sleep.

Once again, Cholan is alone in the world, bereft. His gloom lasts several years after Sophie's death. Once again, channeling saves him: he misses his wife more than anything, but he can at least channel frequently back to their life together.

He often travels back to when they first met in Dr. Liam's office in LA.

> *Cholan notices her hands first. They lightly touch his arm and wrist, as gentle as a butterfly's wing brushing his skin. She is taking his pulse and blood pressure at his annual exam with Dr. Liam. Cholan notices her small, rounded nails, and that may be the moment he falls. He loves hands.*
>
> *After staring at them for a bit, he resists the urge to look up and instead tries to imagine the person who might be connected to such perfect hands . . .*

Sophie is the only thing in his life that ever surpasses channeling. He would have given up channeling without a backward glance if he'd had to choose between it and Sophie.

During this time of profound sadness, the traumas his body endured when he was ten come back in a real way—perhaps because he is spending so much time sitting on the couch in stillness, channeling his way back to Sophie. Whether it is from those long periods of stillness or just old age catching up with him, his bad leg weakens, and the ligaments and tendons that were stretched back to their unburned lengths during all those reconstructive surgeries begin to shrink back like an elastic band that returns to its normal size after every stretch. His leg shortens, which affects his balance, and the tendons cease to control his foot properly. This results in a pronounced drop foot that causes several falls, the last of which results in a broken hip.

Cholan lands in the Brookline Health Facility for several months of rehab. He discovers that it has a lovely assisted-living section, in addition to the rehab hospital, and once he is well enough to live on his own again, he moves into a small apartment there. They provide meals and socialization, if one wants, and even live entertainment on weekends.

He resigns himself to slowly dying and looks forward to joining Sophie in the next life. He imagines melting away, just as he pictured melting into that lumpy mattress all those years ago.

Like back then, it is both his fear and his hope.

Several months later Marta breezes into the Brookline Health facility out of the blue for a visit with Cholan. They hadn't seen each other for thirty years. She is seventy now but looks young and spry.

They sit in one of the alcoves in the community room. She is dressed in a flowing blouse and comfortable pants that look like what one would wear on a safari, and she has a scarf wrapped around her hair.

"I have always been so curious to know what happened with you and Kevin," Cholan admits. "Would you be willing to share your story? Edwin and I had a friendly wager and I would like to know if he owes me money when I see him in the next realm. There better be some sort of currency up there, as I am sure I am the winner of our little bet."

Laughing, Marta says, "I actually have written it all down." She pulls out a large sheath of paper held together with a large clip. "I call it *The Road not Taken*, or *Channels*. I really can't decide which is better." With a papery-thin hand, she wipes away some imaginary dust on the top page. "I put it all down here before it was gone completely. Remembering is becoming a problem and I don't want my story to be lost once my mind disappears."

Cholan raises an eyebrow but doesn't ask the question that hangs in the air.

Marta brightens suddenly. "Sorry for becoming so maudlin. Time enough for that later," Marta says warmly. "Honestly, I've spent the last couple of months trying to find you to do just that—tell you my story—but there are a surprising number of Cholan Kumeras, you know?" Marta teases. "But seriously, I wanted to share it with you, as only you understand mine and Kevin's story. You can read about it later. When I am gone, or my mind is." She pats the pile of white pages.

For a moment she looks pensive, and her eyes dim in the afternoon light. Then she collects herself.

"I was the one that called Kevin first after Edwin shared his phone number. It was only right, since Kevin was the one who called back when we were twenty-three. Our conversation was just like the conversation we had when I channeled. It was like déjà vu—I could feel the energy right through the phone. The connection was wicked strong. But unlike channeling, there was no ripple through time and I didn't have the pressure on my chest or a feeling of some otherworldly being nearby. It was more natural and comfortable; we were, after all, in real time and in the real world. We caught up on what had happened to us since we were fourteen and since we were twenty-three. We described and compared our experiences with channeling. And our conversation was very illuminating—right down to the date of our last channel."

She stares pointedly at Cholan.

Cholan coughs. "So, you found out about the double channel, yes?"

Marta's eyes narrow and she keeps silent.

"It was a bad idea," he admits. "Edwin told me not to do it, but I didn't listen. Look, I am very sorry. I don't know what I was thinking. I certainly never did it again, that's for sure."

Marta's face softens. "As long as you learned your lesson, no harm, no foul. It is what brought us together, right? It was after the bad channel that Kevin and I connected."

Cholan nods, glad that all seems to be forgiven.

She continues, describing their conversation and how they both realized just how unique, just how special, their experiences were.

"To fall in love in eighth grade, nothing too out of the ordinary," she says. "To move apart, still no big deal. To channel—now *that* is something special. And to channel to the same spot? *Unbelievable.* We agreed our story was magical, and it was made possible because of you."

Cholan beams. "I wonder how the previous channeling impacted your real experience," he muses. "Are you both copying interactions from the channel? I am not sure even my quantum physics friends at MIT would be able to theorize an answer."

"Kevin and I discussed that very thing!" she exclaims. "We decided it is just how it is, as we both had slightly different channels, but only very slightly. Both channels couldn't be making up almost the same conversations or the exact feelings. It must be based on something real, or as real as a channel can be, right?"

Cholan shrugs. "As my friend Dr. Lee might say, 'The DNA of the moment had already been cast.' I don't think these things are changeable, whether they occur in a channel or in the 'real' world."

They both fall silent as they absorb the complexity of the question.

"So?" he prompts her. "What happened next?"

She scrunches her face and with a furrowed brow continues, "We delayed meeting in person. We had to weigh real-world issues, both philosophical ones and logistical ones. And there was no good answer to some tough questions."

She reaches for her purse and takes out a packet of letters and pictures. She unties the string holding them together and spreads them out on the table. She picks out one of the photos and hands it to Cholan.

He recognizes Kevin immediately.

"We talked regularly and mailed each other pictures of ourselves and our families," she explains. "I wanted pictures 'cause I was worried Kevin was bald or something. That happens." Her eyes mist up. "Kevin laughed at my worries, as he always used to, and sent me this picture showing his full head of still-blond hair. He scrawled the caption, 'See, all still there!'"

Cholan peers closely at the picture and sees the young man he remembers—slightly unkempt hair, mischievous smile, clear blue eyes staring intently into the camera. He looks joyful.

"I knew when I finally met Kevin again, it would be the end of some things and the beginning of others," Marta continues. "I was ready for that, but Kevin wasn't. He had kids involved, and he, too, knew there would be no turning back once that line was crossed. I didn't push him. It wouldn't have been fair. We both knew that our reunion would be a tidal wave—one that would engulf us and potentially devastate everything around us. So, we agreed to hold off until Kevin's kids were older. It only made sense."

After that first visit, Marta decides to join Cholan at Brookline Health Facility. She recently was diagnosed with Alzheimer's, and Brookline has a top-notch memory care wing.

"I'm hoping that channeling may be able to help me stave off memory loss," she shared with a sad shrug. "No matter what happens, this stupid diagnosis made me finally become the writer I always dreamed of becoming ever since *Harriet the Spy*. So I have it all written down, and as my memory fades, I can keep reading this." She taps the stack of papers proudly.

"Finding the good in even bad things is so important," Cholan says softly, still absorbing the news of Marta's disease.

Cholan hopes his channeling will help. In her channels nothing changes—unlike the real world, which is changing all the time with different nurses, different foods, and different routines. An impaired mind can't keep track of all those changes easily, but in your channel nothing changes. But even if channeling doesn't slow Marta's decline, perhaps it will help erase some of the sadness etched into her being, just as it eases the loneliness of Cholan's life.

CHAPTER 26: Kevin and Marta's Story

2038—Boston, Massachusetts

Cholan wakes up early, as usual, and gets up slowly and carefully. His broken hip healed long ago, but his drop foot is still a bit of a nuisance. At eighty-five, he must do even the simplest of things with careful intention.

Dressed in his white shirt and tan pants, he bends down to tie his clunky orthopedic shoes. Walking down the hallway past the nurses' station, he enters the memory ward. It's been five years since Marta moved in, and he has done this walk a thousand times. Hearing voices inside Marta's room when he approaches her door, he waits just outside the heavy door.

When the aides leave her room, Cholan smiles at them; they smile back with a nod of silent thanks, knowing they will have several hours of peace now, at least as far as Marta is concerned. They have the difficult job of dealing with people who are slowly losing their minds to dementia and Alzheimer's—of watching people turn into someone else before their eyes. Cholan has seen for himself how losing one's grasp on reality can make a person become wildly irrational and very frightened.

Knocking softly, he enters and sees Marta dressed in a flowing robe—the one she brought back with her after her time with the

Peace Corps in Tanzania. She looks younger than her seventy-seven years. Her eyes are cloudy, but they light up when she sees him.

Cholan takes her hand and asks quietly, "Shall we go visit Kevin? Do you have a preference today?"

She tilts her head, then nods firmly.

"Remember when you called Kevin after we channeled together in my office? You were in your yellow house, all was quiet, and you had the piece of paper with his number in your hand."

Marta tilts her head again and asks, "Did Edwin call me with Kevin's number?"

Cholan smiles encouragingly. "Yes. That's it. See, you remember."

"I wanted to be brave enough to finally call Kevin. I was so frightened of so many things back then . . ." She trails off, clearly trying to keep the facts straight.

"That's right," he says. "That's exactly right. Let's go back to Newport when you met."

She looks relieved as she sinks back against the bed and closes her eyes softly. Their hands are clasped, and they shift through time and space with the softest of ripples.

After calling each other and talking and sending letters and pictures for four years, Marta finally meets Kevin in Newport, Rhode Island, on a gorgeous May day in 2007. She moves forward when she spots him and holds out a hand, but when they are within arm's length of each other, some gravitational pull takes over and they just fall into a hug.

Electricity buzzes through Marta, sending sparks across her skin where they touch. Her head fits perfectly into Kevin's chest, his arms are around her, and the feeling is both thrilling and perfectly peaceful, as if an invisible bubble is encasing them, softening everything, shutting out any noise or interference from the world. Coherent thoughts scatter. Their hands clasped, their bodies leaning

into each other, they both pause for a moment in com-
plete stillness—transported elsewhere. Perhaps channels
or multiverses are churning and pulling their conscious-
ness into another time or space.

Kevin is the first to recover. He pulls his body slightly
away, still clasping her hands, looks into her eyes, and
whispers, "I've missed you my whole life."

Her eyes glisten with tears, and as the first tear spills
over, she leans against him like a moth seeking a flame, slides
her hand into her pocket, and withdraws her Breathe rock.

She holds it out to him. He reaches for it and rubs it
lightly with his thumb.

"I told you if you rubbed it enough, it would conjure
me up one day so we would be together," he says, looking
deep into her eyes.

She feels nothing but happiness.

They stroll around the quiet park and end up near
the empty carousel. No one else is around. They agree
that their lives seem to have been leading them to this
moment ever since they left each other the summer after
eighth grade. Marta feels both an electricity and a serenity
following them as they meander. This is what destiny feels
like, she thinks. Giving in and allowing the world to align
itself properly—finally.

They talk about all the plans they made back in eighth
grade: Peace Corps, teaching, kids, and a life together. They
share what they were like in high school and college. Kevin
brought an iPod, and he hands Marta one of the earpieces.
She knows what the song is before she hears the first notes.
Standing perfectly still, they listen to "American Pie"—not
looking at each other at first, just letting the music and the
memories wash over them.

". . . and I knew if I had my chance that I could make
those people dance, and maybe they'd be happy for a while . . ."

Simultaneously, as if the cosmos is directing them to do it, they raise their heads and lock eyes. The connection is immediate and intense. It leaves Marta with the question of how they have lived without each other, and she knows with complete certainty that Kevin is having the same thought.

They begin to walk again, at precisely the same time. It's as if they are one single entity, held together by the music and the pull of the universe that says this is where they belong.

"I always dreamed of you wearing those low-cut flare jeans that were all the rage back in the '70s." Kevin sighs and seems momentarily to go back in time. "God, I loved that style. They weren't really in anymore when I was in high school, but my older cousin Lorraine visited our family one winter break and wore them every day, and I don't think I will ever forget them."

"I'll wear those next time if you wear one of those baseball jerseys," Marta says, her eyes dancing. "You know, the ones with the sleeves a different color than the shirt part? Maybe gray with navy sleeves?"

He chuckles. "I'm good with that. Any preference for cologne?"

She laughs. "Anything except Axe, which you can't go to the mall these days without smelling on every teenage boy. They seem to believe that if a little dab is good, a big splash must be better."

He quirks an eyebrow. "Got it. No bathing in Axe."

She gazes into his blue eyes—a perfect match for the Newport sky that afternoon—and says, "Can I be wearing that musk perfume?" She giggles. "God, it sounds awful now that I say it out loud. But you know the one, you sent me a bottle for Christmas to keep me out of the clink. It may be hard to find, though, as it definitely didn't have *the staying power of Chanel Nº5. What the hell is musk, anyway?" She smirks and shakes her head. "Sounds like a large, shaggy bovine! Hardly the right image for a perfume, but it is what I wore pretty much all through high school. Whenever I get a whiff of it now, it immediately transports me back to high school."*

He whispers conspiratorially, "Go for it. I can almost smell that buffalo when I lean in close to you."

Her eyes flash up at him, and she makes no effort to move away when she realizes he is leaning down toward her. He presses his hands against her shoulders, pushing her gently back against the side of the building they have stopped at.

He murmurs, "I hope the bleachers aren't too cold against your back, but I always wanted to kiss someone behind the bleachers, and I never got the chance."

Marta tilts her head back, engrossed in nostalgia— the feeling of high school and what they both missed as a result of their separation. She leans back, and Kevin's face comes closer. Her mind relaxes its grip on reality and shifts back to those wonderful, awful teenage years that give kids the freedom to begin to explore what it means to be a sexual being.

Kevin's lips press softly against hers and an electric current shoots straight to her gut. She moves her lips ever so slightly, and Kevin pulls back for a moment. She opens her eyes, not remembering closing them. He leans in again and reaches his hand around her neck. She shivers and leans in to meet his mouth, unable to get close enough.

His kiss becomes more demanding as they move their lips against each other's; with eyes partially closed, Marta savors the connection. Nothing else matters but his lips and this kiss. It is breathtaking, and the moment freezes as they shift against each other. Now he is pressing his whole body into hers and she feels the electricity racing along her skin. As the feelings flow through her like the waves she hears nearby, she just . . . lets go. She is raw, free, alive.

Time slows and stutters to a stop, and she is in a daydream she has harbored forever.

They continue to explore each other's lips and mouths. Her arms are pinned to her side; she twists slightly to free them, reaches for Kevin, and twines her hands around his neck and shoulders. She moves again to slip from beneath him, and his body rolls around gently to keep their lips connected.

Now she is leaning into him, and he is the one against the wall. Turning into the aggressor ever so slightly, she presses her mouth hard against his, then rains kisses down his neck. He reaches his hand behind her back to press her even closer.

Perhaps three minutes have passed; perhaps thirty. All she knows is that she is home, and home is a place she has never been before.

Cholan gently removes his hand from Marta's grasp and shifts in his chair. Her eyes flicker open briefly, then close again. With her white hair pulled back in a loose ponytail and a smile of such peace and tranquility on her face, she appears otherworldly—angelic. Cholan basks in the joy they've just shared.

"Thank you for helping me get back to Kevin," she murmurs softly.

Cholan watches as she rubs her thumb against her loosely closed fist. Rubbing and rubbing her imaginary talisman.

Cholan nods, stands, and slowly makes his way out of the room. She will be happy for the next several hours, and so will he.

But as his hand reaches for the door, he hears Marta catch her breath and gasp, "Cholan."

He turns on his heel. It's been years since she's remembered his name. The eyes gazing up at him are clear, no fog clouding them but only the glistening of tears that are beginning to spill down her cheeks.

He moves back toward her bed as quickly as he can and takes her hand. "You remember?" he asks gently.

She dips her head in a yes.

Sitting again, he takes a deep breath and exhales slowly before saying, "Marta, do you remember the bad channel, and how Edwin called you after that and gave you Kevin's number?" He knows by now that it is better to guide Marta gently to the truth in this circuitous way, because if she gets there on her own too abruptly, it is even more painful for her.

The mind, even a damaged one, is so full of mystery, he can't help but marvel, as he braces himself for the difficult task before him.

"Yes. I do." Her brow furrows. "I had his number already, right?"

"Yes, you did. Do you remember what you talked about—your memories from your time together in eighth grade, right?"

"Yes, we had such wonderful memories from that year. We loved talking and sharing what we each took away from that magical year. We were so connected; I could feel it right through the phone. We talked about meeting, but Kevin had kids, and he was hesitant. I didn't want to push him into anything he wasn't ready for. I wanted him to make the decision, as no one else should push someone into doing something that would tear a family apart." Marta stops and ponders that. "We didn't say it, but we both knew if we met, we would not be able to walk away from this thing. If we waited, we could maintain some control. Kevin wanted to wait until his youngest was out of the house, and I agreed. A few more years would be okay, right? We had waited for so long already; what was a few more years? I did insist that we share pictures of each other. I was so worried Kevin would lose his beautiful blond hair." She laughs softly.

Cholan takes a stack of pictures that lay atop Marta's nightstand and hands them to her. She picks through them until she finds the picture of Kevin with the handwritten message pointing to his full head of hair. She smiles wistfully. A tear falls onto the picture, and she quickly wipes it away.

"I never pushed Kevin to meet when we were forty—so Kevin never drove down to Newport? He never kissed me senseless, did he?" Another tear drops onto her bed sheet.

Cholan shakes his head. She is quiet, staring off into space, lost in her real memories. When her eyes refocus on him, he reaches into her bedside table drawer and lifts out the pages clasped together with a large clip. It's titled *The Road Not Taken*. He lays it in her lap and Marta strokes and rubs the pages absentmindedly.

Cholan says quietly, "Six years after your first phone call, Kevin had an accident that ended his channel in this world, and all his alternative ones as well. You never met him in Newport or anywhere."

She squeezes her eyes shut and, in a voice devoid of any emotion, states, "It was a dark February night in 2009. His son was getting ready to head to college, and Kevin was finally going to be ready to meet me and start our life together. His pickup truck rolled off an icy Vermont road." She frowns and her eyes widen. "A pink carnation and a pickup truck. I didn't realize what our song was telling me until it was too late."

Cholan shrugs, not sure what she is referring to. She often travels down vague channels that only she understands, even when she is in her lucid periods.

She weeps quietly with her head down. The only sign of her torment is the periodic heaving of her shoulders. He waits patiently. No words can console her as she faces her fresh loss that happened so very long ago.

After a few minutes, she looks up bleakly. Her eyes are a pool of raw pain. Her pain hits Cholan in the chest, making it hard to breathe. It's like this every time. He wishes he could do something to stave off her reality, but there isn't any rhyme or reason to when her mind snaps into place and when it remains in a blissful, unknowing fog.

She takes a deep, cleansing breath and says, "Breathe, Marta, breathe." She pauses, then continues murmuring to herself, "Why, oh, why didn't I push him to meet? Screw his kids! He might still be alive if I had pushed him. I was such a chicken, and look what happened because I was too scared."

"Marta, we don't know that." He covers her hands with his. "It is awfully hard to fool fate or the cosmos. If his time was up, I don't think you could have changed that. Fate is a tricky thing, and she doesn't like folks that think they can outmaneuver her."

Marta glances up, wiping her tears from her eyes, and straightens her shoulders. "What's done is done. I don't know why I am still crying over something that happened all those years ago. It is my stupid brain that makes me think it was just yesterday. I've wept so many tears, I am surprised there is anything left."

She talks more to herself than to Cholan. She describes the long drive up to Vermont for the funeral. How she held tightly to the stone with the word *Breathe* etched into it and listened to "American Pie" on repeat for hours on end. How she wept for what could have been and for the golden boy of her youth. Angry at the unfairness of life.

"I was so close to Kevin that day in your office. He was just in the next room, channeling back to me when I was doing the same." She looks at Cholan as if seeing him for the first time. She tsks. "That black channel was bad, but I think I'd be willing to chance it again to try to find him in that void." Her voice drops, "Now I won't ever find him. He is lost forever to me."

Cholan shakes his head slowly. "He is not truly lost to you. You can go back and find him in your channels whenever you want or need him. He is there for you, always."

A wry smile twitches on her face. "I should have pushed Kevin to meet me. I held back thinking that was the right thing to do. Jason did that for me all those years ago, so I did the same for Kevin, but Kevin and I were soulmates. That is the difference. So instead, I robbed both Kevin and me of a possible life."

"When I walked into that funeral home on the outskirts of Burlington, all I could think was, *What a waste.*" Marta says. "It smelled of sadness and tears. And the first thing I saw was the bouquet of pink carnations I had sent." Her eyes fill with tears and her voice grows harsh. "I was standing in the long line of fellow mourners that had come to pay their respects, and I wanted to scream and hurt them all. It was so unfair. They'd all had more time with Kevin than I had, and that made me angry enough to spit. I had to tamp down the emotions roiling inside me. I remember clutching my Breathe rock to keep my hands from clenching into fists. I was planning to tuck the rock into the casket, but I was squeezing it so hard in that funeral home line that I honestly thought I was going to shatter it into a million tiny pieces." Her eyes flash with anger. "Then I approached the casket and saw Kevin's face." She exhales, and a calm comes over her. "Suddenly all my anger dissipated, and a feeling of peace enveloped me. I realized Kevin didn't need the stone. But I didn't need it anymore, either. I was going to be brave all on my own from now on."

Marta continues, more subdued, "Standing in front of his casket, a surge of gratitude washed over me like an ocean wave. I thanked God for letting him be part of my life. While our lives may have been physically very separate, but we were always connected over all those years. In so many ways, Kevin shaped me and made me who I am. But I also needed to learn who I was or could be now that I wasn't going to be waiting for Kevin anymore."

"And you have your channel, which is yours and yours alone, and it will go on forever, never-ending," Cholan reminds her. "Your connection impacted both you and Kevin so very profoundly, despite the distance and the separation. Kevin is still a part of your life today—as much, if not more so, than all the people closest to you, right?"

Marta inclines her head. "We had our one magical year, and later our channel that allowed us to find each other after all those years. And it is a spectacular channel, isn't it?"

He nods. "Beyond compare."

She sighs and loses herself in her memories again, then slowly continues.

"On the drive back to New Jersey, I stopped on a bridge over the Hudson River. With the wind whipping against my face, I hurled that stone into the wild water. I imagined the stone tumbling its way to the ocean someday, finding its way home, the word *Breathe* slowly fading away. Becoming what it to was meant to be. I was going to do that for me as well. Become who I was meant to be." Her eyes brighten a little. "I buried a piece of me that day, but I was freed as well. I remember looking up into the crisp sunlight, feeling the warmth on my cheeks. I knew I was going to be all right. I was no longer weighed down by what could have been. I didn't need to wait and wonder any longer. I was forty-six and finally ready to start living my life on my terms."

"And what did that mean for you?" he asks, though he knows the answer.

"I'd been waiting for Kevin to come back to me since I was fourteen, trying to be the girl I thought he would want me to be. But what I really needed was to become myself. I was both that scared Romanian gymnast running routines in her head and the dancing, twirling slice of sunshine Kevin loved. One wasn't necessarily better than the other. They were me and I was them. My love for Kevin was enough to carry me through the rest of my life, but I didn't need to wait for it anymore. It was in me and all around me. I needed to write my own story." She taps the pile of pages on her lap. "I wrote my own story, didn't I?"

Cholan nods. "Yes, you did. Love is not linear. It takes up both time and space, and it is never-ending."

Clasping her papery-thin hand in his, he lets Marta finish telling her story—one he has heard many times by now.

"I needed to be fair to Steve. So, I let him go. He deserved someone that could love him for who he was, not for what he provided or represented. He found a nice woman he worked with who hadn't given away her heart when she was fourteen and never got it back . . ." Marta trails off, and Cholan wonders if she is finding all those alternative channels she has from that time of upheaval, and if she notices them, if she has ever wanted to travel back to see what would have happened if she had chosen a different path. Cholan doesn't think she would. She made the right decisions back then, and she has her Kevin channels she wants to relive.

Marta straightens in her bed and with her clear hazel eyes sparkling says, "Then I got rid of all my lovely, expensive suits." I gave them to a women's charity that helps women in need with interviewing skills and how to dress for success. I had no idea those clothes were weighing me down until I packed them up and gave them away. Oh, the lightness. I hadn't felt such lightness since eighth grade. They were just an illusion of happiness I was desperate to hold on to, but they didn't give me real happiness. Security maybe, but I was done with all that. I wanted to be me and not someone covered in expensive clothes so you wouldn't see who she really was—a scared little girl who was okay with that."

Cholan nods and pictures Marta in comfortable hiking clothes, with a small suitcase heading out into the world. Scared and brave at the same time.

She went off and joined the Peace Corps, traveling to far-off places, finally getting to see the world, as she and Kevin talked about doing when they were fourteen. She found out she was brave on her own and could forge her own path without her father's direction, without a shield of clothes and without the promises of young love. She loved the life she built, despite never finding love with another. She lost her soulmate, and that pain, while bearable, stays etched on her face to this day—even now, as her mind is forgetting the weight of that loss.

When she finishes telling her story, she stares at Cholan with a palpable bleakness.

Squeezing her hand, he declares, "Remember, Marta—despite the pain, this is really a beautiful love story. One that is uniquely yours and Kevin's. And you and I can travel back to your two channels every day to relive your love story. We channel back to Kevin whenever we want. Nothing can take away the love you shared, no matter how short the time you spent with one another may have been. It lives on in your heart and your channels. Sometimes we go back to when you were twenty-three, sometimes to when you were forty—but no matter what channel we choose, it all comes back to Kevin and a love that is greater than time and distance. That is what you tell me and that is all part of your beautiful story, too."

"I do say that." She beams up at him.

But in the very next moment, a cloud passes over Marta's pretty eyes, and she looks at him in confusion. She tilts her head as if she is trying to remember something important; then slumps back against the bed. Suddenly, she sits up, tense and worried, her hand clutching at the sheet in her lap. Then she relaxes and she lifts her open, empty palm toward Cholan.

"I thought I lost my Breathe stone for a minute, but it's right here." She closes her hand around the invisible stone, rubbing her thumb across her fist.

Cholan smiles encouragingly. "Marta, would you like to go visit Kevin today?"

She looks at him with her forehead furrowed in confusion, and after a beat, she nods.

Cholan is happy for the life Marta made for herself, but he, more than anyone, knows just how sad her story is. He feels and sees what might have been if she and Kevin had met in Newport when they first connected after the dark channel, or if she had simply taken the phone from her father back when she was twenty-three. He knows the connection they had and how powerful it was. He's experienced the beauty in their alternative channel, and it is unparalleled.

Still, channeling, though it can't quite measure up to the life Marta almost had, is something. It is real. It allows her to live the life she dreamed of and recapture the spirit of the fourteen-year-old girl she once was. For that, he is grateful. While he is just a guiding spirit in their channel, it is part of who he is now, too. It is his channel as much as it is Marta and Kevin's.

Together, he and Marta spend many an afternoon simultaneously sitting in a sunny spot on the patio of the memory wing and
wandering the narrow streets of Newport. As the blue sky goes on
forever and the sun-drenched waves crash on the shore and the soft
musical strains of "American Pie" play through Marta and Kevin's
headphones, hazel eyes meet dancing blue eyes and love blooms
over and over again.

Hello Reader,
Please consider leaving a review wherever books are sold.
Thank you, Andrea

Book Club Discussion Questions can be found at
https://andreaezerins.com!

Acknowledgements

Having spent the last eighteen years nurturing and developing *Again and Again Back To You*, I came to realize this book is like my fifth child and as with all children, it takes a village. There are many people I need to thank that are part of that village.

To my husband, Edgar, for his unwavering support, encouragement, and laughter (often at my expense). He has kept me sane through this whole crazy journey. I'd like to thank my mother, Erica Bradford, who passed on her love of books to me. She was my most supportive beta reader which is just what I would expect from someone as sweet as her. Thank you to my brother Dave, who provided the best critique when he said, "Well it's not John Grisham, but I can't tell you why." This served as excellent motivation to keep me going back to the grindstone, refining and reworking on the hopes that I move my book a little closer to the venerable John G. To my tenacious alpha reader, my daughter Emily, I was never so grateful to discover her skills included developmental editing. A huge thanks to the rest of my funny, sarcastic, teasing family, Lydia, Alex and Eric and the wonderful author's brunch they gave me in 2022. Sitting around Cape Cod discussing *Again and Again Back To You* is a memory I will treasure forever. And that includes the painting party everyone did of the possible book covers.

The advice, encouragement and support I received from my beta reading friends and family meant the world to me. A heartfelt thank you to Tricia, Michelle, Shaune, Tom, Inta and Taylor for your ideas and suggestions. You were instrumental in getting me to the point where I was ready to share my book beyond the safe confines of my inner circle. Sharing my book is like watching your child climb onto that big yellow bus for the very first time. I was very lucky to find the supportive arms of Katie Walsh who with the most delicate of touches worked with me through countless iterations of the book. She was able to coax a more cohesive, interesting story from the pages. Knowing my book was growing up and perhaps ready for publication, I started the publishing process, and my eyes were opened when I discovered Mary Neighbour, "book shepherd," and her book *Self-Publishing Wizard or Wannabe*. Ultimately, Mary ended up sharpening and polishing my story beyond my expectations. She has been a guiding force as I navigated these new waters. Then, because I am a firm believer that things happen for a reason, my husband's cousin, Michelle Brooks, teacher extraordinaire and beta reader, suggested I send my book to She Writes Press and the stars aligned. A huge thank you to Brooke Warner, Krissa Lagos, Addison Gallegos and the many others that are part of the She Writes Press team that worked with me through this tricky and potentially soul crushing process. You guys are amazing. Meryl Moss, my publicist, has had my back since day one and I'm so thankful to her and her team.

To get this book out into the world, truly took a village and I'm glad I had the She Writes Press village of authors, team members, Meryl Moss Media and my own village of family and friends along for the ride. Thank you all for your faith in me and your understanding and support over these many years.

About the Author

Andrea Ezerins grew up in the small town of Columbia, Connecticut, where she was raised on a small hobby farm that included, at one time or another, pigs, cows, wild ponies, chickens, dogs, cats, and pet mice. She earned a bachelor's degree in business administration at University of Connecticut and went on to spend thirty years working in the insurance industry. She finished *Again and Again Back To You*, a labor of love, thanks in no small part to the pandemic and an empty nest where distractions suddenly were reduced to only a spoiled German shepherd and the many bluebird families that nest in her boxes. Andrea has two daughters and identical twin sons. She resides in Hebron, Connecticut, with her husband.

Author photo © Jeff Yardis Photography

Looking for your next great read?

We can help!

Visit www.shewritespress.com/next-read
or scan the QR code below for a list
of our recommended titles.

She Writes Press is an award-winning
independent publishing company founded to
serve women writers everywhere.